JAVA HEAD

Inscription over the door - a black rock
in the Sunda Strait.

Joseph Hergesheimer

NOVELS
The Lay Anthony, 1914
Mountain Blood, 1915
The Three Black Pennys, 1917
Java Head, 1918
Linda Condon, 1919
Cytherea, 1922
The Bright Shawl, 1922
Balisand, 1924
Tampico, 1926

SHORTER STORIES
Wild Oranges, 1918
Tubal Cain, 1918
The Dark Fleece, 1918
The Happy End, 1919

TRAVEL
San Cristobal de la Habana, 1920

AUTOBIOGRAPHY
The Presbyterian Child, 1923
From An Old House, 1925

JOSEPH HERGESHEIMER

JAVA HEAD

It is only the path of pure simplicity
which guards and preserves the spirit
CHWANG-TZE

ALFRED A KNOPF
New York
1930

To

HAZLETON MIRKIL, Jr.

from

Dorothy

and

Joseph Hergesheimer

JAVA HEAD

JAVA HEAD

I

VERY late indeed in May, but early in the morning, Laurel Ammidon lay in bed considering two widely different aspects of chairs. The day before she had been eleven, and the comparative maturity of that age had filled her with a moving disdain for certain fanciful thoughts which had given her extreme youth a decidedly novel if not an actually adventurous setting. Until yesterday, almost, she had regarded the various chairs of the house as beings endowed with life and character; she had held conversations with some, and, with a careless exterior not warranted by an inner dread, avoided others in gloomy dusks. All this, now, she contemptuously discarded. Chairs were — chairs, things to sit on, wood and stuffed cushions.

Yet she was slightly melancholy at losing such a satisfactory lot of reliable familiars: unlike older people, victims of the most disconcerting moods and mysterious changes, chairs could always be counted on to remain secure in their individual peculiarities.

She could see by her fireplace the elaborately carved teakwood chair that her grandfather had brought home from China, which had never varied from the state of a brown and rather benevolent dragon; its claws were always claws, the grinning fretted mouth was perpetually fixed for a cloud of smoke and a mild rumble of complaint. The severe waxed hickory beyond with the broad arm for writing, a source of special pride, had been an accommodating and precise old gentleman. The spindling gold chairs in the drawing-room were supercilious creatures at a king's ball; the graceful impressive formality of the Heppelwhites in the dining room belonged to the loveliest of Boston ladies. Those with difficult haircloth seats in the parlor were deacons; others in the breakfast room talkative and unpretentious; while the deep easychair before the library fire was a ship. There were mahogany stools, dwarfs of dark tricks; angry high-backed things in the hall below; and a terrifying shape of gleaming red that, without question, stirred hatefully and reached out curved and dripping hands.

Anyhow, such they had all seemed. But lately she had felt a growing secrecy about it, an increasing dread of being laughed at; and now, definitely eleven, she recognized the necessity of dropping such pretense even with herself. They were just chairs, she repeated; there was an end of that.

The tall clock with the brass face outside her door, after a premonitory whirring, loudly and firmly struck seven, and Laurel wondered whether her sisters, in the room open from hers, were awake. She listened attentively but there was no sound of movement. She made a noise in her throat, that might at once have appeared accidental and been successful in its purpose of arousing them; but there was no response. She would have gone in and frankly waked Janet, who was not yet thirteen and reasonable; but experience had shown her that Camilla, reposing in the eminence and security of two years more, would permit no such light freedom with her slumbers.

Sidsall, who had been given a big room for herself on the other side of their parents, would greet anyone cheerfully no matter how tightly she might have been asleep. And Sidsall, the oldest of them all, was nearly sixteen and had stayed for part of their cousin Lucy Saltonstone's dance, where no less a person than Roger Brevard had asked her for a quadrille.

Laurel's thoughts grew so active that she was unable to remain any longer in bed; she freed herself from the enveloping linen and crossed the room to a window through which the sun was pouring in a sharp bright angle. She had never known the world to smell so delightful — it was one of the notable Mays in which the lilacs blossomed — and she stood responding with a sparkling life to the brilliant scented morning, the honey-sweet perfume of the lilacs mingled with the faintly pungent odor of box wet with dew.

She could see, looking back across a smooth green corner of the Wibirds' lawn next door, the enclosure of their own back yard, divided from the garden by a white lattice fence and row of prim grayish poplars. At the farther wall her grandfather, in a wide palm leaf hat, was stirring about his pear trees, tapping the ground and poking among the branches with his ivory headed cane.

Laurel exuberantly performed her morning toilet, half careless, in her soaring spirits, of the possible effect of numerous small ringings of pitcher on basin, the clatter of drawers, upon Camilla. Yesterday she had worn a dress of light wool delaine; but this morning, she decided largely, summer had practically come; and, on her own authority, she got an affair of thin pineapple cloth out of the yellow camphorwood chest. She hurriedly finished weaving her heavy chestnut hair into two gleaming plaits, fastened a muslin guimpe at the back, and slipped into her dress. Here, however, she twisted her face into an expression of annoyance — her years were affronted by the length of pantalets that hung below her skirt. Such a show of their narrow ruffles might do for a very small girl, but not for one of eleven; and she caught them up until only the merest fulled edge was visible. Then she made a buoyant descent to the lower hall, left the house by a side door to the bricked walk and an arched gate into the yard, and joined her grandfather.

" Six bells in the morning watch," he announced, consulting a thick gold timepiece. " Head pump rigged and deck swabbed down? " Secure in her knowledge of the correct answers for these sudden interrogations Laurel impatiently replied, " Yes, sir."

" Scuttle butt filled? "

" Yes, sir." She frowned and dug a heel in the soft ground.

" Then splice the keel and heave the galley overboard."

This last she recognized as a sally of humor, and contrived a fleeting perfunctory smile. Her grandfather turned once more to the pears. " See the buds on those Ashton Towns," he commented. Laurel gazed critically: the varnished red buds were bursting with white blossom, the new leaves unrolling, tender green and sticky. " But the jargonelles —" he drew in his lips doubtfully. She studied him with the profound interest his sheer being always invoked: she was absorbed in his surprising large roundness of body, like an enormous pudding; in the de-

[12]

liberate care with which he moved and planted his feet; but most of all by the fact that when he was angry his face got quite purple, the color of her mother's paletot or a Hamburg grape.

They crossed the yard to where the vines of the latter, and of white Chasselas — Laurel was familiar with these names from frequent horticultural questionings — had been laid down in cold frames for later transplanting; and from them the old man, her palm tightly held in his, trod ponderously to the currant bushes massed against the closed arcade of the stables, the wood and coal and store houses, across the rear of the place.

At last, with frequent disconcerting mutterings and explosive breaths, he finished his inspection and turned toward the house. Laurel, conscious of her own superiority of apparel, surveyed her companion in a frowning attitude exactly caught from her mother. He had on that mussy suit of yellow Chinese silk, and there was a spot on the waistcoat straining at its pearl buttons. She wondered, maintaining the silent mimicry of elder remonstrance, why he would wear those untidy old things when his chests were heaped with snowy white linen and English broadcloths. It was very improper in an Ammidon, particularly in one who had been captain of so many big ships, and in court dress with a cocked hat met the Emperor of Russia.

They did not retrace Laurel's steps, but passed through a narrow wicket to the garden that lay directly behind the house. The enclosure was full of robin-song and pouring sunlight; the lilac trees on either side of the summer-house against the gallery of the stable were blurred with their new lavender flowering; the thorned glossy

[13]

foliage of the hedge of June roses on Briggs Street glittered with diamonds of water; and the rockery in the far corner showed a quiver of arbutus among its strange and lacy ferns and mosses.

Laurel sniffed the fragrant air, filled with a tumult of energy; every instinct longed to skip; she thought of jouncing as high as the poplars, right over the house and into Washington Square beyond. " Miss Fidget! " her grandfather exclaimed, exasperated, releasing her hand. " You're like holding on to a stormy petrel."

" I don't think that's very nice," she replied.

" God bless me," he said, turning upon her his steady blue gaze; " what have we got here, all dressed up to go ashore? " She sharply elevated a shoulder and retorted, " Well, I'm eleven." His look, which had seemed quite fierce, grew kindly again. " Eleven," he echoed with a satisfactory amazement; " that will need some cumshaws and kisses." The first, she knew, was a word of pleasant import, brought from the East, and meant gifts; and, realizing that the second was unavoidably connected with it, she philosophically held up her face. Lifting her over his expanse of stomach he kissed her loudly. She didn't object, really, or rather she wouldn't at all but for a strong odor of Manilla cheroots and the Medford rum he took at stated periods.

After this they moved on, through the bay window of the drawing-room that opened on the garden, where a woman was brushing with a nodding feather duster, under the white arch that framed the main stairway, and turned aside to where breakfast was being laid. Laurel saw that her father was already seated at the table, intent upon

[14]

the tall, thickly printed sheet of the Salem *Register*. He paused to meet her dutiful lips; then with a "Good morning, father," returned to his reading. Camilla entered at Laurel's heels; and the latter, in a delight slightly tempered by doubt, saw that she had been before her sister in a suitable dress for such a warm day. Camilla still wore her dark merino; and she gazed with mingled surprise and annoyance at Laurel's airy garb.

"Did mother say you might put that on?" she demanded. "Because if she didn't I expect you will have to go right up from breakfast and change. It isn't a dress at all for so early in the morning. Why, I believe it's one of your very best." The look of critical disapproval suddenly became doubly accusing.

"Laurel Ammidon, wherever are your pantalets?"

"I'm too big to have pantalets hanging down over my shoetops," she replied defiantly, "and so I just hitched them up. You can still see the frill." Janet had come into the room, and stood behind her. "Don't you notice Camilla," she advised; "she's not really grown up." They turned at the appearance of their mother. "Dear me, Camilla," the latter observed, "you are getting too particular for any comfort. What has upset you now?"

"Look at Laurel," Camilla replied; "that's all you need to do. You'd think she went to dances instead of Sidsall."

Laurel painfully avoided her mother's comprehensive glance. "Very beautiful," the elder said in a tone of palpable pleasure. Laurel advanced her lower lip ever so slightly in the direction of Camilla. "But you have taken a great deal into your own hands." She shifted

[15]

apparently to another topic. "There will be no lessons to-day for I have to send Miss Gomes into Boston." At this announcement Laurel was flooded with a joy that obviously belonged to her former, less dignified state. "However," her mother continued addressing her, "since you have dressed yourself like a lady I shall expect you to behave appropriately; no soiled or torn skirts, and an hour at your piano scales instead of a half."

Laurel's anticipation of pleasure ebbed as quickly as it had come — she would have to move with the greatest caution all day, and spend a whole hour at the piano. It was the room to which she objected rather than the practicing; a depressing sort of place where she was careful not to move anything out of the stiff and threatening order in which it belonged. The chair-deacons in particular were severely watchful; but that, now, she had determined to ignore.

She turned to johnnycakes, honey and milk, only half hearing, in her preoccupation with the injustice that had overtaken her, the conversation about the table. Her gaze strayed over the walls of the breakfast room, where water color drawings of vessels, half models of ships on teakwood or Spanish mahogany boards, filled every possible space. Some her grandfather had sailed in as second and then first mate, of others he had been master, and the rest, she knew, were owned by Ammidon, Ammidon and Saltonstone, her grandfather, father and uncle.

Just opposite her was the *Two Capes* at anchor in Table Bay, the sails all furled except the fore-topsail which hung in the gear. A gig manned by six sailors in tarpaulin hats with an officer in the stern sheets swung with dripping oars across the dark water of the foreground; on the left an inky ship was standing in close hauled on the port tack with all her canvas set. It was lighter about the *Two Capes,* and at the back a mountain with a flat top — showing at once why it was called Table Bay — rose against an overcast sky. Laurel knew a great deal about the *Two Capes* — for instance that she had been a barque of two hundred and nine tons — because it had been her grandfather's first command, and he never tired of narrating every detail of that memorable voyage.

Laurel could repeat most of these particulars: They sailed on the tenth of April in 'ninety-three, and were four and a half months to the Cape of Good Hope; twenty days later, on the rocky island of St. Paul, grandfather had a fight with a monster seal; a sailor took the scurvy, and, dosed with niter and vinegar, was stowed in the longboat, but he died and was buried at sea in the Doldrums. Then, with a cargo of Sumatra pepper, they made Corregidor Island and Manilla Bay where the old Spanish fort stood at the mouth of the Pasig. The barque, the final cargo of hemp and indigo and sugar in the hold, set sail again for the Cape of Good Hope, and returned, by way of Falmouth in England and Rotterdam, home.

The other drawings were hardly less familiar; ships, barques, brigs and topsail schooners, the skillful work of Salmon, Anton Roux and Chinnery. There was the *Celestina* becalmed off Marseilles, her sails hanging idly from the yards and stays, her hull with painted ports and carved bow and stern mirrored in the level sea. There was the *Albacore* running through the northeast trades with royals and all her weather studding sails set. Farther along the *Pallas Athena*, in heavy weather off the Cape of Good Hope, was being driven hard across the Agulhas Bank under double-reefed topsails, reefed courses, the fore-topmast staysail and spanker, with the westerly current breaking in an ugly cross sea, but, as her grandfather always explained, setting the ship thirty or forty miles to windward in a day. She lingered, finally, over the *Metacom*, running her easting down far to the southward with square yards under a close-reefed maintopsail, double-reefed foresail and forestaysail, dead before a gale and gigantic long seas hurling the ship on in the bleak watery desolation.

Laurel was closely concerned in all these. One cause for this was the fact that her grandfather so often selected her as the audience for his memories and stories, during which his manner was completely that of one navigator to another; and a second flourished in the knowledge that Camilla affected to disdain the sea and any of its connections.

Sidsall appeared and took her place with a collective greeting; while Laurel, coming out of her abstraction, realized that they were discussing the subject in which nearly every conversation now began or ended — the solemn speculation of why her Uncle Gerrit Ammidon, master of the ship *Nautilus*, was so long overdue from China. Laurel heard this from two angles, or, otherwise, when her grandfather was or was not present, the tone of the first far more encouraging than that of the latter. Her father was speaking:

" My opinion is that he was unexpectedly held up at

Shanghai. It's a new port for us, and, Captain Verney tells me, very difficult to make: after Woosung you have to get hold of two bamboo poles stuck up on the bank a hundred feet apart as a leading mark, and, with these in range, steer for the bar. The channel is very narrow, and he says the *Nautilus* would have to wait for high water, perhaps for the spring tide. She may have got ashore, strained and sprung a leak, and had to discharge her cargo for repairs."

" That's never Gerrit," the elder replied positively. " There isn't a better master afloat. He can smell shoal water. I was certain we'd hear from him when the *Sorsogon* was back from Calcutta. Do you suppose, William, that he took the *Nautilus* about the Horn and —? " Laurel wondered at the unmannerly way in which he gulped his coffee. " He might have driven into the Antarctic winter," he proceeded. " My deck was swept and all the boats stove off the Falklands in April."

" Gerrit's got a ship," the other asserted, "not a hermaphrodite brig built like a butter box. You'll find that I am right and that he has been tied up in port."

" I made eight hundred per cent on a first cargo for my owners," the elder retorted. " Then there was trading, yes, and sailing, too. No chronometers with confounded rates of variation and other fancy parlor instruments to read your position from. When I first navigated it was with an astrolabe and the moon. A master knew his lead, latitude and lookout then.

" Eight hundred barrels of flour and pine boards to Rio and back with coffee and hides for Salem," he continued; " then out to Gibraltar and Brazil with wine and on in ballast for Calcutta. Tahiti and Morea, the Sandwich Islands and the Feejees. Sandalwood and tortoise shell and *bêche de mer;* sea horses' teeth, and saltpeter for the Chinese Government. I don't want to hear about your bills of exchange and kegs of Spanish dollars and solid cargoes of tea run back direct. Why, with your Canton and India agents and sight drafts the China service is like dealing with a Boston store."

Laurel saw that her father was assuming the expression of restrained annoyance habitual when the elder contrasted old shipping ways with new. " Unfortunately," he said, " the patient Chinaman will no longer exchange silks and lacquer and teas for boiled sea slugs. He has learned to demand something of value."

" Why, damn it, William," the other exploded, " nothing's more valuable to a Chinese than his belly. They'll give eighteen hundred dollars a pecul for birds' nests any day. As for your insinuation that we used to diddle them — I never ran opium up from India to rot their souls. And when the Chinese Government tried to stop it there's the British commercial interests forcing it on them with cannon in 'forty-two.

" Look at the pepper we brought into Salem —" he was, Laurel realized with intense interest, growing beautifully empurpled; "— lay right off the beach at Mukka and did business with the Dato himself. We forded the bags on the crew's backs across a river with muskets served in case the bloody heathen drew their creeses. When we made sail everything was running over with pepper — the boats and forecastle and cabins and between decks."

" Well, father, the heroic times are done, of course; I can't say that I'm sorry. I shouldn't like to finance a voyage that reached out to three years and depended on the captain's picking up six or seven cargoes."

The old man rose; and, muttering a plainly uncomplimentary period about the resemblance of modern ship owners to clerks, walked with his heavy careful tread from the room.

" You are so foolish to argue and excite him," William's wife told him.

Laurel regarded her with a passionate admiration for the shining hair turning smoothly about her brow and drawn over her ears to the low coil in the back, for her brown barége dress with velvet leaves and blue forget-me-nots and tightest of long sleeves and high collar, and because generally she was a mother to be owned and viewed with pride. She met Laurel's gaze with a little friendly nod and said:

" Don't forget about your clothes, and I think you ought to finish the practicing before dinner, so you'll be free for a walk with your grandfather in the afternoon."

Soon after, Laurel stood in the hall viewing with disfavor the light dress she had put on so gayly at rising. In spite of her sense of increasing age she had a strong desire to play in the yard and climb about in the woodhouse. Already the business of being grown up began to pall upon her, the outlook dreary that included nothing but a whole hour at the piano, an endless care of her skirts, and the slowest kind of walk through Washington Square and down to Derby Wharf, where — no matter in

[21]

which direction and for what purpose they started forth — her grandfather's way invariably led.

Janet joined her, and they stood irresolutely balancing on alternate slippers. "Did you notice," the former volunteered, "mother is letting Camilla have lots of starch in her petticoats, so that they stand right out like crinoline? Wasn't she hateful this morning!" Laurel heard a slight sound at her back, and, wheeling, saw her grandfather looking out from the library door. A swift premonition of possible additional misfortune seized her. Moving toward the side entrance she said to Janet, "We'd better be going right away."

It was, however, too late. "Well, little girls," he remarked benevolently, "since Miss Gomes has left for the day it would be as well if I heard your geography lesson."

"I don't think mother intended for us to study to-day," Laurel replied, making a face of appeal for Janet's support. But the latter remained solidly and silently neutral.

"What, what," the elder mildly exploded; "mutiny in the forecastle! Get right up here in the break of the quarter-deck or I'll harry you." He stood aside while Laurel and Janet filed into the library. Geography was the only subject their grandfather proposed for his instruction, and the lesson, she knew, might take any one of several directions. He sometimes heard it with the precision of Miss Gomes herself; he might substitute for the regular questions such queries, drawn from his wide voyages, as he thought to be of infinitely greater use and interest; or, better still, he frequently gave them the benefit of long reminiscences, through which they sat blinking in a mechanical attention or slightly wriggling

[22]

JAVA HEAD

with minds far away from the old man's periods, full of outlandish names and places, and, when he got excited, shocking swears.

He turned the easy-chair — the one which Laurel had thought of as a ship — away from the fireplace, now covered with a green slatted blind for the summer; and they drew forward two of the heavy chairs with shining claw feet that stood against the wall. Smiley's Geography, a book no larger than the shipmaster's hand, was found and opened to Hindoostan, or India within the Ganges. There was a dark surprising picture of Hindoos doing Penance under the Banyan tree, and a confusing view of the Himaleh Mountains.

"Stuff," he proceeded, gazing with disfavor at the illustrations. "This ought to be written by men who have seen the world and know its tides and landmarks. Do you suppose," he demanded heatedly of Janet, "that the fellow who put this together ever took a ship through the Formosa Channel against the northeast monsoon?"

"No, sir," Janet replied hastily.

"Here are Climate and Face of the country and Religion," he located these items with a blunt finger, "but I can't find exports. I'll lay he won't know a Bengal chintz from a bundle handkerchief."

"I don't think it says anything about exports," Laurel volunteered. "We have the boundaries and —"

"Bilge," he interrupted sharply. "I didn't fetch boundaries back in the *Two Capes,* did I?" He thrust the offending volume into a crevice of his chair. "Laurel," he added, "what is the outport of St. Petersburg?"

[23]

"Cronstadt," she answered, after a violent searching of her memory.

"And for Manilla?" he turned to Janet.

"I can't think," she admitted.

"Laurel?"

"Cavite," the latter pronounced out of a racking mental effort.

"Just so, and —" he looked up at the ceiling, "the port for Boston?"

"I don't believe we've had that," she said firmly. His gaze fastened on her so intently that she blushed into her lap. "Don't believe we've had it," he echoed. "Why, confound it —" he paused and regarded her with a new doubt. "Laurel," he demanded, "what is an outport?"

She had a distinct feeling of justifiable injury. A recognized part of the present system of examination was its strict limitation to questions made familiar by constant repetition; and this last was entirely new. She was sure of several kinds of ports — one they had after dinner, another indicated a certain side of a vessel, and still a third was Salem. But an outport — Cronstadt, Cavite, what it really meant, what they were, had escaped her. She decided to risk an opinion.

"An outport," she said slowly, "is a — a part of a ship," that much seemed safe —"I expect it's the place where they throw things like potato peels through."

"You suppose what!" he cried, breathing quite hard. "A place where they —" he broke off. "And you're Jeremy Ammidon's granddaughter! By heaven, it would make a coolie laugh. It's like William, who never would go to sea, to have four daughters in place of a son. I'm

[24]

done with you; go tinker on the piano." They got down from their chairs and departed with an only half concealed eagerness. " Do you think he means it," Janet asked hopefully, " and he'll never have any geography again? "

" No, I don't," Laurel told her shortly. She was inwardly ruffled, and further annoyed at Janet's placid acceptance of whatever the day brought along. Janet was a stick! She turned away and found herself facing the parlor and the memory of the impending hour of practice. Well, it had to be done before dinner, and she went forward with dragging feet.

Within the formal shaded space of the chamber she stopped to speculate on the varied and colorful pictures of the wall paper reaching from the white paneling above her waist to the deep white carving at the ceiling. The scene which absorbed her most showed, elevated above a smooth stream, a marble pavilion with sweeping steps and a polite company about a reclining gentleman with bare arms and a wreath on his head and a lady in flowing robes playing pipes. To the right, in deep green shadow, a charmer was swinging from ropes of flowers, lovers hid behind a brown mossy trunk; while on the left, against a weeping willow and frowning rock, four serene creatures gathered about a barge with a gilded prow.

Still on her reluctant progress to the piano she stopped to examine the East India money on the lowest shelf of a locked corner cupboard. There was a tiresome string of cash with a rattan twisted through their square holes; silver customs taels, and mace and candareen; Chinese gold leaf and Fukien dollars; coins from Cochin China in the shape of India ink, with raised edges and characters; old Carolus hooked dollars; Sycee silver ingots, smooth and flat above, but roughly oval on the lower surface, not unlike shoes; Japanese obangs, their gold stamped and beaten out almost as broad as a hand's palm; mohurs and pieces from Singapore; Dutch guilders from Java; and the small silver and gold drops of Siam called tical.

She arrived finally at the harplike stool of the piano; but there she had to wait until the clock in the hall above struck some division of the hour for her guidance, and she rattled the brass rings that formed the handles of drawers on either side of the keyboard. Later, her fingers picking a precarious way through bass and treble, she heard Sidsall's voice at the door; the latter was joined by their mother, and they went out to the clatter of hoofs, the thin jingle of harness chains, where the barouche waited for them in the street. Once Camilla obtruded into the room. " I wonder you don't give yourself a headache," she remarked; " I never heard more nerve-racking sounds."

Laurel gathered that Camilla was proud of this expression, which she must have newly caught from some grown person. She considered a reply, but, nothing sufficiently crushing occurring, she ignored the other in a difficult transposition of her hands. Camilla left; the clock above struck a second quarter; the third, while she honestly continued her efforts up until the first actual note of the hour.

" Thank God that's over," she said in the liberal manner of a shipmaster. Now only the walk with her grandfather remained of the actively tiresome duties of the day. After dinner the sun blazed down with almost the heat of midsummer, and Laurel felt unexpectedly indifferent, content to linger in the house. Only too soon she heard inquiries for her; and in her gaiter boots, a silk bonnet with a blue scarf tied under her chin and flowing over a shoulder and palm leaf cashmere shawl, she accompanied the old man across Pleasant Street and over the wide green Square to the arched west gate with its gilt eagle and Essex Street.

"Will we be going on Central Street?" she asked.

"No reason for turning down there," he replied, forgetful of the gingerbread shop with the shaky little bell inside the door, the buttered gingerbread on the upper shelf for three cents and that without on the lower for two. She gathered her hopes now about Webb's Drugstore, where her grandfather sometimes stopped for a talk, and bought her rock candy, Gibraltars or blackjacks. It was too hot for blackjacks, she decided, and, with opportunity, would choose the cooling peppermint flavor of the Gibraltars.

The elms on Essex Street were far enough in leaf to cast a flickering shade in the faintly salt air drifting from the sea; and they progressed so slowly that Laurel was able to study the contents of most of the store windows they passed. Some held crewels and crimped white cakes of wax, gayly colored reticule beads with a wooden spoon for a penny measure, and "strawberry" emery balls. There was a West India store and a place where they sold oil and candles, another had charts for mariners; while across the way stood the East India Marine Hall.

Here her grandfather hesitated, and for a moment it seemed as if he would go over and join the masters always to be found about the Museum. But in the end he continued beyond the Essex House with its iron bow and lamp over the entrance, past Cheapside to Webb's Drugstore, where he purchased a bag of Peristaltic lozenges, and — after pretending to start away as if nothing more were to be secured there — the Gibraltars.

They were returning, in the general direction of Derby Wharf, when Jeremy Ammidon met a companion of past days at sea, and stopped for the inevitable conversational exchange. The latter, who had such a great spreading beard that Laurel couldn't determine whether or not he wore a neck scarf, said:

" Barzil Dunsack all but died."

" Ha! " the other exclaimed. Laurel wondered at the indelicacy in speaking about old Captain Dunsack to her grandfather, when everyone in Salem knew they had quarreled years ago and not spoken to each other since.

" He was bad off," he persisted; " a cold grappled in his chest and went into lung fever. Barzil's looking wasted, what with sickness and the trouble about Edward." At a nod, half encouraging, he added, " It appears Edward left Heard and Company in Canton and took ship back to Boston. He's there now for what I know. Never sent any word to Salem or his father. Looks a little as if he had been turned out of his berth. Then one of Barzil's schooners caught the edge of the last hurricane off the Great Bank and went ashore on Green Turtle Key. Used him near all up."

Laurel saw that her grandfather was frowning heavily

and silently moving his lips. The other left them standing and her companion brought his cane down sharply. " Boy and boy," he said. " Barzil was a good man . . . looking old. So am I, so am I. Feet almost useless. Laurel," he addressed her, " I want you to go right on home. I've got to stop around and see an old friend who has been sick." She left obediently, but paused once to gaze back incredulously at the bulky shape of her grandfather moving toward Barzil Dunsack's. That quarrel was part of their family history, she had been aware of it as long as she had of the solemn clock in the second hall; and not very far back, perhaps when she was eight, it had taken a fresh activity of discussion around the person of her Uncle Gerrit, who, it was feared, might now be drowned at sea. What it had all been about neither she nor her sisters knew, for not only was the subject dropped at the approach of any of them but they were forbidden to mention it.

At home she was unable to communicate her surprising news at once because of the flood of talk that met her from the drawing-room. Olive Wibird and Lacy, her cousin, were engaged with Sidsall in a conversation often a duet and sometimes a trio. Laurel took a seat at the edge of the chatter and followed it comprehensively. She didn't like Olive Wibird who would greet her in a sugary voice; but elsewhere Olive was tremendously admired, there were always men about her, serenades rising from the lawn beneath her window, and Laurel herself had seen Olive's dressing table laden with bouquets in frilly lace paper. She had one now, in a holder of mother-of-pearl, with a gilt chain and ring. Her wide skirt was a mass of overdrapery, knots of moss roses and green gauze ribbons; while a silver cord ending in a tassel fell forward among her curls.

Lacy Saltonstone, almost as plainly dressed as Sidsall, was as usual sitting straighter than anyone else Laurel ever saw; she had a brown face with a finely curved nose and brown eyes, and her voice was cool and decided.

" For me," she said, " he is the most fascinating person in Salem."

Olive Wibird made a swift face of dissent. " He's too stiff and there is gray in his hair. I like my men more like sparkling hock. Dancing with him he holds you as if you were glass."

" I don't seem to remember you and Mr. Brevard together," Lacy commented.

" He hasn't asked me for centuries," the other admitted. " He did Sidsall, though, as we all remember; didn't he, love? "

Sidsall's cheeks turned bright pink. Laurel dispassionately wished that her sister wouldn't make such a show of herself. It was too bad that Sidsall was so — so broad and well looking; she was not in the least pale or interesting, and had neither Lacy's Saltonstone's thin gracefulness nor Olive's popular manner.

" It was very noble of him," Sidsall agreed.

" But he was extremely engaged," Lacy assured her with her wide slow stare. " He told me that you were like apple blossoms."

That might please Sidsall, thought Laurel, but she personally held apple blossoms to be a very common sort of flower. Evidently something of the kind had occurred to Olive, too, for she said: "Heaven only knows what men will admire. It's clear they don't like a prude. I intend to have a good time until I get married —"

"But what if you love in vain?" Sidsall interrupted.

"There isn't any need for that," Olive told her. "When I see a man I want I'm going to get him. It's easy if you know how and make opportunities. I always have one garter a little loose."

"Laurel," her sister turned, "I'm certain your supper is ready. Go along like a nice child."

In her room a woman with a flat worn face and a dusty wisp of hair across her neck was spreading underlinen, ironed into beautiful narrow wisps of pleating, in a drawer. It was Hodie, a Methodist, the only one Laurel knew, and the latter was always entranced by the servant's religious exclamations, doubts and audible prayers. She was saying something now about pits, gauds and vanities; and she ended a short profession of faith with an amen so loud and sudden that Laurel, although she was waiting for it, jumped.

It was past seven, the air was so sweet with lilacs that they seemed to be blooming in her room, and the sunlight died slowly from still space. By leaning out of her window she could see over the Square. The lamplighter was moving along its wooden fence, leaving faint twinkling yellow lights, and there were little gleams from the windows on Bath Street beyond.

The gayety of her morning mood was replaced by a dim kind of wondering, her thoughts became uncertain like the objects in the quivering light outside. The palest possible star shone in the yellow sky; she had to look hard or it was lost. Janet, stirring in the next room, seemed so far away that she might not hear her, Laurel, no matter how loudly she called. " Janet! " she cried, prompted by unreasoning dread. " You needn't to yell," Janet complained, at the door. But already Laurel was oblivious of her: she had seen a familiar figure slowly crossing Washington Square — her grandfather coming home from Captain Dunsack's.

Gracious, how poky he was; she was glad that she wasn't dragging along at his side. He seemed bigger and rounder than usual. She heard the tap of his cane as he left the Common for Pleasant Street; then his feet moved and stopped, moved and stopped, up the steps of their house.

She was sorry now that she hadn't known what an outport was, and determined to ask him to-morrow. She liked his stories, that Camilla disdained, about crews and Hong Kong and the stormy Cape. The thought of Cape Horn brought back the memory of her Uncle Gerrit, absent in the ship *Nautilus*. Her mental pictures of him were not clear — he was almost always at sea — but she remembered his eyes, which were very confusing to encounter, and his hair parted and carelessly brushing the bottoms of his ears.

Laurel recalled hearing that Gerrit was his father's favorite, and she suddenly understood something of the unhappiness that weighed upon the old man. She hoped desperately that Janet or Camilla wouldn't come in and laugh at her for crying. In bed she saw that the room was rapidly filling with dusk. Only yesterday she would have told herself that the dragon in the teakwood chair

[32]

was stirring; but now Laurel could see that it never moved. She rocked like the little boats that crossed the harbor or came in from the ships anchored beyond the wharves, and settled into a sleep like a great placid sea flooding the world of her home and the lamplighter and her grandfather sorrowing for Uncle Gerrit.

II

WHEN Jeremy Ammidon sent his granddaughter home alone, and turned toward Captain Dunsack's, on Hardy Street, he stopped for a moment to approve the diminishing sturdy figure. All William's children, though they were girls, were remarkably handsome, with glowing red cheeks and clear eyes, tumbling masses of hair and a generous vigor of body. He sighed at Laurel's superabundant youth, and moved carefully forward; he was very heavy, and his progress was uncertain. His thoughts were divided between the present and the past — Barzil Dunsack, aged and ill and unfortunate, and the happening long ago that had resulted in a separation of years after a close youthful companionship.

It had occurred while Barzil was master of the brig *Luna*, owned by Billy Gray, and he, Jeremy, was first mate. In the exactness with which he recalled every detail of his life in ships he remembered that at the time they were off Bourbon Island, about a hundred and ten miles southwest of the Île de France. The *Luna* was close hauled, and, while Barzil was giving an order at the wheel, she fetched a bad lee lurch and sent him in a heap across the deck, striking his head against the bumkin bitts. He had got up dazed but not apparently seriously injured; and after his head had been swabbed and bound by the steward he returned to the poop. There, however, his

conduct had been so peculiar — among other things send-
ing down the watch to put on Sunday rig against a possible hail by the Lord — that, after a long consultation
with Mr. Patterson, the second mate and the boatswain,
and a brief announcement to the crew, he, Jeremy Ammidon, had taken command in their interest and that of the
owner.

Barzil had made difficulties: Mr. Patterson struck up
a leveled pistol in the master's hand just as it exploded. They had confined him, in charge of the unhappy steward, to his cabin; where, after he had completely recovered from the effects of the blow, and Jeremy
had been upheld by the authorities at Table Bay, he stub-
bornly remained until the *Luna* had been warped into
Salem.

From the moment of their landing they had not ex-
changed a word. Jeremy was surprised to find himself
at present bound toward the other's house. He was not
certain that Barzil would even see him; but, he muttered,
the thing had lasted long enough, they were too old for
such foolishness; and the other had come into adverse
winds, now, when he should be lying quietly in a snug
harbor.

He had never paid serious attention to the threatened
complication two or three years before, when Gerrit had
been seen repeatedly with Kate Dunsack's irregularly born
daughter. He was sorry for the two women. It was his
opinion that the man had been shipped drunk by some
boarding house runner; anyhow, only the second day out
Vollar had been lost overboard from the main-royal yard,
and Kate's child born outside the law. It was hard, he

told himself again, walking down Orange Street, past the Custom House to Derby.

The girl, Nettie Vollar — they had adopted the father's name — was attractive in a decided French way, with crisp black hair, a pert nose and dimple, and, why, good heavens, twenty-one or two years old if she was a week! How time did run. It was nothing extraordinary if Gerrit had been seen a time or two with her on the street, or even if he had called at the Dunsacks'. Barzil's and his quarrel didn't extend to all the members of their families; and as for the Dunsacks being common — that was nonsense. Barzil was as good as he any day; only where he had prospered, and moved up into a showy place on the Common, the other had had the head winds. Through no fault of his own the reputation had fastened on him of being unlucky in his cargoes: if he carried tea and colonial exports to, say, Antwerp, they would have been declared contraband while he was at sea, and seized on the docks; he had been blown, in an impenetrable fog, ashore on Tierra del Fuego, and, barely making Cape Pembroke, had been obliged to beach his ship, a total loss. Then there was Kate's trouble. Barzil was a rigorously moral and religious man and his pain at that last must have been heavy.

Jeremy Ammidon's mind turned to Gerrit, his son; this interest in Nettie Vollar, if it had existed, was characteristic of the boy, who had a quick heart and an honest disdain for the muddling narrow ways of the land. He would have sought her out simply from the instinct to protest against the smugness of Salem opinion. A fine sailor, and a master at twenty-two. A great one to carry sail;

yet in the sixteen years of his commands he had had no more serious accident than the loss of a fore-topgallant mast or splitting a couple of courses. It was Gerrit's ability, the splendid qualities of his ship, that made Jeremy hope he would still come sailing into the harbor with some narration of delay and danger overcome.

He was now on Derby Street, in a region of rigging and sail lofts, block and pump makers, ships' stores, spar yards, gilders, carvers and workers in metal. There was a strong smell of tar and new canvas and the flat odor that rose at low water. Sailors passed, yellow powerful Scandinavians and dark men with earrings from southern latitudes, in red or checked shirts, blue dungarees and glazed black hats with trailing ribbons, or in cheap and clumsy shore clothes. There was a scraping of fiddle from an upper window, the sound of heavy capering feet and the stale laughter of harborside women.

On Hardy Street he continued to the last house at the right, the farther side of which gave across a yard of uneven bricks, straggling bushes and aged splitting apple trees and an expanse of lush grass ending abruptly in a wooden embankment and the water. A short fence turned in from the sidewalk to the front door, where Jeremy knocked. A long pause followed, in which he became first impatient and then irritable; and he was lifting his hand for a second summons when the door suddenly opened and he was facing Kate Vollar. There was only a faint trace of surprise on her apathetic — Jeremy Ammidon called it moon-like — countenance; as if her overwhelming mischance had robbed her features of all further expressions of interest or concern.

[37]

"I heard," Jeremy said in a voice pitched loud enough to conceal any inward uncertainty, "that your father had been sick. Met Captain Rendell on Essex Street and he said Barzil had lung fever. Thought I'd see if there was any truth in it."

"He just managed to stay alive," Kate Vollar replied, gazing at him with her stilled gray eyes. "But he's better now, though he's not up and about yet. Shall I tell him that — that you are here?"

"Yes. Just say Jeremy Ammidon's below, and would like to pass a greeting with him."

He followed the woman in, and entered a large gloomy chamber while she mounted the stair leading directly from the front. The blackened fireplace gaping uncovered for the summer, the woodwork, painted yellow with an artificial graining, and a stiff set of ebonized chairs, their dingy crimson plush backs protected by elaborate thread antimacassars, seemed to hold and reflect the misfortunes of their owner. Jeremy picked up an ostrich egg, painted with a clump of viciously green coconut palms and a cottony surf; he put it down with an absent smile and impatiently fingered a volume of "The Life of Harriet Atwood Newell." She was one of the missionaries who had gone out on the *Caravan*, with Augustine Heard, to India, but forbidden to land there had died not long after on the Île de France.

"Houqua was a damned good heathen," he said aloud; "and so was Nasservanjee." He left the table and proceeded to a window opening upon the harbor, here fretted with wharves. A barque was fast in a small stone-bound dock, newly in, his practiced glance saw, from a blue

[38]

water voyage, Africa probably. Her standing gear was in a perfection and beauty of order that spoke of long tranquil days in the trades, and that no mere harbor riggers could hope to accomplish. The deck was burdened with the ugly confusion of unloading. Jeremy studied the jibs stowed in harbor covers, the raking masts and tapering royal poles over the stolid roofs. Ordinarily seeing no more he could not only name a vessel trading out of Salem, but from her rig recognize anyone of a score of masters who, otherwise unheralded, might be in command.

However, here he was at a loss, and he thought again of the change, the decline, that had overtaken Salem shipping, the celebrated merchants; the pennants of William Gray, he reflected, had flown from the main truck of fifteen ships, seven barques, thirteen brigs and schooners. Ammidon, Ammidon and Saltonstone, in spite of his vehement protests, the counsel of the oldest member of the firm, were moving shipment by shipment all their business to Boston, listening to the promptings of State Street and Central Wharf.

To the right was the sagging landing from which Barzil's schooners sailed trading with the West Indies; and back of it, and of his house, stood the small office. His mind had turned to this inconsiderable commerce when Kate Vollar entered and told him that her father would see him.

Barzil Dunsack was propped up in bed in a room above that in which Jeremy had been waiting. He, totally different from the other, showed his age in sunken dry cheeks, a forehead like an arch of bone, and a thick short gray beard. A long faded lock of hair had been

[39]

hastily brushed forward and an incongruously bright knitted scarf drawn about his shoulders.

Jeremy Ammidon concealed his dismay not only at Barzil's wrecked being but at the dismal aspect of the interior, the worn rugs with their pieces of once bright material frayed and loose, the splitting veneer of an old chest of drawers and blistered mirror above a dusty iron grate. " You have got in among the rocks! " he exclaimed. " Still they tell me you've weathered the worst. Copper bound and oak ribs. Don't build them like that to-day."

Barzil Dunsack's eyes were bright and searching behind steel-rimmed spectacles, and he studied Jeremy without replying. " Well, isn't there a salute in you? " the latter demanded, incensed. " I'm not a Malay proa."

The grim shadow of a smile dawned on Barzil's countenance. " I mind one hanging on our quarter by Formosa," he returned; " I trained a cannon aft and fired a shot, when she sheered off. That was in the *Flora* in 'ninety-seven."

A long silence enveloped them. Jeremy's mind was thronged with memories of ports and storms, mates and ships and logged days. " Remember Oahu like it was when we first made it," he queried, " and the Kanaka girls swimming out to the ship with hybiscus flowers in their hair? Yes, and the anchorage at Tahiti with the swells pounding on the coral reef and Papeete under the mountain? It was nice there in the afternoon, lying off the beach with the white cottages among the palms and orange trees and the band playing in the grove by Government House."

[40]

Captain Dunsack frowned at the trivial character of these memories. He muttered something about the weight of the Lord, and the carnal hearts of the men in ships. Jeremy declared, " Stuff! He'll wink at a sailor man with hardly a free day on shore. It wasn't bad at Cal cutta, either, with an awning on the quarter-deck, watching the carriages and syces in the Maidan and maybe a corpse or two floating about the gangway from the burning ghauts."

" A mean entrance," Barzil Dunsack asserted. " I don't know a worse with the southwest monsoon in the Bay of Bengal and the pilot brigs gone from the Sand Heads. That's where Heard got pounded with the *Emerald* drawing nineteen feet, and eighteen on the bar. Shook the reefs out of his topsails, laid her on her beam ends, and with some inches saved scraped in."

" Pick up the three Juggernaut Pagodas of Ganjam," Jeremy remarked absently.

" ' Thou shalt have no other God —' "

Jeremy, with a glint in his eye, asked, " Wasn't your last consignment of West India molasses marked Medford? "

" You always were a scoffer," the other replied, unmoved.

" How's Nettie? " Jeremy Ammidon inquired with a deliberate show of interest.

Barzil's lips tightened. " I haven't seen her for a little," he replied. " She's been visiting at Ipswich." Jeremy added, " A good girl," but the man in bed made no further comment. His undimmed gaze was fastened upon a wall, his mouth folded in a hard line on a harsh and deeply seamed countenance. An able man pursued by bad luck.

"Nothing's been heard from Gerrit," Jeremy said after a little. Still the other kept silent. His face darkened: by God, if Barzil hadn't a decent word for the fact that Gerrit was seven months overdue, perhaps lost, this was not a house for him. "I say that we've had nothing from my son since he lay in the Lye-ee-Moon Pass off Hong Kong," he repeated sharply.

A spasm of suffering, instantly controlled, passed over Barzil's face. "Gerrit called once and again before he last sailed for Montevideo," he finally pronounced. "I stopped it and he left in a temper. I — I won't have another mortal sin here like Kate's."

"Do you mean that Gerrit's loose?" Jeremy hotly demanded, rising. "A more honorable boy never breathed." Barzil was cold. "I told him not to come back," he repeated; "it would only lead to — to shamefulness." Jeremy shook his cane toward the bed. "I may be a scoffer," he cried, "but I wouldn't hold a judgment over a child of mine! I'm not so damned holy that I can look down on a misfortunate girl. If Gerrit did come to see Nettie and the boy had a liking for her, why you drove away a cursed good husband. And if you think for a minute I wouldn't welcome her because that Vollar fell off a yard before he could find a preacher you're an old fool!"

"Nettie must bear her burden: far better be dead than a stumbling block."

"Well, I'd rather be a drunken pierhead jumper on the Waterloo Road than any such pious blue nose. I'll tell you this, too — I'd hate to ship afore the mast under you for all you'd have the ensign on the booby hatch with prayers read Sunday morning. I don't wonder you got into weather; I'd have no word for a Creator who didn't blow in your eye."

" I'll listen to no blasphemy, Captain Ammidon," Barzil Dunsack said sternly.

" And I'll speak my mind, Captain Dunsack; it's this — your girls are a long sight too good for you or for any other judgmatical, psalm-singing devil dodger." He stood fuming at the door. " Good afternoon to you."

Barzil Dunsack reclined with his gaunt bearded head sunk forward on his thin chest swathed in the gay worsted wrap, his wasted hands, the tendons corded with pale violet veins, clenched outside the checkered quilt beneath which his body made scarcely a mark.

Outside, in the soft glow of beginning dusk, Jeremy blamed himself bitterly for his anger at the sick man. He had gone to see him in a spirit friendly with old memories, forgetful of their long quarrel in the stirred emotions of the past days of youth and first manhood; and he had shouted at Barzil as if he were a lubber at the masthead.

He realized that in order to be in time for supper he must turn toward the Common and home; but his gaze caught the spars of the strange barque; and, mechanically, he made his way over a narrow grassy passage to the wharf. She was the *Cora Sellers* of Marblehead, and he recognized from a glance at the cargo that she had been out to the East Coast of Africa — Mozambique and Zanzibar, Aden and Muscat. A matted frail of dates swung ponderously in air, there were baled goatskins and sacks of

Mocha coffee, sagging baskets of reddish unwashed gum copal carried in bulk, and a sun-blackened mate smoking a rat-tail Dutch cigar was supervising the moving of elephant tusks in a milky glimmer of ivory ashore.

There was a vague murmur of the rising tide, beyond the wharves and warehouses the water was faintly rippled in silver and rose, and a ship was standing into the harbor with all her canvas spread to the light wind. He turned away with a sigh and walked slowly up toward the elms of Pleasant Street. At his front door he stopped to regard the polished brass plate where in place of his name he had caused to be engraved the words Java Head. They held for him, coming into this pleasant dwelling after so many tumultuous years at sea, the symbol of the safe and happy end of an arduous voyage; just as the high black rock of Java Head thrusting up over the horizon promised the placidity and accomplishment of the Sunda Strait. Whenever he noticed the plate he felt again the relief of coasting that northerly shore:

He saw the mate forward with the crew passing the chains through the hawse pipes and shackling them to the anchors. The island rose from level groves of shore palms to lofty blue peaks terraced with rice and red-massed kina plantations, with shining streams and green kananga flowers and tamarinds. The land breeze, fragrant with clove buds and cinnamon, came off to the ship in the vaporous dusk; and, in the blazing sunlight of morning, the Anjer sampans swarmed out with a shrill chatter of brilliant birds, monkeys and naked brown humanity, piled with dark green oranges and limes and purple mangosteen.

JAVA HEAD

In the last few years, particularly with Gerrit away, he had turned more and more from the surroundings of his house — rather it had become William's house — to an inner life of memories. His own active life seemed to him to have been infinitely fuller, more purposeful and various, than that of present existence at Java Head. All Salem had been different: he had a certain contempt for the existence of his son William and the latter's associates and friends. He had said that the trading now done in ships was like dealing at a Boston store, and the merchants reminded him of storekeepers. The old days, when a voyage was a public affair, and a ship's manifest posted in the Custom House on which anyone might write himself down for a varying part of the responsibility and profit, had given place to closed capital; the passages from port to port with the captain, as often as not, his own supercargo and a figure of importance, had become scheduled affairs in which a master was subjected to any countinghouse clerk with an order from the firm: the ships themselves were fast being ruined.

He was in his room, after supper, seated momentarily on a day bed with a covering of white Siberian fox skins, and he pronounced aloud, in a tone of satirical contempt, the single word, " Clipper." Nearly everyone in the shipping business seemed to have been touched by this madness for the ridiculous ideas of an experimental Griffiths and his model of a ship with the bows turned inside out, the greatest beam aft and a dead rise like an inverted roof. That the *Rainbow,* the initial result of this insanity, hadn't capsized at her launching had been due to some freak of chance; just as her miraculous preservation

[45]

through a voyage or so to China could have been made possible only by continuously mild weather.

Even if the *Rainbow* had been fast — her run was called ninety-two days out to Canton and home in eighty-eight — it was absurd to suppose that there had been the usual monsoon. And if she did come in a little ahead of vessels built on a solid full-bodied model, why her hold had no cargo capacity worth the name.

Things on the seas were going to the devil! He moved down to the library, where he lighted a cheroot and addressed himself to the *Gazette;* but his restlessness increased: the paper drooped and his thoughts turned to Gerrit as a small boy. He saw him leaving home, for the first time, to go to the school at Andover, in a cloth cap with a glazed peak, striped long pantaloons and blue coat and waistcoat; later at the high desk in the counting-rooms of Ammidon, Ammidon and Saltonstone; then sailing as supercargo on one of the Company's ships to Russia and Liverpool. He had soon dropped such clerking for seamen's duties, and his rise to mastership had been rapid.

Rhoda, William's wife, entered and stood before him accusingly. "You are worrying again," she declared; "in here all by yourself. It really seems as if you didn't believe in our interest or affection. I have a feeling, and you know they are always right, that Gerrit will sail into the harbor any day now."

He had always liked Rhoda, a large handsome woman with rich coloring — her countenance somehow reminded him of an apricot — and fine clothes. She paused, studied him for a moment, and then asked, " Was your call on Captain Dunsack pleasant? "

" It ought to have been," he confided, " but I got mad and talked like a Dutch uncle, and Barzil went off on a holy tack."

" About Nettie Vollar? "

Jeremy nodded. "Look here, Rhoda," he demanded, " did Gerrit ever say anything to you about her? "

" Yes," she told him; " Gerrit was very frank."

" Did he like the girl? "

" I couldn't make that out. But if there hadn't been, well — something unusual in her circumstances I think he would never have noticed her. Gerrit is a curious mixture, a very impressionable heart and a contrary stubborn will. He was sorry for Nettie, and, at the way a great many people treated her, threw himself into opposition. Nettie's father made him very mad, and Gerrit pretty well damned all Salem before he left in the *Nautilus*. He was excruciatingly funny: you know Gerrit can be, particularly when he imitates anybody. I think being away at sea a great deal, and having absolute command of everything, give men a different view of things from ours. What is terribly important to Salem hardly touches Gerrit; it's all silly pretense, or worse, to him.

" I wouldn't mind that if it weren't for the sense of humor that leads him into the wildest extravagances, and the fact that he'll act on his feelings. You know I'm devoted to him but I give a sigh of relief whenever he gets away on his ship without doing anyone of the hundred insanities he threatens."

[47]

"Gerrit's like me," he said.

"More than William," she agreed. "William is never impetuous, and he's often impatient with his brother. He's a splendid husband, but Gerrit would make a wonderful lover. I'm thankful I never fell into his affections . . . too wearing for an indolent woman."

"You've been a great comfort and pleasure, Rhoda," he told her. "I only wish Gerrit could marry someone like you —"

"But who would give him sons," she interrupted.

"It's just as you say about him, and I've always been uneasy. God knows what he won't do — on land. William's a great deal happier, for all his brother's humor. I joke William, but he's very satisfactory and solid. He'll make port if he doesn't get tied up with newfangled notions. Why, it stands to reason that a ship built like a knife would double up in the seas off the Falklands."

"He has a lot of confidence in Mr. McKay."

"McKay is a good man unsettled. The *May Broughton* is a fine barque, and his packet ships are as seaworthy as any, but —" his indignation increased so that he sputtered, and Rhoda laughed. "Now your girls," he added, "fine models, all of them, plenty of beam, work in any kind of weather."

"That's very complimentary," she assured him, rising. "You mustn't worry about Gerrit. Remember, my predictions never fail."

When she had gone his mind returned to storms he had safely weathered — the gray gales of Cape Horn, black hurricanes and the explosive tempests in eastern straits and seas. He took from the drawer of a bookcase with

[48]

glass doors set in geometrical pattern a thin volume bound in black boards. A paper label was inscribed in a small, carefully formed script, " Journal of my intended voyage from Salem to the East Indies in the Ship *Woodbine*." He opened at random:

" Comes in with strong wind from SSE with rain squalls. Very ugly sea on. Double reefed the Topsails, reefed the courses and furled the mainsail. At six p.m. shipped a very heavy sea that carried away the bulwarks on the larboard quarter and stove those on the starboard quarter and amidships . . . upper cabin filled with water. Through the night strong gales. . . . Lightning at all points of the compass."

The memory of this night, six days out from Manilla to Hong Kong, was clearer than the actuality of the room in which he sat, an old man with his activity, his strength, his manhood, far behind him, a hulk.

" At ten split the mainsail in pieces. Close reefed the fore and double reefed the main-topsails. Rising gales and heavy head sea. Shipping a great quantity of water and leaking considerable. Bent a new mainsail and set it. Reefed and set the jib. Pumping near two thousand strokes an hour.

" October seventh, Sunday. Comes in with strong gales and a heavy head sea. Both officers crippled and man laid up. Through the night the same. Leaking badly. A great number of junks in sight . . . and so at five p.m. come to anchor."

He had been a good man then, sixteen days on the quarter-deck without going below; insensible to ice or fever or weariness. He had been autocratic, too; and had his boy servant carrying areca nuts, chunam and tobacco in two silk bags, another with a fan and a third holding an umbrella. Such things were all over now, he understood, in this driving age.

His mind continually returned to Gerrit, to dwell on the vast number of perils held in store by the sea; there was always the possibility of scurvy, an entire crew rotting alive in the forecastle and the ship broached to, dismasted; of mutiny; the sheer smothering finality of volcanic waves. He had never realized until now, in the misery of uncertainty, the hellish loneliness of a shipmaster at sea; the pride of duty, the necessity of discipline, that put him beyond all counsel, all assistance and human interdependence. Jeremy, who had arrogantly accepted this responsibility without a question, through so many long years and voyages, now dreaded it, found it an inhuman burden, for his son.

William couldn't be expected to appreciate the difficulties of his brother's position: all the former's experience had been got when, with James Saltonstone and a party of Salem merchants, he ventured to the lighthouse at the entrance of the harbor, had a cold collation, and returned with the pilot or in the Custom House sloop. These occasions of huzzas and salutes and speeches were supplemented with a hasty inspection, now and then, of a vessel lying still at the wharf with sails harbor furled. William guessed little of the long effort through which a ship won from the first of those moments to the last. He was solely concerned with the returns of the cargo.

However, Rhoda was right, and this mooning wouldn't bring Gerrit into port. He turned to the bookcase, where a squat bottle of Medford rum rested beside a tumbler; after a drink he lighted a cheroot and smoking vigorously, with hands clasped behind him, paced back and forth in an undeviating line between the door to the hall and a dark polished secretary he had bought in London.

While he was walking Camilla came into the room and sedately took a seat on one of the formal chairs against the wall. " I guess you think that's the deck of a ship," she said conversationally. He regarded her with a faint threatening glint of humor. Camilla's dignity was stupendous; particularly now, when, he observed, her skirts stood out in a thoroughly grown manner. He liked Laurel best of William's children; she had, in spite of her confusion in regard to outports, a surprising grasp upon many of the details of life on shipboard, and a largeness of manner and expression entertaining in a little girl. Sidsall was the most ingratiating — she had Gerrit's direct kindling gaze; Janet showed no individuality yet beyond an entire willingness to conform to outward circumstance while pursuing deeply secret speculations within. But Camilla impressed the entire family by the rigidity of her correctness in personal and social niceties. At times, he felt, she would be a nuisance but for the firm hand of her mother and his own contribution to their well-being by an occasional sly sally.

" It might be that," he admitted; " if it weren't for the facts that it's a house and library, and I'm an old man, and you're not at all like the second mate."

" I should hope not," she replied decidedly. " A second mate isn't anything, and I am a — a young lady anyhow."

" You'll soon be out at dances."

" I go to parties now; that is, mother let me stay at the Coggswells' on Thursday until the men came at nine for sangaree. And I'm at all the Ballad Soirées."

He made a gesture of pretended surprise and admiration. " I don't suppose they ever have a good chantey with the stuff they play? " he queried. " Dear me, no. Mr. Dempster sings The Indian's Lament, and The May Queen: that's a cantata and it's in three parts."

Jeremy began to hum, and in a moment was intoning in a loud monotonous voice, sweeping a hand up and down:

> " To my hero, Bangedero,
>   Singing hey for a gay Hash girl."

" I don't think that's very nice," she said primly.

" What do you mean — not very nice? " he demanded, incensed. " There's nothing finer with a rousing chanteyman leading it and the watch hauling on the braces. You'd never hear the like at any Ballad Soirée. And:

> " Sweet William, he married a wife,
>   ' Gentle Jenny,' cried Rose Marie,
>   To be the sweet comfort of his life,
>   As the dew flies over the mulberry tree."

" There isn't much sense to it," she observed.

For a little, indignant at her disparagement of such noble fragments, he tramped silently back and forth, followed by a cloud of smoke from the cheroot. No one on land could understand the absorbing significance of every detail of a ship's life. . . . Only Gerrit, of all his family, knew the chanteys and watches, the anxiety and beauty of landfalls — the blue Falklands or Teneriffe rising above the clouds, the hurried making and taking of sail in the squalls of the Doldrums.

"In India," he told her, stopping in his measured course, "female children are given to the crocodiles."

Her mouth parted at this, her eyes became dilated, and she slipped from the chair. "That's perfectly awfully appalling," she breathed. "The little brown girl babies. Oh, father," she cried, as William Ammidon came into the library, "what do you suppose grandfather says, that in India female children are . . . crocodiles." Words failed her.

"What's the sense in frightening the child, father?" William remonstrated. "I wish you would keep those horrors for the old heathen of the Marine Society."

Jeremy had a lively sense of guilt; he had been betrayed by Camilla's confounded airs and pretensions. He ought to be ashamed of himself, telling the girl such things. "The British Government is putting a stop to that," he added hastily, "and to suttees —"

"What are they?" she inquired.

"Never mind, Camilla," her father interposed; "go up with your mother and sisters.

"I suppose it's no good speaking to you," William continued; "but my family is not a crew and this house isn't the *Two Capes*. You might make some effort to realize you're on land."

"I know I'm on land, William; tell that any day from a sight of you. You can afford to listen a little now and then about the sea. That's where all you have came from; it's the same with near everybody in Salem. Vessels brought them and vessels kept them going; and, with the wharves as empty as they were this afternoon, soon there won't be any Salem to talk about."

" The tide's turned from here," the other replied; " with the increase in tonnage and the importance of time we need the railway and docking facility of the larger cities — Boston and New York."

" It's running out fast enough," Jeremy agreed; " and there's a lot going out with it you'll never see again — like the men who put a reef in England in 'twelve."

" You are always sounding the same strings; we're at peace with the world now, and a good thing for shipping."

" Peace! " the elder declared hotly; " you and the Democrats may call it that, but it's a damned swindle, with the British to windward of you and hardly a sail now drawing in your ropes. What did Edmund Burke tell Parliament in 'seventy-five about our whalers, hey! Why, that from Davis Strait to the Antipodes, from the Falklands to Africa, we outdrove Holland, France and England. After the laws and bounties Congress passed in 'eighty-nine what could you see — something like a half million tonnage gained in three years or so. In the war of 'twelve your land soldiers were a pretty show, with the Capitol burning; but when it was finished the privateers had sunk over nine million dollars of British shipping to their sixty thousand. The Chesapeake luggers have gone out with the tide, too. And then, by God, by God, what then: the treaty of Ghent, with England impressing our seamen and tying our ships up in what ports she chose under a right of search! On top of this your commissioners repeal the ship laws and the British allow you to carry only native cargoes to the United Kingdom with a part of the customs and harbor dues off.

"But in spite of Congress and political sharks we went out to India and China direct, with *The George* home from Calcutta in ninety-five days, and the East Indiamen six or seven months on the shorter run to England. I can show you what the London *Times* said about that, it's in my desk: 'Twelve years of peace, and . . . the shipping interest . . . is half ruined . . . thousands of our manufactures are seeking redemption in foreign lands.' It goes on to tell that American seamen already controlled an important part of the British carrying trade to the East Indies. Yet your precious lawmakers open our West India trade to Great Britain, but they wouldn't ask the privilege to carry a cargo from British India to Liverpool or Canada."

"Now, father," William put in, "you are getting excited again. It isn't good for you. We are not all such fools to-day as you make out."

"Look at the masters themselves," Jeremy continued explosively; "gentlemen like Gerrit, from Harvard University, and not lime-juicers beating their way aft with a belaying pin. They could sail a ship with two-thirds the crew of a Britisher with her clumsy yellow hemp sails and belly you could lose a dinghy in. Mind, I don't say the English aren't handy in a ship and that they wouldn't clew up a topsail clean at the edge of hell. What we are on the seas came over from them. But we bettered it, William, and they knew it; and, naturally enough, laid out to sail around us. I don't blame England, but I do our God damn —"

" Father," the other firmly interrupted, " you are shouting as if you were on the quarter-deck in a gale. I must insist on your quieting down; you'll burst a blood vessel."

" Maybe I am," Jeremy muttered; " and it wouldn't matter much if I did. When I see a nation with shipmasters who would set their royals when others hove too, and get there, all snarled up with shore lines and political duffel, I'm nigh ready to burst something."

" Rhoda said that you were at the Dunsacks' this afternoon; I saw Edward in Boston yesterday."

" I don't care if you saw the Flying Dutchman," the other asserted, breathing stormily.

" It's curious about the China service," William went on; " anyone out there for a number of years gets to look Chinese. Edward is as yellow as a lemon, but nothing like as pleasant a color. Thin, too, and nervous; hands crawling all over themselves, never still for a moment. He didn't say why he had left Heard and Company, and I didn't quite like to ask. Edward came on from England in the *Queen of the West,* the Swallow Tail Line. I did ask him if he were going to settle in Salem, but he couldn't say; there was something about a Boston house. It seems that Gerrit carried his chest and things from Canton in the *Nautilus* as an accommodation."

Suddenly Jeremy felt very insecure, his body heavy and knees weak, failing. He stumbled back into the chair by the fireplace, William at his side. " You must pay some attention to what you're told, father," the latter said anxiously. " How are you now? "

" I'm all right," he declared testily, trying to brush away the dimness floating before his eyes.

[56]

" Shall I help you up to bed? "

" I'll go to bed when I've a mind to," Jeremy retorted. " I am not under cover yet by a long reach." To establish his well-being he rose and moved to the secretary, where he got a fresh cheroot, and lighted it with slightly trembling fingers. He grumbled inarticulately, remembering his own exploits in the carrying of sail and record runs under the bluff bows of the Honorable John Company itself. The ebb tide, he thought, returning to William's figure and its amplification by himself. So much that had been good sweeping out to sea never to return. . . . Gerrit long overdue.

Once more he shook himself free of numbing dread; automatically he had fallen back into the passage from the secretary to the hall door. He saw that he had worn threadbare a narrow strip where his feet had so often pressed. It would be necessary for him to see about a fresh case of cheroots soon, primes, too; they needn't try to put him off with the second quality. He was put off a great deal lately; people pretended to be listening to him, and all the time their thoughts were somewhere else, either that or they were merely politely concealing the opinion that he was out of date, of no importance.

His family were always providing against his fatigue or excitement; at the countinghouse the gravest problems, he was certain, were withheld from him. At the occurrence of this possibility a fresh indignation poured through his brain. Fuming and tramping up and down he determined that to-morrow he would show any of the clerks who didn't attend to his wishes or counsel that he was still senior partner of Ammidon, Ammidon and Saltonstone.

III

THE evening was surprisingly warm and still, with an intermittent falling of rain, and the windows were open in the room where Rhoda Ammidon sat regarding half dismayed her reflection in the mirror of a dressing table. A few minutes before she had discovered her first gray hair. It was not only the mere assault upon her vanity, but, too, a realization far deeper — here was the stamp of time, the mark of a considerable progress toward the end itself. Her emotions were various; but, curiously enough, almost the first had been a wave of passionate tenderness for William and her little girls. The shock of finding that arresting sign was now giving place to a purely feminine reaction. She considered for a moment the purchase of a bottle of hair coloring, then with a disdainful gesture dismissed such a temporary and troublesome measure.

She kept an undiminishing pride in her appearance and a relentless care and choice in the details of her dress, pleased by the knowledge that the attention men paid her showed no indication yet of growing perfunctory. She had been much admired both in Boston and London through her youth, and she recalled her early doubts at the prospect of life in Salem; but she realized now that, as her years and children multiplied, she was by imper-

[58]

ceptible degrees returning to a traditional New England heritage.

She was glad, however, that William's wide connections lifted him above a purely local view; William was really a splendid husband. Rhoda was conscious of this together with a clear recognition of his faults, and quite aside from both existed her unreasoning affection. The latter vividly dominated her, shut out, on any occasion of stress, all else; but for the most part she held him in an attitude of mildly amused comprehension.

Gerrit Ammidon she hadn't seen until after her engagement to William, and she sometimes thought of the former in connection with marriage. Gerrit, she admitted to herself, was a far more romantic figure than William; not handsomer — William Ammidon was very good looking — but more arresting, with his hair swinging about his ears and intense blue gaze. An exciting man, she decided again, for whom one would eternally put on the loveliest clothes possible; a man to make you almost as ravishingly happy as miserable, and, therefore, disturbing as a husband.

At this her mind returned to her gray hair and the fact that the metal backlog of the kitchen fire, which supplied the house with hot water, had been leaking over the hearth. A feeling of melancholy possessed her at the turning of younger visions into commonplace necessities, but she dismissed it with the shadow of a smile — it was absurd for a woman of her age to dwell on such frivolous things. Yet she still lingered to wonder if men too kept intact among their memories the radiant image of their youth, if they ever thought of it with tenderness and extenuation.

She decided in the negative, convinced that men, even at the end of many years, never definitely lost connection with their early selves, there was always a trace of hopefulness, of jaunty vanity — sometimes winning and sometimes merely ridiculous — attached to their decline.

Rhoda stirred and moved to a window, gazing vaguely out into the moist blue obscurity. Sidsall, she realized, was maturing with a disconcerting rapidity. Depths were opening in the girl's being at which she, her mother, could only guess. It was exactly as if a crystal through and through which she had gazed had suddenly been veiled by rosy clouds. Sidsall had a charming nature, direct and unsuspicious and generously courageous.

There was a sound at the door, and William entered, patently ruffled. It was clear that he had had another disagreement with his father. " It's shameful how you disturb him," she declared.

" Look here, Rhoda," he replied vigorously. " I won't continually be put in the wrong. It seems as if I had no affection for the old gentleman. I always have the difficult thing to do, and he has been slightly contemptuous ever since I was a boy because I didn't go to sea. The truth is — while I wouldn't think of letting him know — he's a tremendous nuisance pottering about the counting-rooms with his stories of antediluvian trading voyages. And worse is to come — these new clipper ships and passages have knocked the wind out of the old slow full-bottomed vessels. We have about determined to reorganize our fleet entirely, and are in treaty with Donald McKay for an extreme clipper type of twelve hundred tons.

" Of course, he's my parent; but I wonder at Saltonstone's patience. Father won't hear of the opium trade and it's turning over thousand per cent profits. We are privately operating two fast topsail schooners in India now, but it's both inconvenient and a risk. They ought to be put right under our house flag for credit alone. It is all bound to come up, and then he'll go off like a cannon."

" Couldn't you wait till he's dead, William? " she asked. " It won't be a great while now. I can see that he has failed dreadfully from this worry about Gerrit."

" Five years will make all the difference. We are losing tea cargoes every month to these ships making sensational runs. I don't talk much, Rhoda, about, well — my family; but I am as upset over Gerrit as anyone else. Except for a tendency to carry too much sail there's not a better shipmaster out of New England. Not only that . . . he's my brother. It's easy to like Gerrit; his opinions are a little wild, and an exaggerated sense of justice gets him into absurd situations; yet his motives are the purest possible. Perhaps that word pure describes him better than any other, however people who didn't know might smile. As a man, Rhoda, I can assert that he is surprisingly clean-hearted."

" That's a wonderful quality," she agreed; " why anyone should smile is beyond me. William, would you know that my hair is turning gray, do I look a lot older than I did five years ago? "

He studied her complacently. " You've hardly changed since I married you," he asserted; " a great deal prettier than these young cramped figgers I see about. The girls, too, are just like you — good armfuls all of them."

The next day was flawlessly sunny, the slightly stir-

[61]

ring air reminiscent of the sea, and the lilacs everywhere were masses of purple and white bloom. Stepping down from her carriage on the morning round of shopping Rhoda encountered Nettie Vollar leaving one of the stores of Cheapside.

"Why, Nettie," she exclaimed kindly, " it's been the longest time since I've seen you. It is just no use asking you to the house, and it seems, with nothing to do, I never have a minute for the visits I'd like to make." Nettie, she thought, was a striking girl, no — woman, with her stack of black hair, dark sparkling eyes and red spot on either cheek. More fetching in profile than full face, her nose had a pert angle and her cleft chin was enticingly rounded. Later she would be too fat but now her body was ripely perfect.

" I don't go anywhere much," she responded, in a voice faintly and instinctively antagonistic. " I don't like kindness in people; but I suppose I ought to be contented — that's all I'll probably ever get from anybody who is a thing in the world. Mrs. Ammidon," she hesitated, then continued more rapidly, her gaze lowered, " have you had any word about Captain Ammidon yet? Have they given up hope of the *Nautilus?* "

" We've had no news," Rhoda told her, and then she added her conviction that Gerrit would return safely.

" He was better than kind," Nettie Vollar said. " I'm sure he liked me, Mrs. Ammidon, or he would have if everything hadn't been spoiled by grandfather. He thinks I'm a dreadful sin, you know, a punishment on mother. But inside of me I don't feel different from others. Sometimes I — I wonder that I don't actually go sinful, I've

[62]

had opportunities, and being good hasn't offered me much, has it?"

"You are naturally a good girl, Nettie," Rhoda answered simply; "but you must be braver than ordinary. If we think differently from Salem still it is in Salem we must live; I keep many of my beliefs secret just as you must control most of your feelings."

The other responded with a hard little laugh. "Thank you, though. You are more like Gerrit, Captain Ammidon, than Mrs. Saltonstone, his own sister. I hate her," she declared. "I hate all the Salem women, so superior and condescending and Christian. They always have a silly look of wonder at their charity in speaking to me . . . when they do. They act as if it's just a privilege for me to be in their church. I'd rather go to a cotillion at Hamilton Hall any day."

"Of course you would," Rhoda agreed. There seemed to be so little for her to offer or say that she was relieved when they parted. The afternoon grew really sultry, but, when the shadows had lengthened, she encountered Jeremy Ammidon wandering aimlessly about the hall and, his fine palmetto hat and wanghee in her hand, urged him out to the East India Marine Society. "It's much too beautiful a day for the house," she insisted.

"There's nothing remarkable about it," he returned; "wind's too light and variable, hardly enough to hold way on a ship." There were the stirring strains of a quickstep without; at the door they saw the Salem Cadets, preceded by Flag's Band, marching in columns of fours into Washington Square. The white breeches with scarlet coats and brass buttons made a gay showing on the green

Common, the sunlight glittered on silver braid and tassels, gilt and pompons, scaled chin straps and varnished leather.

The old man's face grew dark at the brilliant line drawn up for inspection, and he muttered a period about cursed young Whigs. "Wouldn't have one of the scoundrels in my house if I could help it. Don't understand William; he's too damned mild for my idea of a good citizen.

"Why, it's only reasonable that a country's got to be run like a ship, from the quarter-deck. How far do you suppose a vessel would get if the crew hung about aft and chose representatives from the port and starboard watches and galley for a body to lay the course and make sail?"

"Please, father," she protested, laughing. "Do go along into the sun." She gently pushed him toward the door. Rhoda realized the fact that William was more than half Whig already. That threatened still another point of difference, of departure, from all that his father held to be sacred necessities. Jeremy, like most of the older shipmasters, was a bitter Federalist, an upholder of a strongly centralized autocratic government. He left, grumbling, and the staccato commands of the military evolutions on the Common rang through the slumberous afternoon.

She lingered in the doorway and Laurel appeared, jigging with excitement.

"Can't I get nearer," she begged; "there's nothing to see from here." Her mother replied, "Ask Camilla to take you over to the Square." Camilla appeared indifferently. "I don't know why anyone should be flustered,"

[64]

she observed; " it isn't like the Fourth of July with a concert and fireworks."

As they were going, Sidsall came out in a white tarlatan dress worked with sprays of yellow barley, her face glowing with color, and sat on the steps. " Positively," her mother said, looking down on the mass of bright chestnut hair in a chenille net, " we'll soon have to have you up in braids."

" I wish I might," she responded. " And Hodie is too silly — I can't get her to lace me tightly enough. She says such things are engines of the devil."

" It's still a little soon for that —" Rhoda broke off as a slight erect man at the verge of middle age turned in from Pleasant Street upon them. " Roger," she said cordially as he came quickly up the steps. He greeted her lightly and bent over Sidsall with an extended hand:

" The apple blossoms, I see, are here."

Rhoda wondered what nonsense Roger Brevard was repeating; Sidsall's face was hidden from view. But then Roger was always like that, his manner was never at a loss for the appropriate gesture. He had a great many points in common with her, she thought; neither had been born in Salem, and his rightful setting was in the best metropolitan drawing-rooms. He had been here for a dozen years, now, in charge of the local affairs of the Mongolian Marine Insurance Company; and she often wondered why, a member of a family socially notable in New York, he continued in a city, a position, of comparative unimportance.

She was, she said, going back to the lawn, the glare of Pleasant Street was fatiguing; and she proceeded through

the house with the surety of his following. But on the
close-cut emerald sod there was no sign of him, and she
found a seat in a basket chair by the willow tree beyond.
She waited for Roger with a small but growing impatience;
he must be done immediately with whatever he might say
to Sidsall, and she wished to discuss the possibilities of a
rumor that President Polk intended to visit Salem. There
would be a collation, perhaps a military ball, to arrange;
Franklin Hall would be the better place for the latter.
She heard a faint silvery echo of laughter — Sidsall. It
was extremely nice, of course, in Roger Brevard to enter-
tain her daughter, though she didn't care to have the
child give the effect of receiving men yet.

It was, finally, Sidsall who appeared, unaccompanied,
in the drawing-room window. She came forward to where
Rhoda sat, her face still stirred with amusement. " Mr.
Brevard went on," she said in response to her mother's
look of inquiry. " That's rather odd," the latter commented almost sharply. " He had only a few minutes,"
the girl explained. She sank into a seat and mood of abstraction. Rhoda studied her with a veiled glance. Hers
were exceptional children, they had given her scarcely an
hour's concern; and she must see that in the unsettling
period which Sidsall was now entering she was not spoiled.

Perhaps Laurel entertained her more than the others.
She was a very normal little girl, not thoughtful like
Janet, and without Camilla's exaggerated poise; but she
had a picturesque imagination; and her companionship
with her grandfather was delightful. The latter addressed
her quite as if she were a fellow shipmaster; and she
had acquired some remarkable sea expressions, some de-

plorable and others enigmatic: only to-day, questioned about the order of her room, she had said that it was " all square by the lifts and braces." For this her grandfather had given her a gold piece.

There was, she knew, an excellent school for older girls at Lausanne; and, revolving the possibility of obtaining for Sidsall some of the European advantages she, Rhoda, had enjoyed, the following afternoon she drove to the Cliffords' on Marlboro Street for a consultation with Madra, who had spent a number of seasons on Lake Leman. In a cool parlor with yellow Tibet rugs and maroon hangings she had tea while Madra Clifford, thin and imperious, with a settled ill health like white powder and a priceless Risajii shawl, conversed in a shrill key.

" Caroline has been in bed for a week. That vulgar Dr. Fisk, with his elbow in her bosom, tried five times to extract her tooth, and then broke it to the roots. I hear there is a galvanic ring for rheumatism. The pain in my joints is excruciating; I have an idea my bones are changing into chalk; the right knee will hardly bend." The darkly colored shawl with its border of cypress intensified her sunken blue-traced temples and the pallid lips. She developed the subject of her indisposition, sparing no detail; while Rhoda Ammidon, from her superabundance of well-being, half pitied the other and was half revolted at the mind touched, too, by bodily ill. The fortune accumulated by the hardy Clifford men, flogged out of crews and stained by the blood of primitive and dull savages — the Cliffords were notorious for their brutal driving — now served only to support Madra's debility and a horde of unscrupulous panderers to her obsession.

" Edward Dunsack is in Salem," she continued; " and I've heard he has the most peculiar appearance. Very probably the result of the unmentionable practices of the Orient. Father liked the Chinese though; so many of our shipmasters have, and not always the merchants. . . . What was I saying? Oh, yes, Edward Dunsack. I understand you had a distinct alarm in that quarter, about the girl and Gerrit Ammidon. But I forgot to say how glad I am about Gerrit. You must have been horribly worried —"

" What do you mean? " Rhoda demanded.

" Why, haven't you heard! The *Nautilus* was sighted. News came from Boston. She ought to be in to-day, I believe. I suppose William has been too concerned to get you word at home."

Rhoda Ammidon rose immediately, surprised at the force of the emotion that blurred her eyes with tears. Gerrit was safe! Possibly they had been told at Java Head now, but she must be there with Jeremy Ammidon; surprises, even as joyful as this, were a great strain on him. Neglecting the object of her visit she returned at once to Pleasant Street, urging the coachman to an undignified haste, and keeping the carriage at the door.

Her father-in-law was at his secretary in the library, and it was evident that he had heard nothing of his son's return. " Well, Rhoda," he said, swinging about; " what a bright cheek you have — like Laurel's."

" I feel bright, father," she replied with a nod and smile. " After this none of you will be able to laugh at my predictions. You see, a woman's feeling is often more correct than masculine judgment." His momentary bewilderment

[68]

gave place to a painfully strained interrogation. " Yes," she told him, " but we are none of us surprised — Gerrit is almost in Salem harbor." She moved near him and, with a veiled anxiety, laid her hand upon his shoulder.

" A splendid sailor," he muttered. It seemed as if Rhoda could really hear the dull rising pounding of his shaken heart. But his excitement subsided, gave way to a normal concern, a flood of vain questions and preparation to go down to the wharf. In the midst of this a message came from the countinghouse of Ammidon, Ammidon and Saltonstone that the *Nautilus* would dock within an hour.

A small crowd had already gathered on Derby Wharf when Rhoda and her companion made their way past the warehouses built at intervals along the wharf to the place where the *Nautilus* would be warped in. The wharfinger saluted them, William Ammidon joined his wife, and beyond she could see James Saltonstone conversing with the Surveyor of the Port.

The afternoon was serene, a faint air drew in from the sea; and with it, sweeping slowly inside Peach's Point, was the tall ship with her canvas towering gold in the western sun against the distance of sea and sky. As Rhoda watched she saw their house flag — a white field checkered in blue — fluttering from the main royal truck.

" The royals are coming in! " Jeremy Ammidon exclaimed, gripping Rhoda's arm. " He is lowering his topgallant yards and hauling up the courses! My dear, there's nothing on God's earth finer than a ship."

The *Nautilus* slipped along surprisingly fast. Rhoda could now see the crew moving about and coiling the gear.

[69]

"Look, father, there's Gerrit on the quarter-deck."

The shipmaster, shorter than common, with broad assertive shoulders in formal black, was easily recognizable. A woman with a worn flushed face pressed by Jeremy. "Andrew's there, too," she told them, "Mr. Broadrick, the mate."

The ship moved more slowly, under her topsails and jibs, in a soundless progress with the ripples falling away in water like dark green glass, liquid and still. She was now but a short distance from the end of the wharf. Mr. Broadrick was forward between the knightheads with the crew ranged to the starboard and at the braces, while Gerrit Ammidon stood with one hand on the quarter-deck railing and the other holding a brass speaking trumpet to his lips:

"Let go your port fore and after braces, Mr. Broadrick; brace the fore and mizzen yards sharp up, leave the main braces fast, and lay the main topsail to the mast. As she comes to the wind let the jibs run down." He turned to the man at the wheel, "Helm hard a starboard."

"Hard a starboard, sir."

The ship answered quickly and rounded to while her weather fore and mizzen yards flew forward until they touched the starboard backstays and the men hauled in the slack of the braces. With the main yard square to check her way the jibs drooped down along the stays. "Mr. Broadrick, you may let go the starboard anchor and furl sails." The mate grasped a top maul and struck the trigger of the ring stopper a clean blow, the anchor splashed into the water with a rumbling cable, and the *Nautilus* was home.

Gerrit Ammidon walked hurriedly to the companionway and went below, while the mate continued, " Stand by to let go your topsail halliards and man the gear. Sharper with the mizzen sheets and unbend those clew lines and garnets . . . stow the clews in a harbor furl." At a rhythmic shout the bunts of the three topsails came up together.

The wind had died away and the flags hung listlessly from the main truck and spanker gaff. The water of the harbor was unstirred except for the swirls at the oar blades of an incoming quarter boat and the warp paying out at her stern. The voice of the mate, the chantey of the crew heaving at the capstan bars, came to Rhoda subdued:

> " The times are hard and wages low,
>   Oh, leave her, Johnny, leave her.
> I guess it's time for us to go,
>   Oh, leave her, Johnny, leave her.
> I thought I heard the old man say,
>   Oh, leave her, Johnny, leave her.
> To-morrow we will get our pay
> . . . . . . leave her."

Rhoda Ammidon discovered herself leaning forward tensely, her hands shut in excitement and emotion; and she relaxed with a happy laugh as the *Nautilus,* with her yards exactly square and rigging taut, her sides and figurehead and ports bright with newly laid on paint, moved to the wharf.

It seemed to her that Gerrit, descending a short stage from the deck, looked markedly older than when he had last sailed. Yet he had a surprisingly youthful air still;

partly, she thought, from the manner in which he wore his hair, falling in a waving thick line about his cheeks. His mouth was at once fresh and severe, his face clean shaven, and his eyes — if possible — more directly blue than ever.

" I'll take the ship's manifest to the Collector," he said, greeting them and impatiently waving aside the vendors after the cook's slush, the excited women and runners and human miscellany crowding forward. " Then Java Head." He paused, speaking over his shoulder: " I'd be thankful if you would send the barouche down in an hour or so."

Driving back, her hand on Jeremy Ammidon's knee, Rhoda wondered at Gerrit's request. It was entirely unlike him to ride in the barouche; rather he had always derided it in the terms of his calling. However, unable to find a solution for her surprise, she listened to the other's comments and speculations:

" I suppose William's first question will be about the cargo, and, of course, I hope the ship has done well. But I'm just glad to have Gerrit back; I am for a fact, Rhoda."

" We all are," she assured him, " and William as happy as any. You mustn't be misled by his manner, father. I hope the supper will be good and please you."

" Gerrit will be satisfied with anything," he chuckled. " Probably he's been out of beans even for a month. Did you notice that fore-royal mast and yard? They were rigged at sea: Gerrit carried them away. It hurts him to take in a sail. Some day I tell him he'll drag the spars out of his ship. His confounded pride will founder him." He made these charges lightly, with a palpable underlying pride; and, Rhoda knew, would permit no one else to criticize his son.

She found her daughters in a state of gala excitement on the front steps. " Uncle Gerrit in the *Nautilus*," Laurel chanted; and it was evident that Camilla herself was thrilled. They all went up to put on holiday dress. Rhoda turned to the coachman, " Have the barouche at the head of Derby Wharf in an hour."

Gerrit's unusual demand again puzzled her. A fantastic possibility lodged in her brain — perhaps he was not alone. She pulled the bell rope for her maid, changed into black moiré with cut steel bretelles, and selected the peacock coloring of a Peri-taus shawl. She found her husband with his father in the library. " I understand it's a splendid cargo," William remarked. Jeremy nodded triumphantly at her, and she expressed a half humorous resentment at this mercenary display. " He ought to be here," the younger man declared, consulting his watch. As he spoke Rhoda saw the barouche draw up before the house. She had a glimpse of a figure at Gerrit Ammidon's side in extravagantly brilliant satins; there was a sibilant whisper of rich materials in the hall, and the master entered the library with a pale set face.

" Father," he said, " Rhoda and William, allow me — my wife, Taou Yuen."

Rhoda Ammidon gave an uncontrollable gasp as the Chinese woman sank in a fluttering prostration of color at Jeremy's feet. He ejaculated, " God bless me," and started back. William's face was inscrutable, unguessed lines appeared about his severe mouth. Her own sensation was one of incredulity touched with mounting anger and feeling of outrage. The woman rose, but only to sink again before William: she was on her knees and, supported by her hands, bent forward and touched her forehead to the floor three times. Gerrit laughed shortly. "She was to shake your hands; we went over and over it on shipboard. But anything less than the *Kû l'on* was too casual for her."

She was now erect with a freer murmur of greeting to Rhoda. The latter was instantly aware of one certainty — Chinese she might be, she was, but no less absolutely aristocratic. Her face, oval and slightly flat, was plastered with paint on paint, but her gesture, the calm scrutiny of enigmatic black eyes under delicately arched brows, exquisite quiet hands, were all under the most admirable instinctive command. Rhoda said:

"I see that I am to welcome you for Gerrit's family." The other, in slow lisping English replied:

"Thank you greatly. I am humbled to the earth before your goodness."

"You will want to go to your room," Rhoda continued mechanically. "It was only prepared for one, but I'll send a servant up at once." She was enraged at the silent stupidity of the three men and flashed a silent command at her husband.

"This is a decided surprise," the latter at last addressed his brother; "nor can I pretend that it is pleasant." Jeremy Ammidon's gaze wandered blankly from Gerrit to the woman, then back to his son.

Never before had Rhoda seen such lovely clothes: A long gown with wide sleeves of blue-black satin, embroidered in peach-colored flower petals and innumerable minute sapphire and orange butterflies, a short sleeveless jacket of sage green caught with looped red jade buttons and threaded with silver and indigo high-soled slippers crusted and tasseled with pearls. Her hair rose from the back in a smooth burnished loop. There were long pins of pink jade carved into blossoms, a quivering decoration of paper-thin gold leaves with moonstones in glistening drops, and a band of coral lotus buds. Pierced stone bracelets hung about her delicate wrists, fretted crystal balls swung from the lobes of her ears; and clasped on the ends of several fingers were long pointed filagrees of ivory.

" Taou Yuen," Gerrit repeated shortly, with his challenging bright gaze. " That means Peach Garden. My wife is a Manchu," he asserted in a more biting tone; " a Manchu and the daughter of a noble. Thank you, Rhoda, particularly. But I have always counted on you. Will you go up with her? That is if — if my father has a room, a place, for us."

" This will always be your home, Gerrit," Jeremy said slowly, with the long breath of a diver in deep waters.

IV

IN the room that had been his since early maturity Gerrit Ammidon gave an involuntary sigh of relief. Taou Yuen, his wife, was standing in the middle of the floor, gazing about with a faint and polite smile. Her eyes rested on a yellow camphor chest — one of the set brought home by his father — on a severe high range of drawers made of sycamore with six legs, on her brilliant reflection in the eagle-crowned mirror above the mantel, and the sleigh bed with low heavily curved ends.

The situation below, however brief and, on the whole, reasonably conducted, had been surprisingly difficult. At the same time that he had felt no necessity to apologize for his marriage he had known that Taou Yuen must surprise, yes — shock, his family. She was Chinese, to them a heathen: they would be unable to comprehend any mitigating dignity of rank. Where they'd actually suffer, he realized, would be in the attitude of Salem, the stupid gabble, the censure and cold pity caused by his wife.

Personally he regarded these with the contempt he felt for so many of the qualities that on shore bound the interests of everyone into a single common concern. It gave him pleasure to assault the authority and importance of such public prejudice and self-opinion; but, unavoidably implicating his family, at once a part of himself and Salem, he was conscious of the fact that he had laid them all open to disagreeable moments. He was sorry for this, and his regret, principally materialized by his father's hurt confusion, had unexpectedly cast a shadow on a scene to which he had looked forward with a distinct sense of comedy. Where the realities were concerned he had no fear of Taou Yuen's ability to justify herself completely. He possessed a stupendous admiration for her.

He watched her now with the mingled understanding and mystification that gave his life with her such a decided charm. Her gaze had fastened on the mirror-stand above the drawers: she must be wondering if she would have to paint and prepare herself for him here, openly. He knew that she considered it a great impropriety for her face to be seen bare; all the elaborate processes of her morning toilet must be privately conducted. He recognized this, but had no idea what she actually thought of the room, of his family, of the astonishing situation into which her heart had betrayed her.

One and then another early hope he saw at once were vain. It had seemed to him that in America, in Salem, she might become less evidently Chinese; not in the incongruous horror of Western clothes, but in her attitude, in a surrender to superficial customs; he had pictured her as merging distinctively into the local scene. In China he had hoped that in the vicinity of Washington Square and Pleasant Street she would appear less Eastern; but, beyond all doubt, here she was enormously more so. The strange repressed surrounding accentuated every detail of her Manchu pomp and color. The frank splendor of her satins and carved jades and embroidery, her immobile striking face loaded with carmine and glinting headdress, the flawless loveliness of hands with the pointed nail protectors, were, in his room, infinitely dramatized.

The other, less secure possibility that she might essentially change perished silently. In a way his wish had been a presumption — that a member of the oldest and most subtle civilization existing would, if she were able, adopt such comparatively crude habits of life and thought.

She moved slowly up to the bed, examining it curiously; and again he understood her look of doubt — in China beds were called *kang*, or stoves, from the fact that they were more often than not a platform of brick with an opening beneath for hot coals. She fingered the ball fringe of the coverlet, and then turned with amazement to the soft pillow. A hand with the stone bracelet falling back from her smooth wrist rose to the complicated edifice of her headdress.

" Your pillow is coming along from the ship," he told her; " the women here do up their hair every morning."

She considered this with geranium lips slightly parted on flawless teeth, and nodded slowly. The westering sun striking through the window overlooking the Common illuminated her with a flat gold unreality.

" I'll have a day bed brought for you," he continued, realizing that, as the result of fortunate chance, she understood most of what he said without an actual command of the individual words. In reply she sank before him in the deep Manchu gesture with one knee sweeping the floor, the humility of her posture dignified by grace. He touched the crystal globe of an earring, pinched her chin, in the half light manner by which he instinctively expressed his affection for her. She was calm and pleased. "Taou Yuen," he continued, "you miss Shanghai, with the wall of ten gates and the river Woosung stuck full of masts. You'll never think Salem is a paradise like Soochow."

"This is your city," she replied, slowly choosing the words. "Your ancestors are here." There was not a shade of regret in her voice or manner. He tried once more, and as vainly as ever, to penetrate the veil of her perfect serenity. She never, it became apparent, descended from the most inflexible self-control; small emotions — surface gayety of mood, curiosity, the faintest possible indication of contempt, he had learned to distinguish; the fact that she cared enough for him to desert every familiar circumstance was evident; but beyond these he was powerless to reach.

His own emotions were hardly less obscured: the dominating feeling was his admiration for her exquisite worldly wisdom, the perfection of her bodily beauty, and the philosophy which bore her above the countless trivialities that destroyed the dignity of western minds. He realized that her paint and embroidery covered a spirit as cold and tempered as fine metal. She was totally without the social sentiment of his own world; but she was equally innocent of its nauseous hypocrisy, the pretensions of a piety covering commercial dishonesty, obscenity of thought and spreading scandal. The injustice he saw practiced on shore had always turned him with a sense of relief to the cleansing challenge of the sea; always, brought in contact with cunning and self-seeking men and heartless schemes, with women cheapened by a conviction of the indecency of life, he was in a state of hot indignation. From all this Taou Yuen offered a complete escape.

On the purely feminine side she was a constant delight, the last possible refinement, he told himself, of instinct and effect. She was incapable of the least vulgarity; never for an instant did she flag from the necessity of beauty, never had he seen her too weary for an adornment laborious in a hundred difficult conventions. She was, too, a continuous source of entertainment, even as his wife she never ceased to be a spectacle; his consciousness of her as a being outside himself persisted.

" I must go down and see where our things are," he said, rising. In the hall he stopped before the tall clock whose striking was a part of his early memories. Below, the house seemed empty; and, instead of turning to the front door and his purpose, he went into the drawing-room.

The long glass doors to the garden were open, and the interior was filled with the scent of lilacs. The room itself had always reminded him of them — it was pale in color, cool gilt and lavender brocade and white panels. Nothing had been moved or changed: the inlaid cylinder fall desk with its garlands of painted flowers on the light waxed wood stood at the left, the pole screen with the embroidered bouquet was before the fire blind, the girandoles, scrolled in ormolu and hung with crystal lusters, held the shimmer of golden reflections on the walls.

He had remembered the drawing-room at Java Head as a place of enchanted perfection; in his childhood its still serenity had seemed a presentment of what might be hoped for in heaven. The thought of the room as it was now, open but a little dim to the lilacs and warm afternoon, had haunted him as the measure of all peace and serenity in moments of extreme danger, his ship laboring in elemental catastrophes and in remote seas. Its fragance had touched him through the miasma of Whampoa Reach, waiting for the lighters of tea to float down from Canton; standing off in the thunder squalls of the night for the morning sea breeze to take him into Rio; over a cognac in the coffee stalls of the French market at New Orleans, the chanteys ringing from the cotton gangs along the levees:

> " Were you ever down in Mobile Bay?
> Aye, aye, pump away."

As he left the room he saw Laurel, William's youngest child, and he imprisoned her in an arm. " You haven't asked what I've got for you in my sea chest," he said. Gerrit was very fond of all four of the rosy-cheeked vigorous girls, and a sense of injury touched him at Laurel's reserved manner. She studied him with a wondering uneasy concern. This he realized was the result of bringing home Taou Yuen; and an aggravated impatience, a growing rebellion, seized him. He wouldn't stay with his wife at Java Head a day longer than necessary; and if anyone, in his family or outside, showed the slightest disdain he could retaliate with his knowledge of local pettiness, the backbiting enmities and secret lapses.

God knew he didn't want trouble, all he asked was a reasonable liberty, the semblance, anyhow, of a courtesy toward his wife. Whatever might be said would be of no moment to her — except in the attitude of his father — and Taou Yuen's indifference furnished a splendid example for himself. He wondered why the devil he was continually putting his fingers in affairs that couldn't concern him. No one thanked him for his trouble, they considered him something of a fool — a good sailor but peculiar. The damned unexpected twists of his sense of the absurd, too, got him into constant difficulty.

His father was standing outside the principal entrance; and, as he joined him on the steps, he saw two men from the *Nautilus* carrying his ship's desk by the beckets let in the ends. The wind was blowing gently up Pleasant Street; the men, at his gesture, lifted their burden up the steps, between the direction of the wind and Jeremy Ammidon. The latter rose instantly into one of his dark rages:

" What do you mean, you damned packetrats — coming up a companionway to the windward of me! I'll have no whalers' habits here." He repeated discontentedly that everything on sea and land had fallen into a decline. Others followed with a number of Korean boxes, strapped and locked with copper, and wicker baskets. A man in charge said to Gerrit Ammidon:

" The chest was left for Mr. Dunsack at the foot of Hardy Street, sir, as you ordered. The inspector sent it off complimentary with your personal things." Gerrit asked, " He didn't stop to get a whiff of it then? " The other shook his head. " Edward Dunsack asked me to ship it here and explained that it was only junk he was bringing home, but what it amounts to is about a case of Patna opium. He's lucky."

They turned inside, William was in the library, and

Gerrit instinctively followed his father into the room. William surveyed him with a moody discontent. "What I can't understand," he proceeded; "is why you call it a marriage, why you brought your woman here to us, to Rhoda and the children."

"It's simple enough," Gerrit replied; "Taou Yuen is my wife, we are married exactly as Rhoda and you are. She is not my woman in the sense you mean. I won't allow that, William."

"How can it matter what you will or will not allow when everyone'll think the other? Shipmasters have had Chinese mistresses before, yes, and smuggled them into Salem; but this conduct of yours is beyond speech."

Gerrit Ammidon said:

"Don't carry this too far." Anger like a hot cloud oppressed him. "I am married legally and, if anything, by a ceremony less preposterous than your own. Taou Yuen is not open to any man or woman's suspicions. I am overwhelmingly indebted to her."

"But she's not your race," William Ammidon muttered; "she is a Confucian or Taoist, or some such thing."

"You're Unitarian one day a week, and father is Congregational, Hodie's a Methodist, and no one knows what I am," Gerrit cried. "Good God, what does all that matter! Isn't a religion a religion? Do you suppose a Lord worth the name would be anything but entertained by such spiteful little dogmas A sincere greased nigger with his voodoo must be as good as any of us."

"That is too strong, Gerrit," Jeremy objected. "You'll get nowhere crying down Christianity."

[83]

" If I could find it," the younger declared bitterly, " I'd feel differently. It's right enough in the Bible. . . . Well, we'll go on to Boston to-morrow."

" This is your home," his father repeated. " Naturally William, all of us have been disturbed; but nothing beyond that. I trust we are a loyal family. What you've done can't be mended with hard words."

" She may become very fashionable," Gerrit mockingly told his brother. " It'll be a blow to Camilla," Jeremy chuckled. " Some rice must be cooked."

" Manchus don't live on rice," Gerrit replied. " They don't bind the feet either nor wear the common Chinese clothes. Rhoda will understand better."

Again in his room he found his wife bending over a gorgeous heap of satins, bright mazarines and ornaments. " We'll go down to supper soon," he told her. Already there were signs of her presence about the room: the chest of drawers was covered with gold and jade and green amber, painted paper fans set on ivory and tortoise shell, and lacquer fan boxes; coral hairpins, sandalwood combs, silver rouge pots and rose quartz perfume bottles with canary silk cords and tassels. On a familiar table was her pipe, wound in gilt wire, and the flowered satin tobacco case. An old coin was hanging at the head of the bed, a charm against evil spirits; and on a stand was the amethyst image of Kuan-Yin *pu tze,* the Goddess of Mercy.

Taou Yuen sank on the floor with a little embarrassed laugh at the confusion in which he had surprised her. " Let your attitude be grave," he quoted from the Book of Rites with a pretended severity. Her amusement rose in a ripple of mirth. He opened his desk, rearranging the disorder brought about by its transportation; and, when he turned, she was prostrate in the last rays of the sun. " *O-me-to-Fuh*," she breathed; " *O-me-to-Fuh*," the invocation to Buddha. This at an end she announced, " Now I am grave and respectful for your family."

Supper, Gerrit admitted to himself, promised to be a painful occasion; conversation rose sporadically and quickly died in glances of irrepressible curiosity directed at his wife. She, on the contrary, showed no pointed interest in her surroundings; and, in her hesitating slurred English, answered Rhoda's few questions without putting any in return. Camilla preserved a frozen silence; Sidsall was pleasantly conciliating in her attitude toward the novel situation; Janet, her lips moving noiselessly, was rapt in amazement; and Laurel smiled, abashed at meeting Taou Yuen's eyes.

The recounting of his delayed return offered Gerrit a welcome relief from the pervading strain: " There's no tea to speak of at Shanghai, and I took on a mixed cargo — pongees and porcelain and matting. I got camphor and cassia and seven hundred peculs of ginger; then I decided to lay a course to Manilla for some of the cheroots father likes. The weather was fine, I had a good cargo, and, well — we pleasured out to Honolulu. I was riding the island horses and shipping oil when the schooner *Kahemameha* arrived from the coast with the news of the gold discovery in California. Every boat in the harbor was loaded to the trucks, crowded with passengers at their weight in ginseng, and laid for San Francisco. . . . Well, I was caught with the rest.

" Five thousand dollars was offered me to carry a gen-

tleman and his attendant. Two others would pay three
for the same purpose. Stowage was worth what you asked.
. . . The *Nautilus* made a good run; then, about a day
from land, Mr. Broadrick told me that there wouldn't be a
seaman on the ship an hour after we anchored. They
were all crazy with gold fever, he said. I could see, too,
that they were excited; the watch hung under the weather
rail jabbering like parrots; an uglier crew of sea lawyers
never developed.

" There was one thing to do and I did it — called them
aft and gave them some hot scouse. They'd shipped for
Salem and there they must go. I didn't anchor, but stood
off — the harbor was crowded with deserted vessels like
some hell for ships — and sent the jolly boat in with the
passengers and a couple of men. They didn't come back,
you may be sure. The consignment for San Francisco I
carried out that evening, for I made sail at once."

" You had a pretty time getting a way on her," Jeremy
Ammidon remarked.

" I did," Gerrit acknowledged shortly. " The second
mate's ear was taken loose by a belaying pin that flew out
of the dark like a gull. Mr. Broadrick had a bad minute
in the port forecastle after he had ordered all hands on
deck a third time. The fine weather left us, though, and
that kept the crew busy; we carried away the fore-royal
mast and yard before we were within a thousand miles of
the latitude of the Horn. That hit us like a cannon ball
of ice. You know what it is at its worst," he told his
father; " weeks of snow and hail and fog and gales; and
not for anything can you keep an easting. God knows

how a ship lives through the seas; but she does, she does, and you lose the Magellan clouds astern."

The old man nodded.

Gerrit was relieved, however, when supper ended and his wife formally departed for her room. Immediately slipping a hand inside Rhoda's arm he conducted her to the drawing-room. " I'd like you to know more about it," he said directly.

" It was very extraordinary. A Lú Kikwáng was a high official of the Canton Customs, and when Shanghai was declared an open port in forty-two they made him hoppo there. I remembered him at Canton, a dignified old duck with eighty or a hundred servants to keep anyone from possibly speaking to him of business, but there had been some trouble about foreign vessels selling saltpeter illegally and — he knew some English — we had quite a friendly little consultation. Yet it hadn't prepared me for his coming off to the *Nautilus* at Shanghai with a linguist and an air of the greatest mystery. His manner was beautiful, of course, absolutely tranquil and that made what they said, what he hoped, seem even wilder than it was.

" His son, it appeared, had married and was accidentally drowned in the Great Canal hardly a month after the ceremony. His widow belonged, then, to the husband's family, and from that moment her father-in-law had had nothing but bad luck. He had been robbed, his best stallion died, there had been a flood in his tea which not only spoiled the crop but filled the ground with silt — it was impossible to relate his calamities. He consulted a necromancer at last and learned that it was all caused by the presence of Taou Yuen.

"This, you see, made the difficulty, as it's a frightful disgrace to return a married daughter to her own father's home, and Lú had grown very fond of her. She was extremely clever and virtuous, he said. The other thing was to kill her or force her to commit suicide. He told me very calmly that he would like to avoid this.

"Then, in the linguist's most flowery manner, they went on with what Lú Kikwáng proposed. He had recognized that I was a man of 'superior propriety' and he wondered if I would take Taou Yuen away to America with me. Very secretly though — there would be an uproar if it were known that a Manchu woman had been married to a foreigner. I could see her first in his garden without her knowing anything about it.

"It's needless to tell you that I went with them that afternoon. A meeting was arranged for the next day —" he broke off, sitting forward with elbows on knees, gazing fixedly at his clasped hands.

"You make that very clear, Gerrit," his sister-in-law replied; "I now understand the past almost as well as yourself; but it's the future I'm in doubt about. I saw immediately that your wife was not an ordinary woman; it would be much easier if she were. Certainly you don't intend to stay here, at Java Head; but that is immaterial. Wherever you go in America it will not be suitable for her. She'll be no more at home with your friends than you with hers. I feel terribly sad about it, Gerrit; you were as selfish as only a man can be."

"You are unjust, Rhoda," he protested. "Taou Yuen

was willing to come. She had read about other countries
and saw a great deal of the English wife of a rich Dutch
factor at Shanghai; as Lú Kikwáng said, she's wonderfully intelligent. I think she is happy, too."

"Rubbish! Of course she loves you; I am not talking
about that. How will she get along while you are away
on your long voyages? She couldn't possibly live in the
cabin of a ship, and do you suppose she'd be contented
in Salem with you absent for a year!"

"We have as many chances of success as any other
marriage," he asserted. "The whole business is foolish
enough."

"That opinion might do for a single shipmaster, with
only a month or two out of the year on land. When you
were free, Gerrit, your impatience with convention was
refreshing and possible. But can't you see that you have
given up your liberty! You have tied your hands. However loudly you may cry out against society now you are
a part of us, foolish or not. You'll find that your wife
has anchored you in Salem, Boston or Singapore, no matter where you go: people will reach and hurt you through
her.

"She is very gorgeous and placid, superior on the
surface; but the heart, Gerrit — that isn't made of jade
and ivory and silk."

"I'll bring down your presents to-morrow," he told
her, avoiding any further present discussion of his marriage. "Has father failed, do you think? His tempers
are vigorous as ever."

"He seems baggier about the eyes and throat. He is
just as quick, but it exhausts him more. Things would be

much better if he were only content to let William manage at the countinghouse. Times are shifting so quickly with these new clipper ships and direct passages and political changes."

"There's no longer any doubt about the clippers," Gerrit declared; "the California gold rush will attend to that."

In his room he found Taou Yuen, in soft white silk worked with bamboo leaves, on the day bed, smoking. She rose immediately as he entered; and, coming close to him, ran her cool fingers through his hair. He stood gazing out at the dim oil flares that marked the confines of Washington Square, considering all that Rhoda had said. Strangely enough it led his thoughts away from his wife; they reverted to Nettie Vollar.

He had been, he realized, very nearly in love with her: what he meant by that inaccurate term was that if the affair had continued a little longer he would have insisted on marrying her. Nettie was not indifferent to him. An impersonal feeling had attracted him to her — a resentment of her treatment by the larger part of Salem, particularly the oblique admiration of the men. His supersensitiveness to any form of injustice had driven him into the protest of calling and accompanying her, with an exaggerated politeness, about the streets. It had not been difficult; she was warm-blooded, luxurious, a very vivid woman. Gerrit, however, had made a point of repressing any response to that aspect of their intercourse — the sheerest necessity for the preservation of his disdain.

She had cried on his shoulder, in his arms, practically; he had acted in the purely fraternal manner. But the

thing was reaching a natural conclusion when her grandfather, Barzil Dunsack, had interfered with his unsup-
portably frank accusations and command. The *Nautilus*
had been ready for sea, and his, Gerrit's, imperious resentment had carried him out of the Dunsacks' house —
to Shanghai and Taou Yuen — without another word to
Nettie.

How strangely life progressed, without chart or intelligent observations or papers! He heard the tap of his
wife's pipe; there was a faint sweetish odor of drugged
tobacco and the scent of cloves in which she saturated
herself. Outside was Salem, dim and without perceptible
movement; the clock in the hall struck ten. Taou Yuen
didn't approach him again nor speak; her perceptions were
wonderfully acute.

The sense of loneliness that sometimes overtook him
on shore deepened, a feeling of impotence, as if he had
suddenly waked, lost and helpless, in an unfamiliar planet.
There was the soft whisper of his wife's passage across
the room. In the lamplight the paint on her cheeks made
startling unnatural patches of — paint. The reflections
slid over the liquid black mass of her hair, died in the
lustrous creamy folds of her garment. She was at once
grotesque and impressive, like a figure in a Chinese pan-
tomime watched from the western auditorium of his inheritance. His fondness for her, his admiration, had not les-
sened. He surveyed his position, the presence here, in his
room at Java Head, of Taou Yuen, with amazement; all
the small culminating episodes lost, the result was beyond
credence. His thoughts returned to Rhoda's accusation of
selfishness, the disaster implied in her pity for his wife.

He tried again to analyze his marriage, discover whatever justification, security, it possessed. Was his admiration for Taou Yuen sufficient provision for his part of their future together? It was founded largely on her superiority to the world he had known; and here it was necessary for him to convince himself that his wedding had not been merely the result of romantic accident. He knew that the sensual had had almost no part in it, it had been mental; an act of pity crystallizing his revolt against what he felt to be the impotence of " Christian " ethics. Yet this was not sufficient; for he, like Rhoda, had found under his wife's immobility the flux of immemorial woman.

No, it wasn't enough; but more existed, he was certain of that. No one could expect him, now, to experience the thrill of idealized passion that was the sole property of youth. What feeling he had had for Nettie — he was obliged to return to her from the fact that it was the only possible comparison — had come from very much the same source as the other. The old impersonal motives!

The danger, Rhoda pointed out, had been admitted when his marriage made impossible the continuation of that aloof position. He doubted that it could change him so utterly. The thought of the entertainment his wife would afford him in Salem expanded. He regretted that the best, the calling and comments of the women, was necessarily lost to him, but Taou Yuen would repeat a great deal: she, too, had a sly sense of the ridiculous. He hoped that his sister-in-law didn't suppose her helpless; the impenetrable Manchu control gave her a pitiless advantage over any less absolute civilization. In the darkness before sleep the heavy exotic scents in the room oppressed him strangely.

He rose early, and quietly dressing went out into the garden: buds on the June roses against the high blank fence on the street were swelling into visible crimson; there were the stamping of horses' feet on the cobbles of the stable inclosure, the heavy breathing and admonitions of the coachman wielding a currycomb. The sunlight streamed down through pale green willow and tall lilac bushes, through the octagonal latticed summerhouse and across the vivid sod to the drawing-room door. Gerrit turned, and entered the farther yard, where his father was inspecting the pear trees.

" The *Nautilus* will need new copper sheathing," Gerrit said; " she's pretty well stripped forward."

" Take her around to the Salem Marine Railway at the foot of English Street. A fine ship, Gerrit, with a proper hull. I tell you they'll never improve on the French lines."

" She won't go into the wind with a clipper," he admitted; " but I'll sail her on a fair breeze with anything afloat."

" If you come to that," his father asserted; " nothing handsomer will ever be seen than an East Indiaman in the northeast trades with the captain on the quarter-deck in a cocked hat and sword, the shoals of flying fish and alba-core skittering about a transom as high and carved and gilded as a church, the royal pennant at the mainmast head. Maybe it would be the *Earl of Balcarras* with her cannons shining and the midshipmen running about."

[93]

" Yes," the younger man returned, " and taking in her light sails at sunset, dropping astern like an island. The John Company's ruining British shipping."

Jeremy Ammidon muttered one of his favorite pessimistic complaints. " What did you say her name was? " he demanded abruptly.

" Taou Yuen."

" Taou Yuen Ammidon," the elder pronounced experimentally. " It doesn't sound right, the two won't go together."

" But they have," Gerrit declared. He thought impatiently that he must listen to a repetition of Rhoda's assertions.

" I don't know much about 'em," Jeremy proceeded. " All I saw, when I was younger, was the little singing-girls playing mora and wailing over their infernal three-stringed fiddles something about the moon and a bowl of water lilies."

Taou Yuen did not come down to breakfast, and Gerrit stayed away from their room until her toilet must be finished. It was Sunday; and with the customary preparation for church under way William said:

" I suppose you will go down to the ship? "

The hidden question, the purpose of the inquiry, at once stirred into being all Gerrit's perversity. " No," he replied carelessly; " we'll go with you this morning."

" That's unheard of," William exclaimed heatedly; " a woman in all her paint and perfume and outrageous clothes in North Church, with — with my family! I won't have it, do you understand."

[94]

"No worse than what you see there every week," Gerrit retorted calmly; "corsets and feathers and female gimcracks. Plenty of rouge and cologne too. It will give them something new to stare at and whisper about."

William Ammidon choked on his anger, and his wife laid a gloved hand on his arm. "You must make up your mind to it," she told him. "It can't hurt anyone. She is Gerrit's wife, you see."

Above, the shipmaster said to Taou Yuen: "We are going to church with the family." He surveyed her clothes with a faint glimmer of amusement. She had, he saw, made herself especially resplendent as a Manchu. The long gown was straw-colored satin with black bats — a symbol of happiness — whirling on thickly embroidered silver clouds, over which she wore a sleeve coat fastened with white jade and glittering with spangles of beaten copper. Her slippers were pale rose, and fresh apple blossoms, which she had had brought from the yard, made a headdress fixed with long silver and dull red ivory pins.

She smiled obediently at his announcement, and, with a fan of peacock silks and betel nuts in a pouch like a tea rose hanging by a cord from a jade button, she signified her readiness to proceed.

William had gone on foot with his girls, Jeremy was seldom in church, and Rhoda, Taou Yuen beside her with Gerrit facing them, followed in the barouche. It seemed to the latter that they were almost immediately at the door of North Church. The leisurely congregation filling the walk stiffened in incredulous amazement as Gerrit handed

[95]

his wife to the pavement. Rhoda went promptly forward, nodding in response to countless stupefied greetings; while Gerrit Ammidon moved on at Taou Yuen's side.

Prepared, he restrained the latter from a prostration in the hall of the church. Nothing had changed: the umbrella trough still bore the numbers of the pews, the stair wound gloomily up to the organ loft. He again found the subdued interior, the maroon upholstery, the flat Gothic squares of the ceiling and dark red stone walls, a place of reposeful charm. The Ammidons had two of the box pews against the right wall: his brother and children were in the second, and, inside the other small inclosure, he shut the gate and took his place on a contracted corner bench. Taou Yuen sat with Rhoda against the back of the pew. The former, blazing like a gorgeous flower on the shadowed surface of a pool, smiled serenely at him.

He could hear the hum of subdued comment running like ignited powder through the church, familiar faces turned blankly toward him or nodded in patent confusion. The men, he noted, expressed a single rigid condemnation. The women, in crisp light dresses and ribboned bonnets, were franker in their curiosity. Taou Yuen was a loadstone for their glances. As the service progressed her face grew expressionless. Fretted sandalwood bracelets drooped over her folded hands, and miniature dragon flies quivered on the gold wires of her earrings; the sharp perfumes of the East drifted out and mingled with the Western scents of extracts and powders He only saw that she was politely chewing betel nut. It wasn't, he told himself, reverting to his critical attitude toward Salem,

[96]

that he was lacking in charity toward his neighbors, or that he felt any superiority; but the quality that signally roused his antagonism was precisely the men's present aspect of heavy censure and boundless propriety, their stolid attitude of justifying the spiritual consummation promised by the sermon and hymns.

The long night watches, the anxiety of the sea, the profound mysteries of the wheeling stars and the silence of the ocean at dawns, had given him, he dimly realized, an inarticulate reverence for the supreme mystery of creation. He was unable to put it into words or facile prayer but it was the guarded foundation of most that he was, and it bred in him a contempt for lesser signs. The religion of his birth, the faith of Taou Yuen, the fetishism of the Zanzibar Coast, he had regarded as equally important, or futile — the mere wash of the immensity of beauty, the inexorable destiny, that had seemed to breathe on him alone at the stern of his ship.

He lost himself now in the keenness of his remembered emotion: the church faded into a far horizon, he felt the slight heave of the ship and heard the creaking of the wheel as the steersman shifted his hands; from aloft came the faint slapping of the bunt lines on rigid canvas, the loose hemp slippers of the crew sounded across the deck, the water whispered alongside, the ship's bell was struck and repeated in a diminished note on the topgallant forecastle. The morning rose from below the edge of the sea and the pure air freshened. . . . His thoughts were recalled to the present by the dogmatic insistence of the clergyman's voice, promising heaven, threatening hell. His gaze rested on the chalky debility of Madra Clifford.

The service over, the aisle past the Ammidon pews was filled with a slow-moving inquisitive throng. Rhoda chose to wait until the greater part was past, and then she followed with the unmoved Taou Yuen and Gerrit. "This is my brother's wife," he heard the former say. "Mrs. Saltonstone, Gerrit's sister, Mrs. Clifford and Miss Vermeil. Yes . . . from Shanghai. Overdue. We were worried, of course." Taou Yuen smiled vigorously and flapped the vivid fan. Against her brilliant colors, the carved jade and embroideries, silver and apple blossoms, the other women looked colorless in wide book muslin and barége, with short veils of tulle illusion hanging from bonnets of rice straw and glazed crêpe. Palpably shocked by her Oriental face masked in paint, her Chinese " heathen " origin, yet they fingered the amazing needlework and wondered over the weight of her satins.

The men he knew gave him, for the most part, a curt greeting. They glanced more covertly at his wife; he understood exactly what thoughts brought out this condemnation soiled by private speculation; and his disdain mounted at their sleek backs and glossy tile hats supported on stiffly bent arms.

After dinner he walked through the warm sunny emptiness of the afternoon to Derby Wharf and the *Nautilus*. Standing on the wharf, smoking a cheroot, he leaned back upon his cane, studying the ship with a gaze that missed no detail. There was not a sound from the water; across the harbor Peach's Point seemed about to dissolve in a faint green haze; a strong scent of mingled spices came from the warehouses. There was the splash of oars in the Basin beyond, and the more distant peal of a church bell.

At the sound of footfalls behind him he turned and saw Nettie Vollar and her uncle, Edward Dunsack. A dark color rose in the girl's cheek, and her hand pulled involuntarily at Dunsack's arm, as if she wished to retreat. Gerrit thought that she had aged since he had latest met her: Nettie's mouth, with its full, slightly drooping lower lip, had lost something of its fresh arch; her eyes, though they still preserved their black sparkle, were plainly resentful. Edward Dunsack, medium tall but thin almost to emaciation, had a riven sallow face with close-cut silvery hair and agate-brown eyes with contracted pupils.

"Well, Nettie," Gerrit said, moving forward promptly, "it's pleasant to see you again." Her hand was cold and still. "Dunsack, too."

"I am obliged to you for my chest," the latter told him, unmoved by Gerrit's quizzical gaze.

"Glad to do it for you," the other replied; "it came ashore with my personal things, and so, perhaps, saved you something."

"Perhaps," Dunsack agreed levelly.

Looking down at the cob filling of the wharf, Nettie Vollar said, "You came home married, I hear, and to a Chinese lady."

Gerrit assented. "You'll certainly know her, and like her, too. Taou Yuen is very wise and without the prejudices —" he stopped, conscious of the stupidity of his attempted kindness. Nettie looked up defiantly, biting her lip — a familiar trick, he recalled. Dunsack interposed:

"You will find that the Chinese have none of your little sympathetic tricks. No foreigner could ever grasp the depth of their indifference to what you might call humanity. They are born wise, as you say, but weary. I suppose your wife plays the guitar skillfully and sings the Soochow Love Song."

Gerrit Ammidon studied him with somber eyes and a gathering temper: it was, however, impossible to decide whether the implication was deliberately insulting. He wouldn't have any Canton clerk, probably saturated with opium, insinuate that his affair was on the plane of that of a drunken sailor! "My wife," he said deliberately, "is a Manchu lady. You may know that they don't learn dialect songs nor ornament tea houses."

"Very remarkable," Dunsack returned imperturbably. "We never see them. How did you manage a go-between, and did you send the hour of your birth to the Calculator of Destinies? Then there is so much to remember in a Chinese wedding — the catties of tea and four silver ingots, the earrings and red and green silk and Tao priest to consult the gods." Gerrit heard this with a frowning countenance. If Nettie were not there he would put Dunsack forward with the hypothetical crew to which he belonged. He felt as sorry for Nettie, he discovered, as ever. It moved him to see her vivacity of life, her appealingly warm color, slowly dulled by Salem and the adventitious circumstance of her birth. What a dreary existence she led in the harsh atmosphere of her grandfather and the solemn house on Hardy Street! At one time he had fancied that he might change it . . . when now here was Taou Yuen, detached and superior, waiting in his room at Java Head.

"I stopped for a moment to look at the ship," he said, with the trace of an ungracious bow, "and must get back."

The sunlight flung a warm moted veil over Nettie Vollar. She gave him a startled uncalculated glance of almost desperate appeal and his heart responded with a quickened thud. Edward Dunsack was sallow and enigmatic, with thin pinched lips.

V

"THE stupid bruiser," Edward Dunsack declared in a thin bitterness that startled the girl at his side. " The low sea bully! " He was gazing at the resolute back of Captain Ammidon. A surprising hatred filled him at the memory of the other's intolerant gaze, the careless contempt of his words. He thought, oddly enough, of the delicate and ingenious tortures practiced on offenders in China; the pleasant mental picture followed of Ammidon bowed in a wooden collar, of Gerrit Ammidon bambooed, sliced, slowly choking. . . . With an intense sense of horror he caught himself dwelling on these dripping visions. His hands clasped rigidly, a sweat stood out on his brow, in a realization that was at once dread and a self-loathing.

About him lay the tranquil Salem water, the still wharves, the familiar roofs and green tree tops. This wasn't Canton, he told himself, but America: there was Nettie; only a few streets away was his father's house, his own home, all solid and safe and reassuring. China was a thing of the past, its insidious secret hold broken. It was now only a dream of evil fascination from which he had waked to the reality, the saving substance, of Derby Wharf. " It's his domineering manner," he explained the outburst to Nettie; " all shipmasters have it — as if the world were a vessel they damned from a quarter-deck in the sky. I never could put up with them."

" He is very kind, really," she replied, looking away over the harbor. " It is so queer — marrying a Chinese woman like that. How will he ever get along with her or be happy? "

" He won't," Edward Dunsack asserted. " Leave that to time." He studied her attentively. " Was it anything to you? " he asked.

" It might have been," she acknowledged listlessly, her gaze still on the horizon. " He came to see me two or three times, quite differently from other nice men, and took me to a concert at the Philharmonic Society. He was getting to like me, I could tell that, when grandfather interfered —"

" I see," Dunsack interrupted, " with the immorality of the supermoral."

" Whatever it was he was past bearing. No one could blame Gerrit for getting into a fury. The next day I stood almost in this spot, it was late afternoon too, and watched the *Nautilus* sail away. All the canvas was set and I could see her for a long time. When the last trace had gone it seemed to me that my life had sunk too . . . out there."

" The old man's a fool," he said bluntly of his father. " How do you suppose he got hold of a Manchu? " he shifted his thought, addressing the stillness about them rather than his companion. " Don't imagine for a minute that you are superior to her," he told Nettie more directly. " There is nothing more remarkable. They must be gorgeous," a faint color stained his long cheeks. " What incredible luck," he murmured.

He was thinking avidly of the women of China — the

little gay girls like toys, the momentary glimpses of enameled faces in hurrying red-flowered sedan chairs, faces of ivory stained with carmine, in gold-crusted headdresses. A sudden impatience at Nettie Vollar's obvious person and clothes expanded to a detestation of an atmosphere he had but a minute or so before welcomed as an escape from something infinitely worse than death. Now it seemed impossible to spend a life in Salem. It would have been better, when he had been released by Heard and Company, to have taken the position open in the Dutch Hong.

He was in a continual state of such vacillation, as if he were the seat of two separate and antagonistic personalities; rather, he changed the figure, in him the East struggled with the West. It was necessary for the latter to triumph. The difficulty lay in the fact that the first was represented by an actual circumstance while the other was only a dim apprehension, a weakened allegiance to ties never strong.

He cursed the extraordinary chance that, against every probability, had brought the chest of opium safely to him here. Its purchase had been the result of habit evading his will, he had despatched it — in that seesawing contest — by a precarious route, half hoping that it would be lost or seized; and, when he had seen the chest carried down Hardy Street to his door, a species of terror had fastened upon him, a premonition of an evil spirit flickering above him in a turning of oily smoke. Why hadn't he pitched the thing into the water at the foot of their yard! There was time still: he would take the balls of opium and dispose of them secretly. A sudden energy, a renewed sense of strength, flooded him. This distaste for Nettie changed into a pity at the ill luck that had followed her: she didn't deserve it. Generous emotions expanded his heart. He dreamed of taking hold of his father's small commerce in rum and sugar with the West Indies and turning it into a concern as rich and powerful as Ammidon, Ammidon and Saltonstone.

Why not!

They, too, would have a big white house on Washington Square or Chestnut Street, with servants — Chinese servants — and horses and great ships sailing in, laden with the East. Why not indeed! He, Edward Dunsack, had more brains than Jeremy Ammidon, that stiff old man with a face the color of a damask plum. His niece would go to all the balls at Franklin and Hamilton Halls, the injustice of her position overcome by an impressively increasing fortune. Abstractly he patted her shoulder with a hand as long and gaunt and yellow as his face. All this would come as a result of throwing the opium into the harbor. It was as good as accomplished.

In the face of his prospective well-being he felt already the equal of anyone in Salem. If Gerrit Ammidon had married a Manchu lady it was his privilege, no, duty, to call and put his experience in things Chinese at their command. She would speak only a little if any English; no one here understood the preparation of her food — her delicate necessity for dishes not the property of an entire household; a hundred such details of which the infinitely cruder West must be ignorant. He thought complacently that he would understand her better than anyone else in Salem, in Boston, in America; far better than her husband. She would without doubt learn to depend on him: they would laugh together at the manners and people about them. Ammidon would be away for long periods on the China service —.

His dreams broke off with a sardonic laugh, a repetition of the tone in which he had objurgated the shipmaster. Such visions were the property of youth, and he was forty-two, forty-two and nothing more than a discredited clerk who had fled across the world from a shadow. But he was right — he had seen white men who had caught the breath of China accepting just such opportunities as the one offered to him after his dismissal by Augustine Heard. At the Dutch Hong he'd be expected to talk about his late employer. Such situations, he had realized in a rarely illuminating flash, were only temporary, a descending flight.

These men resembled the fate of, say, a brig sailing into the China Sea in all the perfection of order of the British Marine: at, perhaps, Hong Kong, sold to a native firm, she would be refitted under an extravagant flag, and slowly the order would depart until, in a slovenly tangle of rigging and defilement, she'd be seen yawing on secret and nauseous errands.

A homely chime of bells was repeated from the town; a ship's fast strained resinously with the changing tide. "It will be getting on toward supper," Nettie told him. They walked slowly from the wharf, turned silently into Derby Street and Hardy on their way home. Beyond the inner fence of the garden the thick uneven sod reaching to the water was dark and cool against the luminous flush of evening. A sound of frying and heavy odor came from the kitchen, and Kate Vollar's voice informed them that the meal was ready.

Barzil Dunsack bowed his head over the table and pronounced a grace in startlingly resonant tones, the reverent humility of his words oddly emphasized by a sort of angry impatience. It seemed as if he at once subjected himself to his God and expressed a certain dissatisfaction with His forbearance. Edward Dunsack was plunged in the thought of the resolution he intended to fulfill that evening.

The throwing away of the opium had lost a part of its symbolic meaning. It now seemed even a little rash when he could find an immediate highly profitable market — the opium had cost him seven hundred dollars in China. But he must, he realized, be firm. Afterwards, in his room facing away from the street over darkening yards and gables and foliage, he stood gazing at the chest of mango wood that held the drug. Edward Dunsack unlocked and lifted the lid. On the tray before him were twenty balls, each the size of his two fists, wrapped in a hard skin of poppy leaves, and there was a similar number underneath. It was obvious that he couldn't carry a tray through the house, and he took out two balls, after which he secured the remainder.

He walked quickly down the stair and through the close turning of the lower hall that led through a side door to the yard. A pale rectangle of lamplight fell from the sitting room window over a brick path and ground tramped bare of grass; a clinking of dishes sounded in the kitchen. The sod was damp, and perhaps eight feet below the wooden buttress of the land the water showed impenetrably black.

[107]

Safely there he passed a tense hand over a brow suddenly wet; he was shaking as if in the grip of a chill. His condition needed drastic measures. The cold heavy opium gave out its tantalizing odor. In a minute it would be disposed of and he would go for more. He calculated that this necessitated twenty trips at the present rate — a bag might serve his purpose better. He raised an arm with an opium ball, but his hand remained suspended in air. An inarticulate protest seized him, a suffocating sense of impending loss. He would never be able to get Patna opium here; it was a valuable medical property. His nerves shook at the thought of its delights. Then, as if without his volition and against every intention, his arm described a short arc and his hand was empty. There was the impact of a solid object striking the water, a faint ripple on the motionless expanse, and then absolute silence.

He was aghast at his wanton act, the irreparable waste of a precious substance, and cursed in a low audible Cantonese. Whose concern was it if he did, very occasionally, smoke a " pistol "? How could it possibly matter! The dreams about a great foreign commerce, a white house like the Ammidons', were futile; it was too late. He could expect nothing from life but the unspeakable monotony of his father's dwelling, the bare office. He had worked hard, been as full of splendid early resolutions as anyone, and he wasn't blamable if chance balked his ambition. A soul was nothing more than a twisting leaf in the wind of fate. There remained only to take what escape was offered — golden visions, luxury, beauty beyond all earth.

His contrary determination seemed of less actuality than

the imagined echoing of the splash that still hung in his brain. It was a thing far away, belonging to another time, another man; like the memory of a period of charming ignorance. The thought of it wove a strand of melancholy into his present mature realization like the delicate scent of blossoming trees borne to him on the evening air, barely perceptible and then lost in the pungency of the opium. The latter became, mystically, all China, the irresistible fascination that had gradually possessed his imagination, dulling the associations of his heredity and birth, calling him further and further into its secretive heart.

He returned to his room, where he put back the second ball in the tray of its chest. An extraordinary weariness hung over him, there was a sense of leaden weight in his arms and feet. Flashes of a different perception pierced his apathy; a voice, seemingly outside his being, whispered of danger, evil and danger. . . . A twisting leaf, he told himself again with his deep fatalism.

The memory of Gerrit Ammidon's crisp blue gaze, his vigorous gestures and speech, became an intolerable affront, representing the far lost point of his own departure. His contrary feelings met and grappled in his mind; but in the end the past, Salem, was always defeated, weaker, more faintly perceived. In a great many essentials, he told himself, he had become Chinese in sympathy and fiber.

The lamp threw a smooth gleam over the mango wood chest, and he bent, turning the key in the ornamental brass lock. He could reconsider the disposal of the opium tomorrow; there was no hurry; he had no intention of becoming a victim to the drug. That would be an inconceivable stupidity, the negation of all the philosophy he had gained. Very occasionally —

His thoughts swung to the surprising fact of Ammidon's Chinese wife: if, as he had first suspected, she were a common woman of the port who had made a fool of the dull sailor he perceived the making of a very entertaining comedy. There would be the keenest irony in exposing her to himself before the complacent ignorance of her husband. He knew such women: convicted in Chinese, perhaps before the entire Ammidon family, not a muscle of her face would betray surprise or concern. She might try to murder him, very ingeniously, but never descend to the intrigue, the lies, of a Western woman placed in the same position. She'd stoically accept the situation. These visions ran rapidly, vividly, through his brain; he was accustomed to them; a greater part of his waking life was filled with such pictures, infinitely more alluring, persuasive, than the disappointing actuality. He got out of his clothes, and, in a loose gown of black silk, sat at his open window, his chin sunk in the palm of a hand, his face set against the night.

The next morning, at the breakfast table, he listened with a fleering mouth to his father's long dogmatic grace before meat. His sister sat opposite their parent, her gaze lowered in a perpetual amazement, her entire person stamped with a stupid humility. There was nothing humble, however, in Nettie; the crisp French coloring positively crackled with an electric energy; her mouth was set in a rebellious red blot. Studying her, Edward Dunsack saw that she was prettier than he had first realized on his return to Salem. He speculated over the story she had told him yesterday about Gerrit Ammidon's attachment. What an incredible idiot their father had been: Edward would have relished Gerrit as a brother-in-law; good would have come to them all from such a connection.

If he had been in America at the time no such error would have been permitted. With his counsel Nettie would have caught Ammidon beyond any escape. He wondered if the girl had actually cared for the shipmaster or if the affair had been nothing more than a sop to her wounded pride and isolation. In a way beyond his present understanding this seemed to be considerably important. If she had loved him no one could predict what her attitude might be in any future development of their contact; but if her pride only had been involved, injured, she might readily be an instrument for his own obscure purposes.

The office where Barzil Dunsack conducted the limited affairs of his West India trading was a small one-room building back of the dwelling. There was a high desk at which a clerk stood, or balanced on a long-legged stool, a more formal secretary against the length of the wall, with a careful model of a full ship, the spars and standing rigging slack and the whole gray with dust, a built-in cupboard opposite, a dilipidated chair or so and a ten-plate iron stove for wood. A window looked out acros the grass to the harbor and another opened blankly against a board fence.

There Edward Dunsack made a column of entries in a script fine and regular but occasionally showing an uncontrollably tremulous line. He was conscious of this tendency, growing through the past year; and he surveyed his writing with a feeling of angry dismay. Try as he might, with a frowning concentration, to pen the words and numerals firmly, presently his attention would slip, his hand waver ever so slightly, and a sudden stricken appearance of old age fasten on the characters. . . . By heaven, to-night he'd throw all that stinking stuff away!

Outside the day was immaculate, the expanse of the water was like celestial silk, such sails as he saw resembled white clouds. The early morning bird song had subsided, but a persistent robin was whistling from the grass by the open door. The curd-like petals of a magnolia were slowly shifting obliquely to the ground, he could hear the stir of Derby Street. He was inexpressibly weary of the struggle always racking his being: it seemed to him that in the midst of a serene world he was tormented by some inimicable and fatal power.

He fastened his thoughts on commonplace happier objects, on the page under his hand, the entries of Medford rum and sugar cane and molasses, and the infinitely larger affairs of Ammidon, Ammidon and Saltonstone. There was no reason why he shouldn't call on Jeremy Ammidon's family. The latter had signified by his visit the desire to end the misunderstanding between them. He was as well born as Gerrit Ammidon; only ill chance had made them seem differently situated. Anyhow, unlike Canton, mere exterior position had comparatively little weight in Salem. The shipmasters, the more important merchants, arrogated a certain superiority to themselves: but it broke down before the inborn democracy of the local spirit.

That afternoon, he decided, he'd be in Pleasant Street;

and later he dressed with the most meticulous care. A growing doubt seized him as he mounted the outside steps of the Ammidons' impressive house; but he crushed it down and firmly rapped with the polished knocker on the opened door.

The family, a servant told him, was in the garden; and he followed through a large white-paneled hall into a formal drawing-room and green space beyond. He was again uncertain before the number of people grouped about a summerhouse and apparently watching his approach with cold surprise. But Gerrit Ammidon stepped forward and greeted him with an adequately level civility.

" You know my father," he said, and Jeremy Ammidon, his heavy body in linen above which his face was dusky, put out an abrupt hand. There was a Mr. Brevard, a slender unconcerned person in very fashionable but restrained clothes; William Ammidon's wife, a large woman in India muslin, handsome enough, Edward Dunsack conceded, in the obvious American sense; a daughter of William's, a girl blooming into womanhood, far too vigorous and brightly colored for his taste; and Gerrit's wife.

The latter had been hidden from him at first, and he saw her suddenly, completely: his surprise caused him to stand in an awkward suspense — never had he imagined that a woman, even a Manchu, could be so beautiful! He recognized, in a score of unmistakable details, that she was of irreproachably high birth; her satins were embroidered with the symbols of nobility and matrimonial felicity; the gold fingernail guards, the jade and flowering pearls, her earrings and tasseled tobacco pouch and ivory fan, were all in the most superlative manner.

[113]

A deep pleasurable excitement filled him as he made his greeting in correct Chinese. The long delicate oval of her face showed no emotion at the sound of her native speech and she returned his periods in a slowly chosen mechanical English. Edward Dunsack thought that as he spoke an expression of distaste stamped Gerrit's features. However, he was left in no doubt: "My wife," the other instructed him, "prefers to speak English. That is the only way she has of picking it up."

A contempt filled Dunsack which he was barely able to keep from his voice and manner. He nodded shortly, and subsided into a study of Taou Yuen so open that she must have become aware of his interest. Seated on the bench that circled the interior of the latticed summerhouse she moved so that he could no longer see her face. Brevard was beside her, talking in a low amused voice: there was a ringing peal of laughter from Sidsall Ammidon and a faint infinitely well-bred ripple from Taou Yuen. The brilliant patch of her gown made an extraordinary effect in the Salem garden. Edward Dunsack recognized the scents that stirred from her, more Eastern and disturbing even than opium: there was a subtle natural odor of musk, the perfumes of henna and clove blossoms and santal.

A curious double feeling possessed him in the split consciousness of which he was capable — he had the sensation of having come, in the suave afternoon garden, on overwhelming disaster, and at the same time he was enraged by the play of Fate that had given such a woman to Gerrit Ammidon and denied him, with his special appreciation of Oriental charm, the slightest satisfaction. A more general hatred of Gerrit tightened to a consuming resentment of the other's blind fortune.

One thing was unmistakably borne upon him — in spite of the courtesy he was meeting it was clear that he could not hope to become a customary visitor at the Ammidons'. He was put definitely outside the community of interests in which Brevard easily entered. William Ammidon joined them, and something like astonishment at Dunsack's presence was visible on his complacent face.

He remained, however, in a stubborn resistance to small adverse signs in the hope of gaining some additional facts about Taou Yuen. She had been, he learned, a widow and Gerrit had married her with her father-in-law's consent although the latter was a rich official. He wanted to ask a thousand questions, but he knew that even if the Ammidons were too dense to grasp his curiosity, Taou Yuen herself would comprehend his impoliteness. Nowhere else could be found the wisdom and poise of a Manchu lady.

Jeremy Ammidon, in a lawn chair, a smoking cheroot in his fingers, asked him about affairs of Chinese government and commerce. As the old man talked he flushed darkly with quick indignation. " The English have made our political diplomats look like stuffed gulls! " he declared. " Look at their Orders in Council and the British Prize Courts," he proceeded, waving his cheroot; " stop an American vessel anywhere and pretend to find a deserting English sailor. With the Treaty of Ghent and codheaded commissioners and a Congress that wouldn't know a ship from a bread barge the country's going to hell on greased ways! I've said it a thousand times and any man not a complete ass knows that you can't run a government without a strong head. Locofocos," he muttered.

Edward Dunsack listened to this tirade with an air of polite attention which hid completely the fact that he heard or comprehended scarcely a word. His thoughts were filled by the fragrant vision of Taou Yuen; already he was deep in the problem of how to see her again, to-morrow. It would be excessively difficult. Eastern women never, if they could avoid it, walked; and they were, he knew, entirely without the necessity that drove the women of Salem into a ceaseless round of calling and gossip. It was probable that, except to ride, she wouldn't leave the house and grounds. He cursed the chance quarrel that had set a customary void between the houses of Dunsack and Ammidon, the unfortunate affair of his sister and Vollar inescapably adding to the permanency of the breach; he particularly cursed Nettie. There, however, his mind took up the twisted thread of the vague possibility that the latter might be useful to him: he was amazed at the way in which his premonitions fitted into the pattern of situations yet to be materialized.

Edward Dunsack turned from his contemplation of Taou Yuen to a careful consideration of Gerrit Ammidon. The latter had a countenance which showed strong, easily summoned emotions. It was an intolerant face, Dunsack judged, and yet sentimental; and it was surprisingly young, guileless. At the same time it was unusually determined — an affair of uncomplicated surfaces, direct gaze, marked bone.

He questioned sharply, irritably, the length to which his

projections had reached. What were they all about? The answer was presented by the glittering figure of the Manchu; she had risen and was standing in the entrance of the summerhouse. He thought, with a jerking pulse, of Oriental similes; she was a lotus-woman, a green slip of willow, an ambrosial moon, a mustard flower. Her teeth were white buds, her breasts blanched almonds.

His entire life in China had been a preparation for the realization of the present moment. The sense of danger, of anger at Gerrit Ammidon, perished before the supreme emotion called up by Taou Yuen. He wanted to embrace her satin-shod feet, to cling to her odorous hands, such hands as were never formed out of China, like petals of coral. Not only her bodily charm intoxicated him, but the thought of her subtle mind added its attraction, its shadows never to be pierced by the blunted Western instinct, the knowledge of pleasures like perfumes, the calm blend of the eight diagrams of Confucius, the stoicism of the Buddhistic soul revolving perpetually in the urn of Fate, and of the aloof Tao of Lao-tze.

Brevard left with an easy familiarity, already planning a return, that filled Edward Dunsack with resentful envy. The sun had disappeared behind the house; long cool shadows swept down the garden; it was past time for him to go. A reluctance to move from the magic of Taou Yuen possessed him: he was unable to think how, when, he would next see her. He raged at the prohibition against speaking Chinese; that ability should give him an overwhelming advantage of Gerrit Ammidon. This was, of course, the reason that he had been virtually commanded

[117]

to limit himself to English. Many of the forms of extreme Chinese courtesy were impossible to express in another language.

Finally he rose; in departing he emphasized the importance of Jeremy Ammidon — Taou Yuen should recognize and applaud that. He saw that she was watching him obliquely, her lips in repose, her hands still among the satin draperies. An American would have betrayed something of her reaction to him, he could have discovered a trace, an indication, of her thoughts; but the Manchu's face was as inscrutable as porcelain. William Ammidon nodded, the old man responded to his leave-taking with a degree of warmness, Gerrit at least smiled in a not unfriendly manner. Edward Dunsack bowed to Taou Yuen, and she gravely inclined her head. He had a last glimpse of her glowing in the green light of the inclosure of rosebushes and poplars, emerald sod and tangled lilac trees.

At the supper table his sister's appearance in somber untidy black barége, Nettie's unrestrained gestures and speech, the coarse red cloth and plain boiled fare, all added to a discontent that he could scarcely restrain. With the utmost discrimination in delicate shades of beauty and luxury he was yet condemned to spend his days in surroundings hardly raised above poverty-stricken squalor. Incongruous as it was he could yet imagine Taou Yuen moving with a certain appropriateness about the Ammidons' spacious grounds and house; but he was absolutely unable to picture her here, on Hardy Street.

All the vivid scenes that continually formed and shifted in his mind gathered about Gerrit Ammidon's wife. He

[118]

used this phrase in a contemptuously satirical manner: it was impossible for Ammidon actually to marry a Manchu. Such racial mating, he told himself, could not be consummated; there were too many deep antipathies of flesh and spirit; the man was too — too stupidly normal. Sooner or later he would swing back to his own. With him, Edward Dunsack, it was different; he always had an inner kinship with China; at first sight its streets and sounds, odors and ways, had seemed familiar, admirable.

The realization of this, when his place with Heard and Company collapsed, had sent him back to America, in a strange dread. He remembered how the vague fear had followed him to Derby Wharf. Now he laughed at it, welcoming every Chinese instinct he had. They seemed to throw a bridge across enormous difficulties, bringing him finally to Taou Yuen.

He lingered at the table after supper, his head sunk on his chest, revolving the various aspects of his position. One thing was definite — he must have Taou Yuen; it was unthinkable that she should continue with Gerrit Ammidon. It needed skillful planning, tortuous execution, but in the end he'd get his desire. He had no doubt of that. It was necessary. If she opposed him she would discover that he, too, could be subtle, Oriental, yes — dangerous. None of the stupid inhibitions that, for example, bound his father interfered with the free exercise of his personal wishes. He was beyond primitive morality.

An ecstasy of contemplation ravished his senses.

"Goodness, Uncle Edward," Nettie exclaimed, "you scared me, you looked so like a Chinee."

"There are no such people," he retorted sharply, exasperated by the vulgar error. She was undismayed; and when, in reply to the question, she learned that he had been at the Ammidons' her surprise increased his irritation. He saw from her manner that his calling there had been at least unexpected. Nettie interrupted the preparation of the table for breakfast, and dropped into a chair beyond him, her hands — the sleeves were rolled back to her elbows — clasped before her.

" You must tell me everything," she declared eagerly. " What is she like? Do they seem happy? Did he hold her hand? Do Chinese women kiss? Is she tall or —"

" I can't remember a question out of your rattle," he interrupted her. He was about to give expression to his admiration for Taou Yuen, when he stopped, with tight lips. Here, perhaps, was the lever by which so much was to be shifted.

" She's Chinese," he said indifferently, " and that means yellow." Nettie made a gesture of distaste. " They seem to get along well enough. Of course, it's ridiculous to call it a marriage, and it seems to me very questionable to impose it on the Ammidons as that. The thing is — how long will it last, how soon will he get tired of her and send her back to Canton? "

Nettie Vollar closed her eyes, her hands were rigid. The lamplight, streaming up over her face, showed him that it was tense and pale and answered a question. Her feeling for Gerrit Ammidon had been more than a mere hurt pride. In addition to that he saw beyond any doubt the proof of its existence still. This complicated his problem: inspired only by a resentment that he might fan into hatred she would be far more pliable than in the grip of a genuine affection for Gerrit Ammidon. He understood the processes of the former, a flexible and useful steel; but no one could predict the vagaries, the absurd self-sacrifices, of love. Well, he'd have to work with what offered. That, he realized, was the strength of his philosophy — he accepted promptly, without vain regret, the means that lay at his hand.

" Ammidon seems worn," he said generally; " they were in the garden, and I had a few words privately with him." Nettie glanced swiftly across the table; her lips moved; but she repressed the obvious question trembling on them. " He showed, I think," he continued carefully, " a very improper interest in you."

" How? "

" He asked if you were well and happy. I most certainly told him, for any number of reasons, for pride alone, that you were."

" Then you told a lie," she cried in a tone so hard that it surprised him.

" Of course," he went on smoothly, " I know that you are not, almost all your circumstances prohibit that. But I don't intend to circulate it in Salem. Opinion here may have forced you into a long loneliness, but I shan't give anyone the satisfaction of knowing it. And, after all, you have your grandfather mostly to blame. You would have been married to Gerrit Ammidon now if he hadn't interfered; you would have been walking about the Ammidons' garden with your hand on his arm in place of that Chinese prostitute."

" I don't see why you should make me so miserable," she declared. " I don't care anything about the garden, it isn't that. Why do you suppose he brought such a woman home."

" Pique," he told her; " he couldn't care for her in the way he might for, well — you. As I said, he'll drop her on his next voyage to the East; he will leave her and probably never come back to Salem again. I hear that Ammidon, Ammidon and Saltonstone are planning a new policy — bigger ships, clippers in the China and California trade; and that means removal to Boston. Their facilities here are no longer suitable."

She moved, her chin fell upon her hands, propped up with her elbows on the table. Apparently Edward Dunsack was gazing at the wall beyond her. Her breast gave a single sharp heave. When Nettie looked up her face was flushed. " I wish that I were really a bad woman," she spoke in a low vibrant voice.

" What is bad and what is good ? " He still seemed to ignore her, considering a question that had no personal bearing. " In one country a thing is thought wrong and in another it is the highest virtue. In one age this or that is condemned, when, turn the calendar, and everyone is praising it." He became confidential, the image of kindness. " I'll tell you what I think is wicked," he pronounced, leaning toward her, " and that is the way you two were kept apart; unchristian is what I call it."

" Gerrit doesn't care," she said.

" How do you know ? " he demanded. " I cannot agree with you. I don't find a great deal in him to admire, he is too simple and transparent; but there's no doubt of this, he is faithful. One idea, one affection, is all his head will hold."

" That's a beautiful trait." A palpable wistfulness settled over her.

" It's greatly admired," he agreed; " although not by me. I believe in taking what is yours, what you need, from life. I suppose that I have been away from proprieties so long that they have lost their importance. They seem to me of no greater weight than barriers of straw. But, of course, that mightn't suit you; probably, living in Salem as you have, its opinion is valuable."

" Salem! " she exclaimed bitterly. " What has it ever been to me but an unfair judgment? I owe Salem no consideration; I can't see that I owe any to life."

" I don't want to insist on that," he proceeded deliberately. " The tragedy of your position is that married to Ammidon everything in the past would have been overlooked, forgotten. Even now —" he stopped with a gesture indicating the presence still of large possibilities.

God, what a vacillating fool the girl was! He could say no more at present, and he rose, leaving the room with Nettie staring dully across the table. He went outside, to the grass fronting on the harbor. Here, last night, he had thrown the opium into the water. It seemed to him that he had lived through a complete existence since then: the presence of Taou Yuen had created a new world. He thought she walked to him through the gloom; he saw her slender body grow brighter as she approached; he heard her speak in a low native murmur; their hands caught in an eager tangle.

He put aside, momentarily, the problem of the difficulties of going again to the Ammidons' for an easier one — the bringing of Gerrit Ammidon here. He was confi-

[123]

dent that, thrown together on the still rim of the water, at evening, the emotion born between his niece and the ship-master and prematurely choked would revive. He had no means of knowing Ammidon's present exact feeling for Nettie; he was counting only on a general theory of men and nature at large. He was already convinced, from very wide knowledge, experience, that the other could not form a permanent attachment to the Manchu; and Nettie's great difference, together with the romance of her unhappy position, must have a potent effect on the fellow's evident sentimentality. A dank air rose from the water, like the smell of death; and, with an uncontrollable shiver, he turned back toward the house.

In his room Edward Dunsack recalled that he had promised himself to throw away the remainder of the opium on this and succeeding nights. In view of that his movements were inexplicable: he got out from a locked chest the *yen tsiang*, a heavy tube of dark wood inlaid with silver ideograms and diminutive earthen cup at one end. Then he produced a small brass lamp, brushes, long needles, and a metal rod. Taking off his clothes, and in the somber black folds of the silk robe, he made various minutely careful preparations. Finally, extended on his bed, he dipped the end of the rod into opium the color of tar, kept it for a bubbling moment near the blaze of the lamp, and then crowded the drug into the pipe. He held the bowl to the flame and drew in a long deep inhalation. A second followed and the pipe was empty. He repeated this until he had smoked a mace.

A vivacious and brilliant state of being flooded him; he felt capable of profoundly witty conversation, and laughed at the solemn absurdities of the Ammidons, at his father attempting to call down a blessing out of the empty sky upon their food, at his sister's lugubrious countenance, the childish emotions of Nettie. What a nonsensical strutting business life was.

The confines of his room were lost in an amber radiance that filled all space; it was at once a light and a perfume and charged with a sense of impending rapture. A sparkling crimson shape floated down from infinite skies — Taou Yuen. She wore a bridal costume, cunningly embroidered with the phoenix, a hood of thin gold plate, and a band of red silk about her brow bore the eight copper figures of the beings who are immortal. Her hair was ornamented by the pure green jade pins of summer, her hanging wrists were heavy with virgin silver, while her face was like the desirous August moon flushed in low vapors.

He raised his bony arms — the wide silk sleeves falling back — his emaciated yellow hands. From under his dark eyelids there was a glitter of vision like the sheen on mica . . . Taou Yuen floated nearer.

Edward Dunsack woke suddenly, at the darkest ebb of night, and started hurriedly to his feet. A sickening vertigo, a whirling head, sent him lurching across the room. He came in contact with a chest of drawers, and clung to it with the feeling that his legs were shriveling beneath him. His consciousness slowly returned, and with it a pain like ruthless tearing fingers searched his body. The rectangle of the open window, only less dark than the room, promised a relief from the strangled effort of his breathing, and he fell across the ledge, lifting his face to a starless

[125]

and unstirring heat. Waves of complete physical exhaustion passed over him. An utter horror fastened on his brain.

"Oh, God," he said, with numb lips, "we thank Thee for this, Thy daily blessing —" He broke off with an effort. That was his father pronouncing a grace. "Oh God —" he said again, when it seemed to him that in the darkness he saw the blank placidity of a Buddha carved from gray stone. Tears ran over his sunken cheeks, salt and warm like blood.

VI

THE night was so oppressive, continuing such
an unusually sultry period for the season, that
Sidsall, ordinarily impervious to the effects of
weather, was unable to sleep. Although the door between
her room and her parents' was shut, she heard her father
— his step, at once quick and firm, was easily recognizable — moving about beyond. Her restlessness increased and she got up, crossing the floor to the window
open on the garden, where she knelt, the thick plait of
her hair across her cheek and shoulder, with her arms
propped on the ledge. The depths of sky were hidden
in a darkness like night made visible; and, in place of
moving air, there were slow waves of perfume, now from
the lilacs and now from the opening hedge of June roses.

Her brain was filled by a multitude of minor images
and speculations, but fixed at their back was the presence of Roger Brevard. She approved of him absolutely.
He had exactly the formal manner that gave her a pleasant sense of delicate importance, and his clothes were
beautiful, a sprig of rose geranium in a buttonhole and
his gloves and boots immaculate. She liked rather slight
graceful men, she thought, with the quiet voices of a
polite ancestry. Naturally Olive Wibird preferred less
restrained companions, although Heaven knew that Olive
appeared to make all kinds welcome. Olive's opinion

[127]

of Roger Brevard would have been very different if he had asked her to dance.

Sidsall recalled the quadrille he had led her through at Lacy's party; he had been a perfect partner, at once light and firm. He had been a habitual caller at Java Head before that occasion, and had come in the same manner since. That is, casually viewed, his visits seemed the same; but in reality there were some small yet significant differences. They were all held in his attitude of the afternoon when he had stayed talking exclusively to her on the steps.

She couldn't say just what the change was; when she attempted to examine it her thoughts became confused and turned to a hundred absurd considerations, such as — at present — the loveliness of the night. The scents of the flowers were overwhelming. He got on, too, better than almost anyone else with her Uncle Gerrit's Manchu wife. She had watched them together until it had dawned on her that the two had some important qualities in common — they both appeared to stand a little aside from the world, as if they were against the wall at a cotillion. She thought this in spite of the fact that it was precisely what Roger Brevard never did; it was true in the mysterious way of so much now that came from ideas over which she had no control.

The subject of Uncle Gerrit's wife — she had not yet been told or decided for herself what to call her — was inexhaustibly enthralling. But, before she was again fairly launched in it, she paused to wonder at the presence of the dreadful Dunsack man on their lawn. His hollow yellow cheeks and staring brown eyes which somehow made her think of pain, his restless hands and speech, all repelled her violently. Taou — Taou Yuen hadn't liked him either: when, after the longest time, he had gone, she replied to a short comment from her, Sidsall's, father:

"Rotten wood cannot be carved."

Some one else had mentioned opium. She had intended to ask more particularly about this, but it slipped from her mind. She remembered that her grandfather made one of his familiar exclamations peppered with an appalling word. He was really very embarrassing, and she was glad that Roger Brevard had left. It was a bad example for Laurel, too, who copied him, and only that morning said "My God" to Miss Gomes. Her mind swung back to the consideration of the Manchu:

The latter was the fact upon which Camilla was so insistent, that in this case a Manchu was a noble, almost a princess. Camilla suffered dreadfully from the endless questions put to her outside their house about Uncle Gerrit's wife. She had more than once wept at the public blot laid on them. Laurel was frankly inquisitive and Janet as puzzling as usual.

The clothes of course were enchanting, the richness of the materials and hand embroidery marvellous; her jewelry was never ending. It didn't seem quite like clothing, in the sense of her own tarlatan and crinoline, her waist which Hodie wouldn't properly lace and tulle draping; there was a certain resemblance to the dressing in Van Amburgh's circus; but — in spite of Camilla's private laments — every inch of it was distinguished. The layers of paint upset them, but Uncle Gerrit had explained, a little impatiently, that it was a Manchu custom, adding that the world couldn't be all measured and judged by Salem.

Sidsall liked her rather than not, she decided; and determined to make an effort to know her better. She wanted specially to discover the nature of the bond that held one to the other, and explore, in safety, the depths of love. She could not help feeling that her uncle's affair, extraordinary as it was, must throw light on the whole complicated business of marriage. . . . The clock in the hall struck an indeterminate half hour, it appeared to grow lighter outside, and there was a twittering of martins from the stables. From above came the vigorous harsh cawing of crows. Suddenly sleepy she returned to bed and almost immediately the room was flooded with sunlight.

It was an accepted fact now that Taou Yuen, the Garden of Peaches, stayed in her room until long after breakfast; and when Sidsall, rising from the table, found a servant taking up a pot of hot water for tea, she secured it and knocked carefully on the door above. The slurring hesitating voice said " Come in," and she entered with a diffidence covered by a cheerfully polite morning greeting. She found the other in crêpe de Chine pantaloons wrapped tightly about her ankles and bound over quilted muslin socks with gay brocaded ribbons and a short floating gown of gray silk worked with willow leaves. Her hair was an undisturbed complication of lustrous black, gold bodkins and flowers massed on either side; and her face, without paint or powder, was as smooth as ivory and the color of very pale coffee and cream.

Sidsall saw that she was at her toilet, and she put

down the pot of steaming water, moving toward the door; but Taou Yuen, with a charmingly shy gesture, begged her to stay. She swiftly drew a cup of tea from silvery leaves, filled and lighted the minute bowl of her tobacco pipe, deeply inhaled the smoke; then returned to a mirror.

Fascinated, Sidsall followed every motion.

Taou Yuen polished her face sharply with a hot damp cloth and then dipped her fingers in a jar that held a sticky amber substance. "Honey," she said briefly, rubbing it into her cheeks and palms. Next she attacked her eyebrows, and skillfully wielding a thin silk cord left arches like pencil markings. At times she interrupted her preparations to turn to Sidsall with a little smile so engaging that the girl smiled sympathetically in answer. There were a gilt paper box of rice powder, with which she drenched her countenance, leaves of carmine transferred to her cheeks with a wet finger, and a silver pot of rouge from which she coated her lips. As she gazed approvingly at her reflection Sidsall said:

"It's very beautiful."

Her eyes, drawn up toward her temples, shone gayly; and, close to Sidsall, she touched the latter affectionately on the cheek. The cold sharp contact of the long curving finger guard gave the girl an unpleasant shock. It seemed lifeless, or like the scratching of a beetle. Suddenly the woman's glittering gaze, her expressionless face stiff with paint, the blaze of her barbaric colors, filled Sidsall with a shrinking that was almost dread.

She was even more oppressed by an instinctive feeling of what she could express to herself only as cruelty hidden under the other's scented embroidery. At the same time her curiosity persisted, conquered. She was unable, however, to think of any possible manner of introducing the new subject of her interest, love, and was forced to be content with an indifferent opening.

"We were all quite surprised when Mr. Dunsack called yesterday," she said. "He isn't in the least a friend of the family. Grandfather went to sea with his father, but even they didn't speak for years in Salem. The Dunsacks are a little common."

"I know," Taou Yuen replied. "Mr. Dunsack — a long time in Canton, at the American agents. China is bad for men like him. Black spirits get in them and the ten sins."

"He stared at you in the rudest way."

"He never saw a Manchu lady before. In China the dog would not have passed by the first gate. Here it is nothing to be a Manchu or an honorable wife; it is all like the tea houses and rice villages. Men walk up to you with bold eyes. I tell Gerrit and he laughs. I stay in the room and he brings me shamefully down. This Mr. Dunsack comes and the wise old man talks to him like a son. He touches your mother's hand. He sees the young girls like white candles."

"We wouldn't let him really bother us," Sidsall explained; "probably if he comes again we'll all be out."

Taou Yuen made a comment in Chinese. "A bad thought is a secret knife," she continued; "it is more dangerous than the anger of the Emperor, a sickness that kills with the stink of bodies already dead."

This seemed rather absurd to Sidsall. She considered once more the introduction of the subject of her new concern; but, in spite of Taou Yuen's extravagant appearance, there was a quality of being which made impossible any blunt interrogation. She had a decidedly aloof manner. Her mother, Sidsall recognized, and the older women they knew, had a trace of this; but in the Manchu it was carried infinitely further, a most autocratic disdain. Her feeling for the other shifted rapidly from attitude to attitude.

She watched, she was certain, these same sensations come over her Aunt Caroline Saltonstone, Mrs. Clifford and Mrs. Wibird, who called on Gerrit Ammidon's wife that afternoon. They were sitting with their crinoline widespread against their chairs, gazing with a concerted battery of curiosity at Taou Yuen's shimmering figure in the drawing-room screened against the sun. Mrs. Wibird, Sidsall thought — a woman of fat and faded prettiness, with wine red splotches beneath her eyes, and a voice that went on and on in the relating of various petty emotional disturbances — must have resembled Olive as a girl. It was probable, then, that Olive would look like her mother when in turn she was middle-aged. Mrs. Clifford, unseasonably huddled in her perpetual shawl, more than ever suggested a haggard marble in somberly rich clothes. Aunt Caroline sat with complacent hands and loud inattentive speech. Taou Yuen smiled at them placidly.

"Our men," said Mrs. Clifford, "went out to China for years. It never occurred to them however to marry a Chinese woman; but I dare say they didn't see the right sort."

"Most of the captains like China," Taou Yuen said.

"They are so far away from their families —" she made a brief philosophical gesture, and Madra Clifford studied her with a narrowed gaze. "It would be the same," she continued, "if Chinamen came to America." Mrs. Wibird shuddered. "A yellow skin," she cried impetuously; "I can't bide the thought."

"I'm sure we'd be tremendously interested," Mrs. Saltonstone hurriedly put in, "if you'd tell us about your wedding. A Chinese wedding must be — be very gay, with firecrackers and —"

"My marriage with Captain Ammidon was not beautiful — I was a widow and he foreign. The Manchu wedding is very nice. First there is the engagement ceremony. I sit like this," she sank gracefully to the floor, cross-legged, "on the bed with my eyes shut, and, if I am noble, two princesses come and put the *ju yi*, it's jade and means all joy, on my lap. Two little silk bags hang from the buttons of my gown with gold coins, and two gold rings on my fingers must be marked with *Ta hsi*, that's great happiness."

"I'm told polygamy is an active practice," Mrs. Wibird remarked with a rising interest.

"Yes?" Taou Yuen asked.

"One man — a lot of wives."

"The Emperor has a great many and some Manchus take a second and third. You think that is wrong here. Who knows! The Chinese women are very good, very modest. The Four Books For Girls teach perfect submission; the five virtues are benevolence, righteousness, propriety, wisdom, sincerity. Confucius says, 'The root is filial piety.'"

[134]

" Very admirable," Mrs. Wibird nodded, agitating the small dyed ostrich plumes tipped with marabou of her bonnet; but it was clear to Sidsall that this was not the revelation for which she had hoped. A momentary silence, the edge of an uneasiness, enveloped the visitors.

" What lovely satins," Mrs. Saltonstone commented.

" Please — I have a box full; you will let me give you some? "

" Indeed yes, and thank you."

Mrs. Wibird, growing resentful, said that a cousin of her aunt's had been a missionary to China, " and did a very blessed work too."

Taou Yuen smoothly agreed that it was quite possible. " Our poor have a great many wrong and lustful ideas," she acknowledged; " they tell lies and beat their wives and gamble. The higher classes too, the mandarins and princes, use the people for their own security and rob them. Sometimes the law is not honest, and a man with gold gets free when a laborer is put in the bamboo cage."

Mrs. Clifford said very vigorously, " Ha! "

The silence returned intensified.

" I remember," the Manchu went on, " this will amuse you. My father-in-law, who was in the Canton Customs, told me that some boxes of Bibles came out from America, with other objects, and when they were opened at the Mission they were the wrong ones and filled with rum."

There was not, however, any marked appreciation of this on the part of the Salem women. They rose to leave and Taou Yuen sank on her knee. She gazed without a trace of emotion at the three flooding the door with their belled skirts. "They are the same everywhere," she told the girl. The latter moved out into the garden. There she subconsciously picked a rose and fastened it in her hair; her thoughts turned to Roger Brevard. In his place her Uncle Gerrit came out through the drawing-room window. The usual shadow of the house, lengthening with afternoon, was pleasantly enveloping, and they walked slowly over the grass.

"A flower in your hair," he said, "and by yourself. You have been thinking about true love." She blushed vividly at this unexpected angle on her mind and found it impossible to meet his keen blue eyes. "Love must be a remarkable thing." She raised a swift glance to his face and discovered that he had not spoken to her at all, but, hat in hand, was looking away with an expression of abstraction.

"I mean the unreasonable silly divine kind," he specified, now gazing at her quizzically, as if lost in a mood over which he had no control; "the sort that is as long as life and stronger. It is entirely different and ages older than the reasonable logical love, all proper and suitable and civilized; or the love that is the result of a determination, the result of a determination," he repeated, frowning darkly at their feet. Sidsall held her breath, thrilled by the wealth of what she had heard, fearful of diverting what might be yet revealed. But he moved away abruptly, in a manner that enforced solitude, and stood apparently examining the rockery.

Her brain rang with the splendid phrase, "Love as long as life and stronger." It seemed to clarify and state so much of her lately confused being. Hodie, artfully drawn into the consideration of earthly affection, was far less satisfactory than Gerrit Ammidon. She dwelt on the treasure beyond moth or rust, lost in an ecstasy of contemplation expressed in her customary explosive amens. At the same time she admitted that lower unions were blessed of God, and recommended Sidsall to think on " a man who has seen the light and by no means a sea captain." Sidsall replied cuttingly, " I think you must forget where you are."

" I forget nothing," Hodie stoutly maintained; " I'll witness before anyone." She settled the flounces of Sidsall's skirt with a deft hand.

Walking toward the Saltonstones' for tea, with a mulberry silk parasol casting a shifting glow on her expanse of clear madras, Sidsall wondered at the sudden change of almost all her interests and preoccupations. It was very disturbing — she fell into daydreams that carried her fancy away on a search that was a longing, a soft confusion of opening her arms to mystery. This varied with a restless melancholy; the old securities of her life were hidden in a mist of uncertainty in which her consciousness was troubled by nameless pressures; something within her held almost desperately back from further adventuring. But all the time a latent fascination was drawing her on, putting aside the curtain for her better view.

The Saltonstones' dwelling on Chestnut Street was one of a pair — a large solid square of brick — with two identical oval white porticoes and rows of windows keyed in white stone. Within the staircase swept up to a slender pillared opening, through which Lacy, calmly dressing, waved a deliberate hand. Mrs. Saltonstone was seated by the tall gilt framed mirror on a low marble stand between long front windows. "As usual," she said, in connection with her daughter, "Lacy's as cool as a water monkey; gets it from James; they wouldn't hurry if —" She searched in vain for an expression of her family's composure. "Now I am an impetuous woman." She promptly exhibited this quality in the vigor with which she met the wrong canister of tea brought by a servant. She didn't intend to serve Padre Souchong to a lot of people who apparently confused afternoon tea with an invitation to dinner.

In the small press which followed Sidsall stopped in the dining room with Lacy and Olive Wibird. Olive was still discussing men. "He sat holding my hand right on that bench by your hedge, Sidsall, and said that nothing could keep him from coming back for me, but he died of yellow fever in Batavia." She left in the company of a beau of fifty anyhow, with a glistening bald head, a silly smirking bow and flood of compliments. Lacy moved away and Sidsall found herself facing Roger Brevard.

"That looks remarkably like a garden," he said, waving toward an open door. The sun had become obscured in a veil of cloud, drooping until it almost seemed to rest on the bright green foliage; her companion's mood, too, was shadowed. "I thought you'd be here," he added outside, "and looked for you at once."

"There was something special you wanted to say?"

"My dear child," he replied, "can't you guess how absolutely refreshing you are? No, I have nothing special. But you'll soon get used to men around with no more reason than yourself."

She studied this seriously; and, as its complimentary intent emerged, a corresponding color stained her cheeks. Her gaze rested on him for the fleetest moment possible and, to her surprise, she saw that he was frowning.

" I came here just to see you. No," he corrected his period, " only to see you." His manner was surprisingly abrupt and disconcerting. " I can quite realize," he went on, " that I shouldn't say any of this. Yet, on the other hand, it is the most natural thing in the world. I have been listening to the conventional babble of teas and cotillions for so long that you are like a breath of lost youth. Certainly that is appropriate. I think," he told her, " that you are the youngest thing alive." Then he laughed, " So young that I have annoyed you."

" I feel a great deal older than I did, well — last month," she said.

" That is a tragedy." She felt that if he were still amused at her she was furious, but he was even graver than before. " To tell you helps hurry the charm to an end. That is what might be complained against me. Yet flowers will open, you know, and it might as well be in an honest sun."

" I don't understand," she admitted, troubled.

" Why, it means, Sidsall, that I am offering you an experienced hand, that I'm certain I can do you more good than harm —"

" That's silly," she interrupted. " If you mean that we might be friends, really confidential friends, it would help me awfully. But then it's so one-sided."

[139]

" You'll have to overlook that," he answered; " probably all that I can give you, experience, isn't worth the smallest of your feelings. Probably you won't need me for an instant. Certainly the pleasure will be mine."

" You didn't understand," she told him, with dignity; " it's the other way round. I am not a particle interesting and everyone agrees that I'm too healthy. But I can't help it if my cheeks are red and mother won't let me have powder." It was obviously impossible to explain about Hodie and the lacing.

" I like it," he insisted. " I'll admit that I am unfashionable there. I think we'll hit on a great deal to share privately." There was a faint patter among the leaves, and a cold drop of rain fell on Sidsall's arm. Others struck Roger Brevard but he continued without apparently noticing them. " You must understand that I am entirely at your service. Sometimes, although they won't come yet, there are things a — a friend can do better than one's family. You'll ask me, Sidsall? "

" Yes," she said solemnly. More rain struck her; she could see it now plainly, falling between them. Roger Brevard's face was dark, the frown still scarred his forehead. Personally she was happier than she remembered ever being before and she wondered at his severity of bearing. " But you must go in at once," he cried, suddenly energetic, his familiar self; " you are getting wetter every minute."

The clouds dissolved into a late sunlight that streamed in long bars through the canopies of elms on the streets. From her windows Sidsall saw a world of flashing greenery and limpid sky. Usually when she was happy she sang unimportant bits of light song, but her present state was serious and inarticulate. The indeterminate questions, the disturbing vague moods, of the past days somehow combined and took on the tangible shape of Roger Brevard. Her curiosity about love was resolved into a sudden inner shrinking from its possibilities and meaning.

She was lost in her aloofness from mundane affairs: Taou Yuen in whispering silk, her grandfather's rotund tones, Laurel and Camilla and her mother, were distant, immaterial. In the evening she sat on the front steps, a web of white, dreamily intent on the shimmering sweep of Washington Square. After a little she was joined by Gerrit Ammidon. He wore linen trousers and a short blue sea jacket; and the wavering delicately lavender trail of smoke from his cheroot was like her floating thoughts.

" Already," he said, " I am full of getting back on my ship."

She smiled at him absently.

" The land doesn't do for a sailor," he continued. " They are always into trouble on shore. I can't say why it should be so but it is. If there's not one kind there is another; rum and such varnish for the able seaman, and — and complications for a master. I suppose that's because there are so confounded many unexpected currents and slants of wind, as you might say. On shipboard everything pretty much is charted; a thing will be followed more or less by a fixed consequence. The waves break so and so on coral or rocks or sand; there is usually the sun for an observation; a good man knows his ship, how many points she'll hold on the wind, how a cargo must be stowed, when to take in the light canvas. You can give the man at the wheel a course and turn in or stay on deck and beat your way through hell. It's exact, you know, but on shore —" he made a hopeless gesture.

"There are no regulations," he observed moodily; "or else nobody follows them: collisions all the time, sinkings and derelicts drifting round, awash and dismasted. But they are everywhere. That fellow, Edward Dunsack —" he stopped, lost in speculation. Then, " He seems harmless enough," he resumed, "even pitiful; but he sticks in your head. I wish I'd never brought his damned chest to Salem. A fool would have known better. I'm worse — a childish fool. A derelict," he said again. "You are smashing over a swell at twelve knots or more, everything spread, when, in a hollow, there it is squarely across your bow. No time to shift the wheel, and a ship's missing, perhaps in a hundred fathom. It might be the best ship afloat, the best master and stoutest crew, but in a minute she's only a salty tangle."

He laughed uneasily at the vividness of his fancy. "If it's hard for us what must it be for Taou Yuen?" he demanded. "Married to me! Here! That's courage for you." He tramped down the steps, across Pleasant Street, with his bare head sunk, and vanished into the obscurity of the Square. She caught a last glimmer of white trousers, a faint rapid gleam where his lighted cheroot described the arc of a passionate gesture on the night.

The spring, like the full buds of the hedge roses in the

Ammidons' garden, passed swiftly into early summer. The flowers against the house showed gay perennial colors, the stocks and larkspur and snapdragons succeeded the retreating flood of the lilacs. The days were still yellow pools of heat, or else cooled by the faintly salt sea wind drawing down the elms and chestnuts, followed by purple-green nights of moonlight. They seemed to Sidsall to hold everything in a pause. She saw less and less of Taou Yuen who now scarcely came out of her room except for an occasional ride in the barouche with Mrs. Ammidon or a contemplative hour in the garden, usually at dusk. Apparently content with the elaborate rearrangement of her headdress, she sat for long periods, gazing out over Washington Square, idle except for the regular tap of her pipe emptying the ashes of the minute bowl.

Yet Sidsall's first interest in her had almost completely shifted to Gerrit Ammidon. He evidently preferred her company to that of the other members of his family, and they often took short largely silent walks, usually down to the Salem Marine Railway where the *Nautilus* was undergoing repairs. His protracted silences were broken by the sudden vehement protests against the generally muddled aspect of affairs or longer monologues of inner questioning and search. He almost never referred to her or made her part of a conversation; she was free to dwell on her own emotions while he, with a corrugated brow, went on in his tortuous and solitary course.

On an afternoon when they had walked to the foot of Briggs Street, and were gazing out over the tranquil water of Collins Cove, Gerrit Ammidon asked abruptly:

" Have you seen Nettie Vollar lately?"

Sidsall was unable to remember exactly when that had been. She rather thought she had caught a glimpse of her in Lawrence Place with books under her arm which she was probably taking from the Athenæum for her grandfather. Anyone, she told herself privately, could see that Nettie Vollar wouldn't care for books.

Something had occurred, or threatened to occur, between her uncle and Nettie; what it was she had never been told; but she realized that only one thing could really happen between a man and girl — they must have been in love. In the interest of this she recalled Nettie Vollar's appearance, but was unable to discover any marked attractions. The elder had a good figure, rather full for her age, and totally different from her own square solidity. Her hair was coarse and carelessly arranged, her clothes noticeable for a love of brightness rather than care in the spending of a small sum.

Gerrit Ammidon had the strangest tastes!

He was standing immobile, looking across the Cove as if he were on a quarter-deck searching for a hidden land. His legs were slightly spread, firmly planted in a manner to defeat any sudden lurching. She grew a little impatient at him staring like a block at nothing at all; she felt older than he, superior in the knowledge of life; he seemed hardly more than an absurd boy. Sidsall had a desire to shake him. He was so — so impracticable. " Don't you think we'd better be going? " she asked finally. Gerrit Ammidon turned and followed her obediently.

There were lights in the rope walk on Briggs Street;

through a window she could see a man pacing down the long narrow interior laying a strand of hemp from the burden on his shoulders. It made her shudder to think of the monotonous passage forward and back, an eternity of slow-twisting rope. Yet life was something like that — she took the happenings of each day and wove them into a strand dark and bright: a strand, she realized, that grew stronger as it lengthened. . . . That would be true of everyone — of her companion and grandfather and Hodie.

They reached the house as the family were gathering in the dining room, when Sidsall found Roger Brevard unexpectedly staying for supper. She met his direct greeting and smile with a warm stir of pleasure and sat in a happy silence listening to the voices about the table. Her uncle had brought his wife down and the candles glittering among the lusters on the walls spread their light over the Manchu's strange vivid figure. Everything about life was so confusing, Sidsall thought. The night flowed in at the open windows drenched with magic: here were candles but outside were stars. The port in its engraved glass decanter seemed to burn with a ruby flame. " Bah! " her grandfather was exclaiming. " I'll put a thousand dollars on Gerrit and the *Nautilus* against any clipper built; but mind, in all weathers."

" Voyage by voyage," William Ammidon insisted, " he would be left in the harbor. The California gold deposits —."

Later a crowd, slowly collecting, recalled the fact that the Salem Band was to play that night in the Square. " Oh, mother, look," Laurel cried; " they've got lamps in

their hats." Small wavering flames were being lighted
on the musicians' hats; there were melancholy discon-
nected hoots from bassoons and the silver clear scale
of a bugle. "Can't I get nearer, mother?" Laurel implored as usual. "Can't I go and see the little lamps on
their heads?"

"Sidsall and I will look after her," Roger Brevard
put in, and almost immediately the three were entering
Washington Square. The throng was thickest directly
behind the band, radiating in thinning numbers to the
wooden boundary fence. Laurel led them to an advan-
tageous position, where they could watch the curious effects
of the ring of lights above intent faces drawn hollow-
cheeked by the vigorous blowing of instruments. The
leader, in the center of the flickering smoky illumination,
now beat with his arms in one direction, now in another.

A second selection followed, and a third, during which,
in surprising pauses, the band shouted a concerted
"Hurrah!" Sidsall was infinitely contented. How
splendidly erect and calm and distinguished Roger Brevard was! She hated younger men, they were only boys,
who kept up a senseless talk about college humor. He
saw instantly that the people were crushing her skirts,
and firmly conducted them out of the crowd. It was
nicer here beyond the wavering dark mass: a waltz flowed
about her so tender and gracious that her eyes filled with
tears.

But Laurel had to be taken home; and, clasping Mr.
Brevard's hand, the little girl talked volubly as they
moved away. "And so," she said, "I told her to keep
her topsails full."

" What? " he demanded.

" She was falling off, you know — losing way. Hell's hatches —"

" Laurel," Sidsall corrected her sharply. " No, you mustn't laugh at her."

Only Gerrit Ammidon was on the steps, the other men were in the library; her mother had gone up with Janet. Laurel left them, and, without speech, they walked through the house to the lawn. The stars had apparently retreated to new infinities of distance and night, there was a throb of music so faint that it might be only an echoing memory; Roger Brevard's face was pale and strained. He asked:

" Have you forgotten that we are friends? "

" No," she returned seriously, lifting her look to his. He was very close to her and her heart beat unsteadily. She had a choking premonition of what was about to occur, but she stood without the slightest attempt to prevent his kiss. It affected him even more than herself, for he stepped back sharply with his hands clenched. Roger was silent for so long that she said, timidly:

" I didn't mind, so much."

" Thank you," he replied almost harshly. " There's no need for you to regret it. No need, no need. But if it were only a year more —."

" We all grow older," she told him wisely.

" So we do, Sidsall, and we change. But you should stay exactly as you are now, white and young and fragrant. Never the fruit but always the blossom, and always a night in early summer. The afterwards is an indifferent performance."

" I don't understand," her voice was shadowed.

" Sidsall for a moment.   Don't move — opening petals, shy pure heart . . . loveliness. . . ."

" I don't understand," she repeated, but the trouble had vanished.   She even smiled at him: she was filled with an absolute security in her vision of Roger Brevard. Why, she had no need to question; it was an instinct beyond search and above knowledge; perhaps, she thought as they turned toward the house, its name was love.

VII

THE days, to Nettie Vollar, seemed to be both unutterably dull and colored by a possibility of excitement like an undercurrent of hardly perceptible fever. Her mother, it was true, took on herself most of the duties of Barzil Dunsack's house; but there were still a large number of little things that returned unvaried with every morning, noon and night for the girl's attention. The cause of any impending excitement — except the mere presence of Gerrit Ammidon in Salem, now surely of no moment to her — she was unable to place. The feeling that pervaded her most was the heavy conviction that her life was a complete waste, she had the sensation of being condemned to stay in surroundings, in a service, that never for a moment represented her desire or true capabilities. Her family, as she had grown into maturity, seemed strange, her place there an unhappy accident.

At her brightest periods she pictured being suddenly, arbitrarily, removed into happier appropriate regions. For a time that vision had assumed the tangible shape of Gerrit Ammidon; then this comfortable figure had abruptly left her to an infinitely more seldom return of her faint indefinite hope.

Through the inordinate number of hours when she was potentially alone she had developed a strain of almost painful thought out of keeping with the whole of her naturally unreflective being. In moments such as the present — she was sitting in her room overlooking Hardy Street on its landward reach — she followed the slow turnings of her mind in the manner of a child spelling out a sentence. Two things seemed to her of the first importance — the existence into which she had been forced by the circumstance of her birth, and her unknown father himself: unknown, that is, except for vague promptings and desires which, for need of a better reason, she traced to his personality. That he was superior, in that he had had a distinct measure of gentle blood, she was assured by her mother on one of the rare occasions when the subject was touched between them. To that she credited the greater part of her obscure dissatisfaction with conditions which she described as mean.

The latter evidently didn't disturb her mother or grandfather; she realized that the long-drawn silent severity of the old man had crushed what spirit her mother may have had. It was clear that the elder woman had been very pretty, with wide fluttering eyes which made you think of gray moths, and delicately colored cheeks; but all that had been crushed, too. She was meek in a way that filled her daughter with determined resentment and fear. The resentment sprang from the silent assertion that she wouldn't be worn down like that; the fear followed the realization of the rigid power of the old man and the weight of all that held her powerless to escape. Naturally she was rather cheerful than somber, an involuntary gayety rose from her in the drabbest moments; she even defied Barzil Dunsack with ribbons and flowers on her bonnet.

The prospect from her window offered no relief from the interior; it was true that in the other direction she could catch glimpses of the harbor, by leaning out she could get the comparatively full sweep at the bottom of the street; but there were usually things ugly and restraining between her and the freedom of the horizon. Her favorite place had been at the edge of the grass above the tide; but, since his return, Edward Dunsack had hit upon it too, and his proximity made her increasingly uneasy. For one thing he talked to himself out loud, principally in Chinese, and the sliding unintelligible tongue, accompanied by the sight of his gaunt yellow face, his inattentive fixed eyes, gave her an icy shiver. It was almost worse when he conversed with her in a palpable effort at an effect of sympathy.

She rose and wandered finally to the embankment of the garden. The water shimmered under the full flood of afternoon; she was gazing at the distance in an aimless manner that had lately fastened on her when she heard a stirring of the grass behind her and Edward Dunsack approached. He was livid in the pitiless light, and seemed terribly fragile, a thing that a mere clap of thunder might crumble to nothing; she felt that she could sweep him away with a broom; yet at the same time there were startling gleams of inner violence, a bitter energy, an effect of deepness, that appalled her.

" If you should ask me," he declared, " if my opinion is of any value, I'd say that Ammidon owed you considerable. He led you to expect something better than his running away without a word; I'd have an explanation out of him. Of course, if he had come back married —

this affair with a Chinese woman isn't that — it would be all over. But, somehow, with things as they are, I can't believe that it is."

" Do you expect me to go to their house, like you did? " she replied resentfully.

He turned such a malicious face on her that instinctively she moved back. For a moment he was silent, his meager leaden lips drawn tight over dark teeth in a dry grin, his fingers like curved wires; then, relaxing, he cursed the entire house of Ammidon. " The truth is," he ended, " that you were a little fool; you had everything, everything, in your hand and threw it away." His gaze strayed from her to the surface of the water, a short distance from the land. " Threw it away," he repeated; " it can't be got in this country either."

He was, she thought, crazy. However, all that he said about Gerrit lingered in her mind; it fanned to new life the embers of her rebellion. If a chance should come she would let Gerrit Ammidon know something of the wrong he had done her. As her uncle had pointed out, the Chinese woman was different from an American, a white woman. Their entire position, Gerrit's and her own, was peculiar, outside ordinary judgments.

She saw him occasionally from a distance, as she must continue to do while he was in Salem, since no opportunity had been made for them to exchange words. That must come from Gerrit.

Her mother called her, and she went in, finding the elder in the kitchen. " I can't get enough heat to bake," she worried; " you can bear your hand right in the oven. Your grandfather won't have his sponge biscuit for supper." Nettie declared, " I certainly wouldn't let it bother me. Just tell him and let him say what he likes." Her mother turned palpably startled. " But —" she began weakly.

" I know exactly what you're going to say," Nettie cut in, " he has it every night and he'll expect it. How much, I'd like to ask, have you been expecting all your life and getting nothing? And now I am the same. I don't believe we're as wicked as grandfather lets on, and I'm certain he's not so good as he thinks. I don't admit we are going to hell, either; if I did I can tell you I'd be different. I'd have a good time like some other girls I see. I guess it would be good, anyhow, with silk flounces four yards around. I'm what I am because I don't listen to him; I don't pay any attention to the pious old women who make long faces at us."

" You mustn't talk like that, Nettie," her mother protested anxiously. " It has a right hard sound. Your grandfather is a very upright religious man. It's proper for those who sin to suffer in this world that they may be humble for the next."

" I don't want to be humble," Nettie told her. " The Ammidons aren't humble. Mrs. Saltonstone isn't." A pain deepened visibly on the elder's pale countenance. " You mustn't think it doesn't hurt me, Nettie, to — to see you away from all the pleasure. It tears at my heart dreadful. That is part of the punishment." The girl made a vivid gesture, " But you sit back and take it! " she cried. " You talk of it as punishment. I won't! I won't! I'm going to do something different."

" What? " her mother demanded, terrified.

"I don't know," Nettie admitted. "But if I had it to do over I'd kiss Gerrit Ammidon as soon as he looked for it."

"Nettie, do you — do you think he wanted to marry you?"

"Yes," she answered shortly. "He's like that. Whatever you might say against him he's honest."

Her mother began to cry, large slow tears that rolled out of her eyes without a sound. She sat with lax hopeless hands in her lap of cheap worn dress stuff. Nettie Vollar felt no impulse toward crying; she was bright with anger — anger at what Barzil Dunsack had done with her mother, at the harm he had worked in her. "You are a saint compared to Uncle Edward," she asserted. "I don't know what's wrong with him, but there is something."

"I've noticed it too: times his eyes are glazed like, and then his staring at you like a cat. It's a fact he doesn't eat right, and he forgets what's said as soon as a body speaks. Might he have some Chinese disease, do you think?"

"It's not like a real sickness. . . ."

The evening in the dreary sitting room with only the reddish illumination of one lamp was almost unendurable. Her grandfather sat with broad wasted hands gripping his shrunken knees, his eyes gazing stonily out above a nose netted with fine blue veins and harsh mouth almost concealed by the curtain of beard. Edward rose uneasily and returned, casting a swelling and diminishing shadow — obscurely unnatural like himself — over the faded and weatherstained wall paper. Her mother was bowed, speechless. Nettie wanted to scream, to horrify them all with some outrageous remark. She would have liked to knock the lamp from the table, send it crashing over the floor, and see the flames spread out, consume the house, consume . . . she stopped, horrified at her thoughts.

She didn't want things like that in her mind, she continued, but the echo of dancing, of music, of the Salem Band marching up Essex Street with Mr. Morse playing his celebrated silvery fanfare on the bugle. She wanted to laugh, to talk, yes — to love. Why, she was young, barely twenty-one; and here she was in a house like the old cemetery on Charter Street. Before they went to bed her grandfather would read out from the Bible, but always the Old Testament. Finally he rose and secured the volume, bound in dusty calf, its pages brown along the edges. His voice rang in a slow emphasized fervor:

" ' Hast thou not procured this unto thyself, in that thou hast forsaken the Lord, thy God, when he led thee by the way?

" ' And now what hast thou to do in the way of Egypt, to drink the waters of Sihor? or what hast thou to do in the way of Assyria, to drink the waters of the river?

" ' Thine own wickedness shall correct thee, and thy backslidings shall reprove thee; know therefore and see that it is an evil thing and bitter, that thou hast forsaken the Lord thy God, and that my fear is not in thee, saith the Lord God of hosts.

" ' For of old I have broken thy yoke, and burst thy bonds; and thou saidst, I will not transgress; when upon every high hill and under every green tree thou wanderest, playing the harlot.

[155]

" ' Yet I had planted thee a noble vine, wholly a right seed: how then art thou turned into the degenerate plant of a strange vine unto me?

" ' For though thou wash thee with nitre —' "

Nettie was impressed, intimidated, in spite of the contrary resolution in the kitchen: the words seemed to burn into her mother, herself, like boiling fat from a pan; and a great relief flooded her when she could escape again to the temporary relief of her room. It was hot, the windows were up, and she made no light that might attract mosquitoes or force her to draw the close shades. She stood undressed luxuriating in the sense of freedom of body. She was richly white in the gloom: her full young beauty gave her a feeling of contentment and strength, and, equally, a great loneliness. It wasn't corrupt, a " degenerate plant," she thought with a passionate conviction like a cry.

She determined to say no prayer to such a ruthless Being; yet, soon after, in her coarse nightgown, she found herself kneeling by the bed with hard-clasped hands. It was a prayer for which Barzil Dunsack would have had nothing but condemnation: she implored the dark, the mystery of Augustness, for carnal and light things, yes — for waltzes and quadrilles and songs and pleasure, young pleasure, all the aching desires of her health and spirit and nature and years; but most for love. She said the last blindly, in an instinct without definition, with the feeling that it was the key, the door, to everything else; and in her mind rose the image of Gerrit Ammidon. She saw his firm direct countenance, the frosty blue eyes and human warmth. He needn't have come at all, she added, if it had been only to double the dreariness of her existence.

She wondered a little, her emotion subsiding, at the interest her uncle showed in her affairs. It wasn't like what else she had gathered of him; and she searched, but without success, for any hidden reason he might have. He actively blackened the name of Ammidon while he was lost in too great an indifference to be moved by any but extraordinary pressures. Everything left his mind, as her mother had said, almost immediately. Suddenly weary, she gave up all effort at understanding.

A wind moved in from the sea, fluttering the light curtains, and brought her a sense of coolness and release. It came from the immense free sweep of ocean to which her sinking consciousness turned in peaceful recognition and surrender.

Altogether, in the days that followed, she realized a greater degree of mental freedom than before her revolt. She had removed herself, it appeared, a little outside the family, almost as if she were studying them calmly through a window: a large part of the terror her grandfather had possessed for her had disappeared, leaving for her recognition a very old and worn man; she was sorry for her mother with a deep affection mixed with impatience. At first she had tried to put something of her own revived spirit in the older woman but it was like pouring water into a cracked glass: her mother was too utterly broken to hold any resolution whatever.

Nettie's feeling for Edward Dunsack became an instinctive deep distrust. It was almost impossible for her to remain when — as he so often did now — he approached her to talk about the injustice of her mode of life and the debt Gerrit Ammidon owed her. He would stand with his fingers twitching, talking in a rapid sharp voice, blinking continuously against any light brighter than that of a shaded room or dusk. He seldom left the office or went out through the day; his place at the dinner table was far more often empty than not. But after their early supper, in the long late June twilights, he had an inexhaustible desire for her to stroll with him. She occasionally agreed for the reason that they invariably passed in the vicinity of Washington Square and Pleasant Street, and saw the impressive block of the Ammidon mansion. However, they never met any of its inmates. Once they had walked directly by the entrance; some girls, perhaps a woman, certainly two men, were grouped in the doorway: it was growing dark and Nettie couldn't be certain.

Edward Dunsack clearly hesitated before the bricks leading in between the high white fence posts topped with carved twisting flames; and, in a sudden agony at the possibility of his stopping, Nettie hurried on, her cheeks flaming and her heart, she thought, thumping in her throat.

Her uncle followed her. There was a trail of intimate merriment from the portico, a man's voice mingling gayly with those of the girls. "That was the Brevard who's in the Mongolian Marine Insurance Company," Edward Dunsack informed her. "I hear he's a great hand for leading cotillions and balls — the balls you ought to take part in." On and on he went with the familiar recital of her wrongs. It carried them all the way over Pleasant

and Essex and Derby Streets home. The next day, however, he was forced to go about the town, and returned
for dinner in a state of excitement evident to anyone.

He ate without attention whatever was before him, and
extravagantly pleasant, related how he had conversed with
Mrs. Gerrit Ammidon in the family carriage in front of
the countinghouse of Ammidon, Ammidon and Saltonstone on Liberty Street. Nettie was surprised that his
concern was caused by such a commonplace event. " The
women of China —." Words failing him, he waved a
thin dry hand. His father frowned heavily. Then,
abruptly, as if he had been snatched out of his chair
by an invisible powerful clutch, he started up and disappeared.

The afternoon passed the full and Nettie, bound in
preparation for supper for Redmond's, the Virginia Oys-
terman's at Derby Wharf, stood waiting for some money.
" I can't think where I left my reticule," her mother
called, " unless it's in Edward's room where I cleaned
this morning. Just run up and see. . . . He'll be at the
office."

Above, Nettie found the door closed, but it opened
readily as she turned the knob: she went in without hesitation. The interior she naturally thought was empty;
and then, with an unreasoning cold fear, she saw that
Edward Dunsack was lying on the bed. Some of his
clothes were tumbled on the floor, and he wore his black
Chinese gown. The room was permeated with a heavy
smooth odor; on a stand at her uncle's hand was a curious
collection of strange objects — a little brass lamp with a
flickering bluish flame, a black and silver object like a

swollen unnatural pipe, stained bodkins, a lump of what she took to be tar —

Her attention was caught by Edward Dunsack's face: it had fallen back with his pinched chin pointing toward the ceiling, it was the color of yellow clay, and through his half-opened eyelids was an empty glimmer of gray-white. She shrank away involuntarily, and the word "Dead" formed just audibly on her trembling lips. In an instant she was in the hall, calling in a panic-stricken voice, her icy hands at her throat; and her grandfather mounted the stair with surprising agility, followed by his daughter Kate.

"Uncle Edward," Nettie articulated, waving toward the room from which she had fled. The two women followed the rigid advance of Barzil Dunsack. As he saw the figure of his son there was a stabbing gasp of his breath. He halted for a moment, and it seemed to Nettie Vollar that suddenly his determined carriage crumbled, his shoulders sagged; then he went forward. The bed had high slender posts that at one time supported a canopy, but now they were bare, and an old hand held to one as he bent over.

"Is he dead?" the older woman asked.

Barzil Dunsack made no immediate reply; his gaze turned from his son to the stand, the fluttering lamp and its accessories. His head moved slowly in the act of sniffing the pungent haze swimming in the interior. Nettie could see his face, and she was appalled by an expression grimmer than any she remembered; it was both harsh, implacable, and stricken, as empty of blood as the countenance on the bed. The hand on the post tightened until it, too, was linen white. She drew close to her mother's side, putting a supporting arm about the soft shaking shoulders.

"No," said Barzil Dunsack, in a booming voice, "not dead, and yet dead forever. Go downstairs," he commanded. They backed confused to the door. "If Edward is sick —" Kate Vollar began. The old man's face blazed with intolerable pain and anger. "Woman," he demanded, "can you cure what God has smitten?" His eyes alone, hard and bright in the seamed and hairy face, drove them out into the hall. Below in the sitting room Nettie exclaimed, "He might have told us something!"

"Whatever it is," her mother returned, "it's dreadful bad. I've felt that all along about Edward; he's never been himself this last time." Mechanically she found her reticule beside the painted ostrich egg from Africa. "You'll have to get the oysters anyhow," she told her daughter, maintaining the inevitable pressure of small necessities that defied all tragedy and death.

Nettie escaped with an enormous relief into the sunny normal tranquility of the afternoon. The house had become too horrible to bear; and even on the thronged length of Derby Wharf, like a street robbed of its supports and thrust out into the harbor, she was followed by the vision of Edward Dunsack's peaked clayey face.

She got the oysters, and in an overwhelming reluctance to return walked out to the end of the wharf, where a ship was discharging her cargo — heavy plaited mats of cassia with a delicate scent, red and blue slabs of marble, baskets of granular cakes of gray camphor, rough brown logs of teak, smooth dull yellow rolls of gamboge, bags with sharp conflicting odors, baled silks and half chests of tea wrapped in bamboos and matting painted with the ship's name, *Rose and Rosalie.*

There Nettie found herself beside a little girl clasping the hand of a bulky old gentleman in pongee and a palm leaf hat and following every operation with a grave critical regard. " I guess," she said to her companion, " it's only the cheap sort of tea, a late picking, or it would be in canisters." She was, Nettie realized, the youngest Ammidon child with her grandfather. The latter looked round and recognized Nettie Vollar. " How's Barzil Dunsack? " he asked immediately.

She was at a loss for an answer, since she could not describe the subject of the inquiry as all right nor explain their unhappy condition. " Intend to stop in," Jeremy Ammidon continued; " last time I was there I went up like a rocket." Laurel — that was the child's name, she remembered — gazed at her intently. " I was saying to grandfather," she repeated precisely, " that this wasn't really much of a cargo. Nothing like the one Uncle Gerrit brought back in the *Nautilus.* We were having an argument about Salem too. But, of course, all the big cargoes are going into Boston," she sturdily confronted the flushed old man.

" You're William all over again," he asserted, almost annoyed. Both their expressions grew stubborn in a manner that, in view of their great difference in age and experience, Nettie thought quite absurd. What a beautiful dress the child had on — Porto Rico drawn work, with pale yellow ribbons to her bonnet. " I wish you'd stay here a minute with Nettie Vollar," Jeremy told her, " while

I see the wharfinger." He went unhurried along the wharf, and Laurel Ammidon drew closer to her.

"She's not much of a ship either," Laurel said, indicating the *Rose and Rosalie.* "She's built like — like grandfather. They're different now. I went to New York to see the *Sea Witch* launched, and she's the tallest vessel afloat, with three standing skysail yards and ringtail and water sails. She's black and has a gilded dragon for a figurehead; and, although she went out in a gale, got to Rio in twenty-five days. I talked to Captain Waterman, too; he commanded the *Natchez,* you know."

How the child ran on! "You've studied a lot on ships," Nettie commented. "I know the main truck from a jewel block," Laurel replied complacently. "But Camilla's a frightful lubber. I should think she'd make Uncle Gerrit sick. She does me." Nettie Vollar was seized by the temptation to question Laurel about Gerrit Ammidon, about his wife — anything that touched or concerned him. A wave of emotion swept over her, a loneliness and a desire the cause of which she would not face. She wanted to take Laurel's hand in hers, and with the old ponderous comfortable gentleman go up to the serenity of their gardens and wide happy house. She wanted Gerrit Ammidon to smile at her with his eyes blue like a fair sea. . . . His father was returning.

Laurel again grasped the large hand and they turned to leave. Jeremy Ammidon nodded to Nettie. Nothing remained for her but the place on Hardy Street; then she saw that the others had stopped and were signaling for her. "Captain Dunsack . . . old friend," the elder said abruptly. "Stubborn as the devil. No worse than me,

[163]

though, no worse than me. Confounded proud, too. You let me know if there is anything, that is, if you need —" he paused, breathing stormily, glaring at her in an assumed angry impatience.

"Thank you," she answered, "but there's nothing."

What most shocked her on the return home was the manner in which their life callously continued when she felt it should have been shattered by their suffering in Edward Dunsack's room; yet not so much theirs as her grandfather's. He took his place at the head of the table, the grace went up as loudly as ever above their heads; but in spite of that she saw that the old man suddenly looked infinitely spent. His knife slipped insecurely and scraped against the plate in fumbling and palsied hands. All at once she had a feeling of gazing straight into his heart, and finding — like a burning ruby hidden in earth — such an agony beneath his schooled exterior that she choked thinking about it.

Nettie wondered what he would do if she put an affectionate arm about his neck and told him of their sympathy. She knew now that her Uncle Edward had been smoking opium, and that it was a worse vice, more hopeless and destructive, than drink. But she was certain that he'd repel her; he looked on them all, Edward Dunsack, her mother and herself, as sinful, "degenerate plants." Even now, she realized, there was no weakening of his spiritual fibers such as had plainly overtaken his physical being. He had a blasting contempt for the unrighteous flesh.

When they had risen from the table, Edward Dunsack appeared and sinking weakly into a chair demanded a cup of tea. He knew nothing of their discovery, of the fact that they had stood above his revolting insensibility. After the tea he seemed to revive; he lighted a cheroot and said something about going out. It wasn't possible, however; his knees sagged walking the length of the floor; in the sitting room he fell into a leaden apathy. Nettie Vollar's gaze rested on the volume of the life of the missionary who had died at such an early age on the Île de France. The lamplight spread over the depressing mustard yellow paint of the woodwork with its obviously false graining and deepened the blackness of the fireplace. Throughout the reading of the Scripture Edward Dunsack never shifted his slumped position; his face, with smudged closed eyes, seemed fixed in a skeptical smile. The hollows of his temples were green. The reading finished, old Barzil said:

" I wish to speak to Edward alone."

The latter straightened up. " Eh! " he exclaimed. " What? " He resettled his stock and crossed a knee with a show of ease. Nettie followed her mother from the room. Her last impression was that of a startling resemblance between the young man and old — her uncle's face was as ruined as the other's — between father and son. " I wish he'd go away," her mother surprisingly asserted; " I won't sleep for thinking of him lying there like a corpse."

" He'll not," Nettie replied, musing; " something is holding him we still don't know of."

She had lately begun to realize a great many things of which only a month before she had not been aware — that sudden illuminating grasp of old Barzil's inner pain, of her mother's wasted spirit, and the sense that some unguessed potent motive was at the back of her Uncle Edward's apparently erratic strolling and reiterations. Nettie stopped to wonder a little at the change in herself: she was more alive, more included. There were no reasons that she could see why this should be so; never had the present, the entire future, been darker. With her deeper consciousness, too, came an increased shrinking from life, a greater capacity for injury; and there could be no doubt that it was an older Nettie Vollar who, in her mirror, returned the questioning in the resentful black eyes.

No further mention was made of the opium, no hint escaped from the two men of what Barzil Dunsack had said to his son after the evening reading of the Bible. An evidence of the miserable episode was visible for a while in the difficulty of any attempted general conversation; then that died away and everything was seemingly as it had been before. But the rising gayety and widespread public preparations at the approach of the Fourth of July made her existence drabber than ever. There was, too, unusual planning, for later in the month President Polk was to be in Salem.

The various military organizations drilled incessantly: the Salem Light Infantry, the Mechanic Light Infantry, the Salem Cadets and Independents and a squad of the Salem Artillery might be seen at any hour of the morning or early evening smartly marching and countermarching, led by Flag's or the Salem Band. Strange constructions of light wood climbed in Washington Square — the set pieces of the celebrated pyrotechnist secured at a " staggering expense." Preliminary strings of firecrackers were exploded by impatient boys and the dawn of the holiday was greeted with a sustained uproar of powder.

All this was communicated to Nettie in the form of a determination to forget the dreariness of home and for once anyhow be a part of the careless holiday town. Edward Dunsack opened the day by deprecating what fireworks Salem could show and recalling the extravagant art of China in that particular. No one, he said, of the least moment would be abroad in the rabble; and he intended to spend the day over the invoice of a schooner returned from Curaçao. She was glad of this, for it left her free to get an uninterrupted pleasure from the morning parade, the floats and fantasies, the afternoon drilling in Washington Square, and see the last colored disk of the fireworks. Maybe, she told herself, tying the becoming ribbon of her bonnet beneath a round chin with a lurking dimple, maybe she wouldn't come back home once during the entire day! She ignored, in the rush of her spirits, even her mother's lonely labors: for once they'd have to do without her. Nettie took a scarlet merino shawl for the cooler evening, shook forward the little black curls about her face, and hurried away from Hardy Street.

She was swept along in the crowd on Essex Street until, before the office of the Salem *Register,* she found a place that commanded the parade. There Nettie lost all memory of the dreariness that pressed upon her; she became one of the throng, applauding the members of the East India Marine Society carrying the palanquin from the Museum in native dress, or stood with sentimental tears blurring her vision. The parade ended, and currents of people swept toward dinner; but she stopped at a baker's and got a paper of seed cakes, made in the shape of oak leaves and sat contentedly eating them in the Common.

The thought of Gerrit Ammidon, with all the other deeper aspects of her life, was thrust into the back of her consciousness; she was existing as she breathed — without will; the instinctive lighter qualities had her in full possession. She felt that her cheeks were glowing and hummed the refrains of the music she had heard. One by one the military companies marched into the Square. She was fascinated by the tall leather helmets and silver straps under severe young lips. The Newburyport men were in a new scarlet uniform, that was the Boston Brass Band — it was painted on the bass drum — with the Independents; there were the Beverly Taylor Guards. The massed onlookers filled the broad plain.

The drilling and countermarching proceeded and the afternoon waned. At the dispersal of the spectacle, when for an hour or two Washington Square was comparatively deserted, when the sun sank lower and lower over the roofs of Brown Street and the gold haze thickened, turning to blue, Nettie became quieter but no less happy. The time sped; never was she conscious of being lonely, by herself in a multitude composed of grouped families and friends. It was all such a beautiful relief to the other constant dwelling on somber and hopeless facts! Already people were streaming in under the wooden arched gates for the evening display; already she could see a star in the clear-shining green east.

The fireworks, the papers said, were to be in two parts, ending with a bombardment of Vera Cruz, five hundred feet long, and a series of triumphant arches with full-length portraits in colored lights of celebrated Americans. There was a sudden salute of artillery, and a flight of rockets soared upward in long flaming curves, dissolving in showers of liquid emerald and ruby and silver against the night. Bengola lights casting a blue glare over the standing mob and farther house fronts were followed by a great Peruvian Cross, a silvery fountain of water and Grand Representation of Bunker Hill Monument.

With this the first came all too soon to an end, and Nettie was folding the shawl about her shoulders when almost the entire Ammidon family were upon her. . . . In an instinctive confusion she saw William Ammidon and his wife with their daughters, the old man, Jeremy, and Gerrit.

They stopped before her in an assured, not unkindly inquisitiveness, the girls fresh and bright-faced, with crisp lovely clothes; their mother, in a smart mantle and little bonnet with knots of French flowers, greeted her with a direct question tempered by a smile. William Ammidon, smoking, was unconcerned; while Gerrit stayed obscured outside the group. " Whom are you with, Nettie? " Rhoda Ammidon asked; and when she admitted that she was alone the elder, with visible disapproval, asserted:

" That won't do at all in this rough assembly. I must see that you are taken care of." She hesitated, with a slight frown on her handsome brow. " But you will want to see the rest of the fireworks. Yes, what you must do is to come over to our steps, the view from there is fairly good, and then some one can walk home with you."

They moved resolutely forward, giving Nettie Vollar

no opportunity for protest, the expression of what she might prefer; and, with so many determined minds, she dropped silently into their progress. She was beside Rhoda Ammidon, the girls trooped on before, and the men — Gerrit Ammidon — followed. Her peace of mind had been broken into a hundred half-formed doubts and acute questions. She wished that she had declined to go with them: the invitation, no, command, had been a criticism, really. Now, after so long, it wasn't necessary for them to become suddenly responsible for her.

The happiness of the day sank a little, thoughts of her mother and grandfather and Uncle Edward returned. But, at the same time, she realized that she was near Gerrit once more. This made a confusion of her emotions that hid what she most felt about him. It wasn't a proximity that meant anything, however; it had been utterly different when he came to see her before his marriage. Yet, just the fact of his being close behind her, and that she would be on the steps at the Ammidons' with him, undoubtedly had a power to stir her heart.

It brought, like her carefree excursion, a certain momentary glow, a warmth, without relation to what had gone before or might follow; there was the same quality of momentary rest, refreshment, complete and isolated as a jewel in a ring. She didn't analyze it further; but drifted with the vigorous chattering tide of the Ammidons.

They arrived at the impressive entrance open on a high dim interior. Jeremy and William Ammidon went in, Rhoda lingered while a chair was brought for her, and Sidsall and Camilla, Laurel and Janet ranged themselves facing the Square. Gerrit hung silent in the doorway.

"Perhaps Taou Yuen will come down," Rhoda Ammidon suggested, and Nettie's throat was pinched at the possibility of seeing Gerrit's Chinese wife. But he answered shortly in the negative. Taou Yuen preferred to stay in her room; the view from her window was better than this. The latter was easily possible, for here the set pieces were almost unintelligible: an impressive beehive could be seen surrounded by swarming golden bees, a pyramid of Roman candles discharged their rushes of colored balls and streamers; but the bombardment of Vera Cruz was a cause of bitter complaint to the children.

The fireworks had ceased to have the slightest significance for Nettie; she was luxuriating in the suavity of the Ammidon steps and company. It seemed to her that an actual air of ease rolled out over her from within. Seen from her place of vantage the great throng in the Square was without feature, the passers-by on Pleasant Street — as Edward Dunsack and herself had been — were unimportant. The massive portico and dignified fence, the sense of spaciousness and gardens and lofty formal ceilings, the feeling of fine silks and round clear direct voices, of servants for everything, everyone, transcended in force all her speculations. She was familiar — who wasn't in Salem? — with the meaning of the house' name, Java Head. It was more, quite heaven.

Thoughts of Gerrit winged in and out of her mind like wayward birds. She turned with studied caution and glanced swiftly but intently at as much of his countenance as she could see. Her memory vividly supplied the rest. There wasn't another like it — one so clear and compelling to read — in the world.

The past in which he had had a part seemed like an impossibly happy dream. She was hardly able to believe that he had been in their sitting room, walked with her in the evening to the grassy edge of the harbor, or held her fingers in his hard cool grasp. Now she wondered if he were contented. She couldn't quite decide from glimpses of his face; but something that had nothing to do with vision disturbed her with the certainty that he was troubled. It might mean unhappiness, but she wasn't sure.

"Now there go the arches!" a young voice exclaimed, "and I just can't see anything. You'd never know at all it was a temple of eight columns. Oh, look — there's a number coming out, 'July fourth, seventeen seventy-six.'" A tide of hand clapping swept over the dark masses. "No," Laurel continued, "that's Salem. . . . It's Washington, no, General Taylor."

The amazing day, Nettie realized, was over, the people flowed back through the gates like a lake breaking in streams from its bank; there was a stir on the steps. Looking up she saw that the stars were obscured, and a low rumble of thunder sounded from a distance, a flash lit the horizon. Now she must go back, return to Hardy Street, to her bitter grandfather like an iron statue eaten by rust and storms, to Edward Dunsack following her with his dragging feet and thin insinuating voice, to her hopeless mother.

"It's the powder, she heard, about what she had no conception. Rhoda Ammidon turned decidedly to her. "It was nice to have you, Nettie," she declared; "but we must see about getting you safely home. The carriage

[172]

would be best since it's threatening rain." She didn't, she replied, want to give them so much bother, she often went on errands after supper, she'd be all right —

" Nonsense," Mrs. Ammidon interrupted impatiently. Then Gerrit advanced from the doorway. " I'll walk down with her," he said almost roughly. " No need to take the horses out so late." Nettie Vollar thought that his sister-in-law's mouth tightened in protest, but he gave them no chance for further argument. He descended the steps with a quick grinding tread, and she was forced to hurry through her acknowledgments in order to overtake him.

The night at once absorbed them.

The air, charged with the fumes of gunpowder and rumbling with low intermittent thunder, was oppressive and disturbing. Gerrit's head was exactly opposite her own, and she could see his profile, pale and still, moving on a changing dark background. He walked with the short firm stride men acquire on the unsteady decks of vessels, swinging his arms but slightly. Neither spoke. The rain, Nettie saw, was hanging off; probably it would not reach Salem. Washington Square was already empty except for a small obscure stir by the scaffolding for the fireworks. A murmur of young voices came from a door on Bath Street. Such minute observations filled her mind; beneath their surface she was conscious of a deep, a fathomless, turmoil. It was a curious sensation, curious because she couldn't tell whether it was happiness or misery. One now exactly resembled the other to Nettie Vollar.

She grasped, however, one difference — it was happiness

now, the misery belonged to to-morrow. But suddenly that last unrealized fact — at once immaterial and the most leaden reality of all — lost its weight. The greater freedom she had lately grown into became an absolute in-difference, a half willful and half automatic shutting of her eyes to everything but the present, the actuality of Gerrit Ammidon walking by her side. She wanted him to speak, so that she could discover his thoughts, feelings; yet she was reluctant to have their companionship of silence broken: words, almost all the possible terms she could imagine, would only emphasize the distance between them.

She was thinking of one now — a word he had never pronounced, but which she felt had been, however obscurely, at the back of the attention he had paid her: love. It was a queer thing. It seemed to be — everyone agreed that it was — of the greatest, perhaps the first, importance; and yet all sorts of other considerations, some insignificant and others mean and more, yes — cowardly, held it in check, drove it back out of sight, as you might hurriedly shut some shabby object into a closet at the arrival of visitors.

"How have you been?" he demanded in the abrupt voice of the expression of his determination to see her home. Well enough, she assured him, if he meant her health. He glanced at her with somber eyes. "Not altogether," he admitted; "it included your family, things generally."

"They are as bad as possible," she told him. She admitted this frankly, a part of her entire surrender to the moment, careless of how it might affect him. "They would be," he muttered savagely. " It's a habit . . . here." The " here," she knew, referred to life on shore; his gloomy attitude toward the management and affairs of the land had caused her a great deal of precious laughter. He had revealed a most astonishing ignorance of necessities that she had understood instinctively when hardly more than a child; and this simplicity had, as much as anything, brought her affection for him to life. At the same time she in particular had felt the justice of a great many of his charges. But no one could reasonably hope for the sort of world — a world as orderly and trim as that of a narrow ship — he thought should be brought about by a mere command. Nettie wished that it could! She sighed, gazing at him.

" Then it's no better than before? " he asked, adding, with a descriptive gesture: " the town and people? "

" I hardly speak to ten in a year, outside the stores and like that. Of course they nod going into church, or a lady, I mean really, your sister-in-law, will say something nice, even do what you saw to-night. Though it's the first time anything like that has happened."

She caught a repressed bitter oath.

" I suppose I'll get used to it," she continued. " No, I won't," she added differently; " never, never, never."

" If you were a man now —" he said with an incredible stupidity.

She wondered angrily if he'd rather have her a man; there had been a time, Nettie reflected, when such a possibility would have stirred him to violent protest. And this brought out the reflection that, while at one time he might have cared for her, now perhaps he was merely sorry for her unhappiness. Yes, this must be it. She had a momentary fatal impulse to throw back at him scornfully any such small kindness. She didn't, she told herself, want condescending sympathy. What silenced her was the sudden knowledge that she did; she wanted anything whatsoever from Gerrit Ammidon. The fact that he had a Chinese wife was powerless to alter her feeling in the smallest degree. On the contrary, she was shocked to find that it had increased immensely, it was growing with every minute.

She wondered drearily if her stubborn love — the term took its place without remark in the procession of her thoughts — for Gerrit didn't, in spite of her protest to the contrary, stamp her as quite bad. Perhaps her grandfather was right about them all — her mother and Uncle Edward and herself, and they were wicked, lost! The energy with which she had combated this charge now faced by the circumstance of her realized affection for a man married to some one else, even Chinese, wavered. All the cheerful influences of the day, rising to the supreme tranquil hour on the Ammidon porch, sank to dejection; it was like the flight of the rockets.

She walked listlessly, her brain was numb; she was terribly tired. Gerrit Ammidon's head was bent and she was unable to see his expression. He might even have forgotten, by the token of his self-absorbed progress, that she was at his side.

"There's going to be a stir in Ammidon, Ammidon and Saltonstone," he said presently, "when my father hears of the new program. Everything is turning to the fastest California runs possible. William and James Sal-

[176]

tonstone want me to take command of a clipper. But I find I'm like my father, Nettie; all my experience has been in the East and the China service. I'm used to it. I'd never get on navigating a passenger boat, a packet ship, from Boston to San Francisco and San Francisco to Boston. The other's in my blood, too — running the northeast trades to Brazil and coming up into the southwest passage winds for the Cape of Good Hope. A long reach nearly to Australia and then north again to the Indian Ocean and southeast trades.

"I'm fit for that, for long voyages, a blue-water sailor and all it means; but battering back and forward round the Horn with my deck cluttered up by prospectors and shore crews the mates would have to slam into the rigging —!" His exclamation refused every face of such a possibility. She understood his necessity completely; and the brief account of such far happy journeys, safe from everything that Salem had come to mean for her, filled her with longing.

"I'm beginning to see," he took up again the self-examination, "that I am to blame for a good deal that I've found fault with in others. I mean that I'm a different variety of animal, and, naturally, no judge of the kinds of holes they live in or the way their affairs are managed."

"You are worlds better!" she cried.

He turned to her, obviously startled, and she held for a long breath his unguarded intense gaze. "Not very useful, I am afraid," he replied at last; "not to-day, anyhow. I belong to a life that is dying, Nettie; mark my words, dying if not already dead. And I'm newfangled to my father. It goes as quickly as that."

This was a fresh mood to all her knowledge of his impatient arrogance, and one that sent her to him in a passionate unperceived emotion. They had arrived at her home and were waiting aimless and silent. Beyond, the gate to the yard was standing open, and Nettie saw that his discovery of the fact had occurred at the identical moment of her own. She made an involuntary movement forward and he followed her through to the blurred tangle of bushes and bare trodden earth. Mutely they turned to the sod spread at the harbor.

The thunder had died away, but pale sheets of reflected lightning hovered at short intervals low in the sky. Directly above them stars shone again. The window of the sitting room still bore the illumination of the lamp within; and Nettie could picture her mother, with stained and rough hands loose on their wrists, opposite Barzil Dunsack's gaunt set countenance.

" You said something about things as bad as possible."

In a level voice she told him about her discovery of Edward Dunsack unconscious in his black wrap on the bed. " I thought he had died," she repeated almost monotonously; " he had such a yellow gone look."

" But that can't be allowed! " he cried. " You mustn't see it. Indecent, worse. The beast will have to be removed. No one will hear of his staying about with two women and a fanatical old man." She was afraid that he would go into the house at once and appear with her uncle, very much in the manner of a dog with a rat. Her sense of a worldly knowledge, a philosophy of realization, far deeper than his own returned. Things couldn't be disposed of in that easy manner; it was probable that they couldn't be disposed of, righted, at all. Her mother, with her help, must continue to keep Barzil's home: there was no other place for Edward Dunsack to go. "He won't hurt us," she said vaguely. "It's principally bad for him. Then, at first, I didn't know. You get used to so much."

He, Gerrit Ammidon, wouldn't have it, he asserted in a heated return of his familiar dictatorial manner. The fellow would be out of there to-morrow. It was a damned unendurable outrage!

She smiled softly and laid a momentary hand on his sleeve. "That's nothing, Gerrit; nothing compared to the rest, to me." He frowned down at her out of the gloom.

"What am I to do?" she asked.

He again cursed Salem and the world with which he had proclaimed himself out of date and sympathy. This, while it communicated to her a certain warm comfort, resolved nothing, made no reply to her question. To-morrow offered precisely the same hopeless outlook of yesterday. No answer from Gerrit, Gerrit married, was possible. She saw that.

"I'm not fit to go around on land blundering and setting tongues to clapping," he declared. "I ought to be locked in my cabin when the ship's in port, and let out only after sail's made again."

She heard a slight movement in the grass; and turning sharply caught the vague outline of a man, the thin unsubstantial shape of Edward Dunsack. He vanished immediately; Gerrit, absorbed in bitter thought, had missed him. Strangely her uncle only filled her mind with the image of China, the China that had ruined him, and

[179]

which, too, in the form of a woman, a Manchu, had destroyed the hope of any acceptable existence of her own.

"Great pretensions and idiotic results," he went on; "no ballast. Take what your grandfather said to me — nothing in that unexpected or to drive a man off. Yet off I go and —" he halted oddly, just as her breath was suspended at the admittance which she was certain must follow. But he fell into another glooming silence.

After all, she couldn't expect him to continue that development. A different man might; and Nettie wasn't sure of her refusal to listen . . . to the end. But she was familiar with Gerrit's unbending conception of the necessity of truth alone. If he married a woman, yellow, black, anything, he would perform the obligation to the entire boundary of his promise. Good and bad seemed equally united against her. Little flashes of resentment struck through her leaden conviction that all this was useless.

"I must be of some use to you."

But, Nettie realized, there was only one way in which he could help her; only one thing she wanted — could take — from him. She was terrified at the completeness with which love had possessed her, making every other fact and consideration of little interest or importance. Suddenly it seemed as if she were being swept by an overwhelming current farther and farther out from safety into a bottomless immensity that would claim her life.

"Yet," he cried, "if I lift a hand, here, in Salem, if I as much as cross the street to speak to you — the clapping tongues! I can do you nothing but harm. Though Rhoda might —"

" I don't want your Rhoda! " she interrupted passionately. " I've managed without them all up to now." He raised his arms in a hopeless gesture. " Nothing's to be done," she concluded. " I saw that all along; that is, this last time."

" It's late," he muttered absently; " you have had a day." He turned mechanically and moved away from the indefinite black rim of the harbor. The lamp in the sitting room had been extinguished, the house was dark. A brief embarrassment seized her as he stood trying vainly to find something confident, even adequate, to say for farewell. And as the stir of his footfalls died away up Hardy Street the memory of his last futile words mocked her laboring heart.

She turned and faced Edward Dunsack, advancing from an obscurity deeper than the rest. He murmured approvingly, she caught words of commendation and unspeakable reassurance. She hurried away blindly, sick to the inmost depths of her being. The morning, when she had tied her gay bonnet ribbons and started out with the scarlet merino shawl on her arm, seemed to belong to a long, long time ago, to a girl. . . . The popping of a final string of firecrackers died outside.

VIII

THE dejection, the sense of a difference that held from him any comprehension of the vast maze of shore life, persisted as Gerrit Ammidon walked toward home. It was such an unusual feeling that he was conscious of it; he examined and speculated upon his despondency as if it had been something actually before him. The result of this was a still increased disturbance. He didn't like such strange qualities arbitrarily forcing their way into his being — he had the navigator's necessity for a clear understanding of the combined elements within and without which resulted in a harmonious, or at least predictable, movement. He distrusted all fogs. In a manner the course before him was plain — married to Taou Yuen, shipmaster in his family's firm, he had simple duties to perform, no part of which included sailing in strange or dangerous waters; yet though this was beyond argument he was still troubled by a great number of unpleasant conditions of mind and obscure pressures.

Gradually, however, his normal indignation returned, the contempt for a society without perceptible justice, centered principally in what Nettie Vollar had had from life. This, he assured himself, wasn't because he was in any way involved with her; but because it was such a flagrant case. She was a very nice girl. It was entirely allowable that he should admit that. As a fact, he warmly felt that he was her friend; the past justified, no, insisted on, that at least. He wondered exactly how fond he had been of her — in other words, how near he had come to marrying her. It had been an obvious possibility, decidedly; but the desire had never become actual. No, his feeling for her had never broken the bounds of a natural liking and a desire to secure decent treatment for her. The last had been vain.

If his mental searching had ended there it would have presented no difficulties, created no fog; but, unfortunately, there was another element which he admitted with great reluctance, an inborn discomfort. Although he had been clear about what had actually happened with Nettie there was reasonable doubt that the same limitations had operated with her. Briefly she had missed him more than he had realized. He explained this to his sense of innate masculine diffidence by the loneliness of her days. She had missed him . . . something within whispered that she still did. Women, he remembered hearing, were like that.

In the light, the possibility, of this he saw that he had done her a great wrong.

It had been his damned headlong ignorance of the dangerous quality of life, the irresponsibility of a child with gunpowder. With all this in his mind it seemed doubly imperative that he should do something for her; he owed her, he was forced to admit, more than a mere impersonal consideration. His thoughts returned unbidden to the fact that she — she had liked him. He insisted almost angrily on the past tense, but it surprised him and gave him a perceptible warm glow. Nettie was very pleasing: he inferred that she was a creature of deep emotions, affections.

[183]

At this he shook himself abruptly — such things were not permissible. Gerrit felt a swift sense of shame; they injured Nettie. His mind shifted to Taou Yuen. He found her asleep on the day bed she preferred, her elaborate headdress resting above the narrow pillow of black wicker. He could distinguish her face, pallid in the blue gloom, and a delicate, half-shut hand. He was flooded with the intense admiration which increasingly formed his chief thought of her; this, with the obvious racial difference, put her, as it were, on an elevation — a beautifully lacquered vase above his own blundering person. She was calm, serious and good, in the absolute Western definitions of those terms; she had her emotions under faultless control. Taou Yuen should be an ideal wife for any man; she was, he corrected the form sharply. All that he knew of her was admirable; the part which constantly baffled him didn't touch their relationship.

It was reasonable to expect small differences between her and Salem: at times her calm chilled him by a swift glimpse of utter coldness, at times he would have liked her gravity to melt into something less than ivory perfection; even her goodness had oppressed him. The last hadn't the human quality of, for example, Nettie Vollar's goodness, colored by rebellion, torn by doubt, and yet triumphing.

If he only understood the three religions of China, if he were an intellectual man, Gerrit realized, he could have grasped his wife more fully. He was completely ignorant of Chinese history, of all the forces that had united to form Taou Yuen. For instance: he was unable to reconcile her elevated spirit with the " absurd superstitions " that influenced almost her every act — the enormous number of lucky and unlucky days, the coin hung on his bed, the yellow charm against sickness and red against evil spirits; only yesterday she had burnt a paper form representing thunder and drunk its ashes in a cup of tea. She was tremendously in earnest about the evil spirits — they were, she maintained, lurking everywhere, in all shapes and degrees of harm. Edward Dunsack was possessed, she declared; but he had pointed out that opium was a sufficient explanation of anything evil in him, and that it was unnecessary to look for a more fantastic reason.

He lay awake for a comparatively long while, as he had several times lately, divided between his consciousness and the regular breathing of his wife. If the past had brought Nettie Vollar to depend on him in some slight degree Taou Yuen did so absolutely: except for him she was lost in a strange world. Yet Taou Yuen didn't seem helpless in the manner of Nettie. He had once before thought of the former as finely tempered metal. Her transcendent resignation, with its consequent lack of sympathetic contact with the imperfect humanity of — well, Nettie, gave Taou Yuen a dangerous freedom from all that bound Salem in comparative safety.

He dressed first, as usual, in the morning, while she stirred only enough to get her pipe and tobacco, on the floor at her side. Outside, the elms were losing their fresh greenness in the dusty film of midsummer; the Square held an ugly litter from the fireworks of last evening. William, too, was about, but he was uncommunicative, his brow scored in a frown. Their father, always down before the others, had returned from the inspection of his trees, and was tramping back and forth in the library.

[185]

The elder seemed unrested by the night, his skin, as Rhoda had pointed out, was baggy.

"Now that the *Nautilus* is afloat again," Jeremy Ammidon said, "you'll want to be at sea." Examining this natural conclusion, Gerrit was surprised, startled, to find that it was no longer true. For the first time in his memory he was not anxious to be under sail. This of course was caused by a natural perplexity about Taou Yuen's comfort and happiness.

"I don't know what the firm's plans are for me," he answered cautiously. "There is some talk of taking me out of the China trade for the California runs. I shouldn't like that."

Jeremy was turning at his secretary, and he stopped to pound his fist on its narrow ledge. "It's that damned Griffiths again and his cursed jackknife hull!" he exclaimed. The dark tide suffused his countenance. Gerrit studied him thoughtfully: he didn't know just how much William had yet told their father about the sweeping changes taking place in Ammidon, Ammidon and Saltonstone. He did see, however, that it was unwise to excite the old gentleman unduly.

"I was saying only yesterday," he put in pacifically, "that you and myself are getting to be old models —" he broke off as William entered the library. The latter evidently grasped at once the subject of their discussion, for he went on in a firm voice somewhat contradicted by a restrained but palpable anxiety:

"Now, father, this was bound to come up and you must sit down and listen quietly." The elder, on the verge of a tempestuous reply, constrained himself to a painful attention. " It's useless to point out to you the beneficial changes in sea carrying, for you are certain to deny their good and drag out the past. So I am simply forced to tell you that after careful consideration we have decided to line the firm with the events of the day and hold our place in the growing pressure of competition. This may sound brutal, but it was forced on us by the attitude you have adopted. Shortly, this is what we intend, in fact are doing:

" Orders have been placed with George Raynes at Portsmouth and Jackson up in Boston for clippers of a thousand and twelve hundred tons and another is almost ready to be launched from Curtis' Chelsea shipyard. It oughtn't to be necessary to call your attention again to the fact that the *Sea Witch* has brought the passage from Hong Kong to something like three months. The profits of the California trade will be enormous and depend entirely on speed.

" I'll admit that this is a big thing, it will cut sharply into our funds — something like a quarter of a million dollars. But, if you will be patient for a little only, I can promise that you'll see astonishing returns. At the same time we have no intention of giving up China and India, but we'll limit ourselves more closely in the nature of the cargoes, practically nothing but tea unbroken from Canton to Boston. I'll be glad to go into all this in detail at the countinghouse, where we have the statistics and specifications."

To Gerrit's surprise Jeremy Ammidon sat quietly at the end of William's speech; he wasn't even looking at them, but had his gaze bent upon the floor. There was a commanding, even impressive, quality in his silence that forced the respect of both his sons. More — it made Gerrit overwhelmingly conscious of his affection, his deep admiration, for his father. He recalled the latter's memorable voyage in the little *Two Capes* — the barque of two hundred and nine tons — into the dangers, so imminent to a master, of uncomprehended waters and thousands of miles with, for the most part, only the sheerest dead reckoning. Jeremy Ammidon said finally:

" If it's done it's done. I used to think there were two Ammidons in the firm, not to mention Gerrit; but it seems there's only one. A man who has never been to sea." He rose and marched, slower and more ponderous than ever before, to the cupboard where he kept the square bottle of Medford rum; there, with trembling hands, he poured himself out a measure. He shut the glass door, but stood for an oppressive space with his back to the room, seeing what old vision of struggle or accomplishment.

" I suppose I've been a damned nuisance about the countinghouse for a long time," he pronounced, turning. William rose. " You made it," he said; " it's you. God forgive me if I have been impatient or forgetful of all we owe you." There was a stir of skirts in the doorway, and Rhoda entered. " Breakfast —" she stopped, and with a quick glance at her husband and Gerrit went at once to Jeremy Ammidon. " They've been bothering you again," she declared, and turned an expression of bright anger on the younger men. " Ah, how hard and hateful and blind you are! " she cried.

William, with a hopeless gesture, walked from the room. Gerritt moved to a window facing the Square; but he saw nothing of its sultry yellow-green expanse — he was remembering how as a child, his mother already dead, a nurse had held him up on Derby Wharf to see his father sweep into port from the long voyage to the East. He caught again the resonant voice, as if sounding from a hold of ribbed oak, the tremendous vigor of the arm that swept him up to a bearded face. He couldn't bring himself to move now and see an old haggard man clinging with tremulous emotion and tears to the sympathy, the strength, of a woman.

Later in the morning, to his immense relief, Jeremy Ammidon regained a surprising amount of composure. At first determined never to return to Liberty Street, toward noon Gerrit found him in the hall with his broad hat and wanghee. " I'll just have a slant at those specifications," he remarked. " Like as not they've left off the hatch coamings." Gerrit suggested, " Since it's so hot why don't you have the carriage round? " The other voiced his customary disparagement of that vehicle. " If I see that I'm going to be late for dinner," he added, " I'll get one of the young men to fetch me something. I don't want to give Rhoda any trouble."

Still, on the steps, he lingered, gazing pridefully up at the bulk of the house he had built; his eyes rested on the brass plate, engraved with the words Java Head, on the dignified white door. " A lot of talk when I had that done," he commented; " people said they'd never heard of it, ought to have my name there for convenience if nothing else. They didn't know. It would take a sailor for that. Don't forget to tell Rhoda not to wait if I'm late. All those girls of hers get hungry. I expect William consulted Laurel about this new move," he ended with a gleam of humor. " She's a great hand for a clipper since she talked to Captain Waterman." He was down the steps, starting deliberately across the street. There was a last mutter of doubt. The bulky slow figure in yellow Chinese silk moved away and Gerrit returned to the shadowed tranquillity of the library.

More than any other place in the house it bore the impression of his father. He wandered about the room, lost in its associations, stopped in front of the tall narrow walnut bookcase and took out one of the small company of Jeremy Ammidon's logs, reading disconnectedly in the precise script:

" Tuesday, December 24. 132 days out. All this day gentle breezes and cloudy. Saw kelp, birds, etc.

" Tacked ship to the eastward under short sail. At daylight made all sail to SW. Gentle breezes and clear pleasant weather. Saw huge shoals of flying fish."

" May 19, 11 days out. Hainan in sight, bearing from W by N to NNW. At sunset the breeze died away and hauled off the land. All night light breezes. Made all possible sail to the SSW. At the same time set the extremity of Hainan which bore NW by N to N. Past three Chinese vessels steering NNE. Saw much scum on the water and at 11 A. M. lost sight of land."

" November 14, 65 days out. These twenty-four hours commences with variable breezes at west and smooth sea. Saw brig steering to the Eastward. The land of Sumatra bearing SW by W to SE by S. Tied rips."

He returned the log to its resting place with a quiet smile at the last period. It was all incredibly simple —

[190]

a lost simplicity of navigation and a lost innocent wonder at the Mare Atlanticum of old fable.

Neither William nor Jeremy Ammidon was present for dinner. They were, Gerrit concluded, submerged in the effort to bring the changing activities of the firm into the latter's comprehension. His foot was on the stair leading up to his wife, when there was a violent knocking on the front door. It sounded with a startling abruptness in the shut hall, and Gerrit instinctively answered without waiting for a servant. The flushed and breathless young man before him was evidently perturbed by his appearance. He stammered:

" Captain Ammidon, you — you must come down to the countinghouse. At once, please! "

His thoughts, directed upon his father, gathered into a chilling certainty. " Captain Jeremy is sick? " he demanded instantly. The hesitation of the other seemed to confirm an infinitely greater calamity. " Dead? " he asked again, in a flooding misery of apprehension. The clerk nodded:

" In a second, like," he continued. " All we know they were talking in Mr. William Ammidon's room — one of the boys was out that minute getting the old gentleman some lunch — when we heard a fall, it was quite plain, and Mr. Saltonstone —"

" That will do," Gerrit cut him short. He turned into the house, rapidly considering what must follow. He'd go, certainly; but first he must warn Rhoda, she would have the girls to prepare. . . . Rhoda had always been exceptionally considerate and fond of Jeremy Ammidon. He found her at the entrance to her room, and said, " My father is dead." Her warm color sank and tears filled her eyes.

Hurrying over Bath Street to Liberty his grief was held in check by the pressing actualities of the moment. He had time, however, to feel glad that he had spent the morning largely in warm thoughts of the dead man.

He passed rapidly into the entrance of the establishment of Ammidon, Ammidon and Saltonstone. Immediately on the right there was an open railed enclosure of desks in the center of which a group of clerks watched him with mingled respect and curiosity as he continued to the inner shut space. It was a large light room with windows on Charter Street. William's expansive flat-topped desk with its inked green baize was on the left, and, under a number of framed sere ships' letters and privateersmen's Bonds of the War of 1812, Gerrit saw the heavy body extended on a broad wooden bench, a familiar orange Bombay handkerchief spread over the face.

Never in all the memory of his brother had William Ammidon been so stricken. As he entered James Saltonstone left studying a list hastily scribbled on a half sheet of the firm's writing paper. He nodded silently to Gerrit, who advanced to the covered face and lifted the handkerchief. There were still traces of congestion, but a marble-like pallor had taken the place of the familiar ruddy color. Something of the heaviness of his old age, the blurring thickness of long inactivity, had vanished, giving his still countenance an expression of vigor, resolution, contradicted by an arm trailing like the loose end of a heavy rope on the floor. William, with a clenched hand on his desk, spoke with difficulty:

[192]

"You must know this, Gerrit; and then I'll ask you never to allude to it again. It might be argued that — that James and I killed him, but absolutely without intention, by accident. Gerrit, I loved him more than I took time to know. Well, you may or may not have heard that we own two topsail schooners in the opium trade, between India, Ningpo and Amoy, but you do know how father detested anything to do with the drug. We said nothing to him about this; it seemed necessary, no — permissible. But to-day when we were coming to a peaceable understanding about the new contracts he stumbled over one of the schooner's manifests. Mislaid, you see — a clerk! It swept him to his feet in a rage, he couldn't speak, and — and he had walked, it was hot. . . ."

Gerrit Ammidon made no answer; there was nothing to be said. He was shaken by a burning anger at the cupidity, the ugly commercial grasping, to which his father had been sacrificed. A gulf opened between him and his brother and James Saltonstone; he was as different from them as the sea was from the land, as the wind-swept deck of the *Nautilus* was from this dry building with its stifling papers and greed. He might be in the service of the firm — Gerrit was not incorporated in the partnership — he might carry their cargoes for the multiplication of the profit, but his essential service and responsibility, his life, were addressed to another and infinitely higher and more difficult consummation than the stowed kegs of Spanish dollars, the bills of sale. This was composed of the struggle with the immeasurable elements of the seas and winds, the safety of lives, the endless trying of his endurance and will and luck.

"Now," he spoke with a perceptible bitterness, "you can have your way without interference, without his mixing up your papers or making the blunders of a slow sort of honesty."

"I am under no obligation to your judgment or opinion," William replied stiffly. "There are always complications you will never penetrate nor carry. At present your assistance is more necessary than any display of temper."

The funeral gathered and ebbed in a long procession of carriages through a sultry noon, the services at the grave concluded by the symbolic dropping of the earth on Jeremy Ammidon's coffin lowered into the deep narrow clay pit. The large varied throng lingered for a breath, as if unable to take their attention from the raw opening that had absorbed the shipmaster, and then there was a determined and reassuring commonplace murmur, a hurrying away into the vital warmth of the day.

The evening was the loveliest summer and the garden of Java Head could afford: a slow moon disentangled itself from the indigo foliage at the back of the stable and soared with an increasing brilliancy, bathing the sod and summerhouse and poplars, the metallic box borders and spiked flower beds, in a crystal clearness. The Ammidons sat about the willow, Rhoda with a hand affectionately on her husband's arm, the children — Laurel and Janet staying without remark long past their accustomed hours for bed — still and white under the blanching moon. Gerrit intently studied his wife, Taou Yuen, in a concentrated manner. She, too, was in white, the Chinese mark of sorrow.

Suddenly in the face of his suffering and memories

she had appeared startlingly remote, as if, from standing
close beside him, she were moving farther and farther
away. The image was made profoundly disconcerting by
the fact that they acted without their own accord; it took
the aspect of a purely arbitrary phenomenon over which
they had no control. At the same time Nettie Vollar was
surprisingly near, actual — he could see every line and
shading of her vivid face; he felt the warm impact of her
instant sympathy. He had caught a glimpse of Barzil
Dunsack at the funeral; but the other was immediately
hidden by the crowd, and Gerrit had been unable to discover whether his son and daughter or Nettie had accompanied him.

His thoughts turned in a score of associations and questions to Nettie; but when he found himself trying to picture her exact employment at the present moment he was
angrily aroused. He had, he realized, considered nothing
else for the past hour, and his preoccupation was growing
more intense, personal. He stirred abruptly, and fixed his
mind on the imminent changes from his father's death.
First the possibility would develop of his becoming a
member of the firm; but to this, he silently declared, he
would not agree. His gaze rested with a faint underlying
animosity on William, seated upright in a somber absorp-
tion, and a disparagement of the latter's activities and
scale of values. Gerrit saw that there must be a pacific
legal knot to untangle; the division of Jeremy's estate
would require time — he had somewhere heard that such
affairs often dragged on for a year; and now he was again
in a fever of impatience to be away, safe, at sea. He
added the more portentous word with the vague self-

assurance that it was only the customary expression of his notable ignorance of land; but it echoed with an ominous special insistence in his mind.

The *Nautilus,* he recalled, was once more afloat, repaired; and a plan occurred to him that seemed to dispose of all his difficulties, even of the distasteful possibility of the California clipper service. He could take the ship as part of his inheritance; and, though ostensibly sailing her in the interest of the firm, make such voyages and ports, carry such cargoes, as his independence dictated. The *Nautilus,* with a cargo out of tin and dyes and cotton manufactures, and forty or fifty thousand trade dollars, would represent a sum of nearly two hundred thousand; but as a family they were very rich; he'd have more than that; and bank the remainder intact to the credit of his wife.

There were many practical aspects of his marriage that he had not stopped to weigh in its precipitant consummation. The problem, pointed out by Rhoda, of his absence from Taou Yuen on cruise could not be solved with the facility he had taken for granted. It was as impossible to leave her happily here — he was aware of her growing impatience with Western habit — as it would be for him to become a contented part of Chinese home life; and not only was she uncomfortably cramped and sick on shipboard, but he doubted whether he could persuade his crews to sail with her. Superstitious able seamen balked at the presence of even a normal wife aft; and a Chinese would be regarded as a sign of certain disaster.

He would have to establish her somewhere in the East Indies; and he viewed with a new dislike all such tropical settings. His entire life threatened to become an affair of damnable palm trees and Oriental stenches. Gerrit Ammidon broke into a cold sweat at the realization of the far more direct implication that had taken substance in his mind. The thing was going entirely too far! He wondered irritably at the obscure cause for such violent inner agitations.

Rhoda Ammidon with a dim smile rose, gathering her daughters about her, and departed in a pale cloud of muslin. Taou Yuen, with her murmuring formal politeness, moved away too, leaving the brothers together. Whatever sympathetic intercourse they might otherwise have had, whatever shared memories of their boyhood and their father, were made impossible by William's admission of the immediate cause of the elder's death.

"The Saltonstones are going into Boston this fall," William said abruptly. "It is necessary for one of us to live there; and Caroline has always had a hankering for wider society. Rhoda, I was surprised to learn, wishes to remain here at Java Head for a year or so anyway. She has a very real affection for the place. But I tell her when the girls are older Boston, or perhaps New York, will give them far greater opportunities. Sidsall, stranger still, was in tears at the whole thing; she seemed ridiculously upset about leaving."

The vision of Nettie Vollar persisted, bright and disturbing. Once he was at sea, Gerrit told himself, on the circumscribed freedom of his quarter-deck, he would lose the unsettling fever burning at that instant in his veins. But the memory of long solitary passages with nothing to distract his mind through week upon week after the ship

[197]

took the trades, when hour upon hour his thoughts turned inward on themselves and reviewed every past act and feeling, made doubtful even that old release. The trouble was that he instinctively avoided any square facing of the difficulty that had multiplied with such amazing rapidity — like a banyan tree — about the present and the shadowed future. This he was forced to admit, but grimly added that there could be only one answer to whatever he might lay bare — the adherence to the single fundamental duty of which he never lost sight. No port was gained by changing blindly from course to course, that way lay the reefs; a man could but keep steadily by the compass. That, at least, was all he could see, propose, for himself, being rather limited and lacking the resources which others of greater knowledge so confidently explored.

After breakfast on the following morning he mounted the dignified staircase, with the sweeping railing of red narra wood and high Palladian window at the turn, to his wife. In their room he was bathed in a cold sweat of dismay at a sudden detached view of Taou Yuen in her complete Manchu mourning for his father. An unhemmed garment of coarse white hemp hung in ravelings about slippers of sackcloth; what had been an elaborate head-dress was hidden under a binding of the bleached hemp; she wore no paint nor flowers; her pins and earrings were pasted with dough, and her expression was drugged with the contemplative fervor of what had evidently been a religious ceremonial.

"For the wise old man, for your father," she said. She was exhausted and sank onto the day bed; but almost immediately her hand reached out in the direction of her pipe, and she smiled faintly at him. He clenched his sinewy hands, the muscles of his jaw knotted, as he gazed steadily at the woman, the Manchu woman, he had of his own free accord married. It sickened him that, for the drawing of a breath, he had regarded Taou Yuen with such appalling injustice — injustice, the evil he hated and condemned more than any other. What, in the name of God, was he made of that he could sink so low!

"We'll leave here soon," he declared abruptly; "the *Nautilus* will be ready for sea almost any time."

He could recognize, from his slight knowledge of her, that Taou Yuen welcomed the news. "Shanghai?" she asked. He nodded. It came over him that he was no longer young. His father had retired from the sea within a few years of his own present age and built Java Head, the house that was to be a final harbor of unalloyed happiness. No such prospect awaited him; he had one of the premonitions that were more certain than the most solid realities — as long as he lived he must sail in ships, struggling with winds and calms, with currents and cockling and placid seas. Well, that was natural, inevitable, what he would have chosen. At the same time he dwelt, with a sensation of loneliness, on the green garden and drawing-room filled in June with the scent of lilacs, on Rhoda surrounded by her girls.

When the question of the division of Jeremy Ammidon's estate came up, he was, as he had foreseen, urged to become a partner of the firm; and, when that failed, told that it was his vested duty to continue in his present capacity as a shipmaster in all their interests. He was seated with Saltonstone and William in the countinghouse and he could tell from his brother's ill-restrained impatience that the other considered him hardly more than a clumsy-witted, stubborn fool before the mast of the facts of actual life.

His gaze, above their heads, rested on the framed pass of the ship *Mocha,* one of his father's last commands, over the bench where he had lain dead. It was given by the President, James Monroe, in 1818, its white paper seal embossed on the stained parchment. It had an engraving of a lighthouse and spired town on the dark water's edge, and above, a picture of a ship with everything drawing in a fair wind, the upper sails torn off on a dotted wavering line for the purpose of identification with its stub.

" No," he told them quietly, " I'll go my own way as I said; with the *Nautilus,* if that can be arranged." He rose with a nod of finality, and James Saltonstone remarked, " Jeremy to the life." Gerrit replied, " I'd not ask anything better."

Through the evening he heard little but the discussion of Mr. Polk's approaching visit to Salem. The President was to leave the train at the Beverly Depot at three P. M. and be fetched with Secretary Buchanan and Marshal Barnes in a barouche with six horses and met at the outskirts of Salem by the city authorities.

There would be a Beverly cavalcade, the city guard was ordered to muster at the armory; while an evening parade at five o'clock and the military ball in Franklin Hall were to follow.

But when the day and occasion actually arrived it was spoiled by a succession of unforeseen mishaps. The train was late and the presidential party in a fever of haste —

the procession, hurrying through the massed public-school children and throngs of Chestnut Street, gave a perfunctory attention to the salutes and short address of the mayor. The President's reply, hardly more than a few introductory phrases, cut short, the barouche was sent plunging over its route with the Secretary crying, "Drive on! Drive on!" and Marshal Barnes swearing and expectorating in callous profusion.

Some of the crowd, the Ammidons heard, had been knocked down and injured in the pell-mell of the rush. Gerrit's countenance showed his contempt of what he held to be a characteristically ludicrous farce. After all, his wishes in regard to the *Nautilus* had been easy of execution, the ship was now his; he was already contracting for a cargo. He had been to see Mr. Broadrick, his first mate, and the latter was assembling the chief members of the crew. As always at the prospect of sailing he was unsettled, concerned with countless details of departure — like a vessel straining at her last anchor.

Seated in the library with Taou Yuen — he had called her aside from her fixed passage to their room from the garden — he was recounting his main plans for the near future, when he became aware of an arrival on the steps outside. He heard a servant's voice, and, immediately after, the woman appeared in the doorway; but she was forced aside by Edward Dunsack. Gerrit's quick resentment flared at such an unmannered intrusion, and he moved ungraciously forward. The servant explained impotently, "I told him I would see —"

"Yes?" Gerrit Ammidon demanded.

Dunsack bowed ceremoniously to Taou Yuen, then he

faced the other. On the verge of speech he hesitated, as if an unexpected development made inadequate whatever he had been prepared to say; then, with a sudden decision, he hurried into an emotional jumble of words. "I can tell you in a breath — Nettie was badly hurt in that cursed rabble yesterday. It looks as if she was actually struck by one of the horses. She was unconscious, and then delirious; now she is in her right mind but very weak; and, since she wished to see you, I volunteered to put our pride in my pocket and carry her message."

An instant numbing pain compressed Gerrit's heart; he felt that, in an involuntary exclamation, he had clearly shown the depth of his dismay. Damn the fellow, why had he burst out in this public indecent manner! The situation he had plausibly created, the thing he managed to insinuate, was an insult to them all — to his wife, Taou Yuen, coldly composed beyond, himself and to Nettie. He stood with his level gaze fixed in an enraged perplexity on Edward Dunsack's sallow countenance, deep sunk on its bony structure, conscious that there was no possibility of a satisfactory or even coherent reply.

"Something was said about this afternoon," the other added. That period, Gerrit realized, was nearly over. But above every other consideration rose the knowledge that he would have to see Nettie Vollar, badly injured, as she desired. The common humanity of that necessity left him no choice.

He turned to Taou Yuen with a brief formal explanation. A friend, their families had been associated for years, had been hurt and sent for him. . . . Return im-

[202]

mediately. He paused, in the act of leaving, at the door of the library, waiting for Edward Dunsack to join him; but the other had resolutely turned his back upon Gerrit. He showed no indication of departure. Gerrit Ammidon was at the point of an exasperated direction; but that, in the light of Dunsack's purpose there, appeared ridiculously abrupt; and confident of his wife's supreme ability to control any situation he continued without further hesitation to the street, hurrying in a mounting anxiety toward the Dunsacks'.

Dwelling on his conduct in the library, at the sudden announcement of Nettie's accident, he felt that he had acted in a precipitant if not actually confused way. As a fact, it had all been largely mechanical; his oppression, his dread for Nettie, had made everything else dim to see and faint to hear. Dunsack's grimacing face, the immobile figure of his wife, the familiar sweep of the room, had been things of no more substance than a cloud between him and the only other reality existing. He had no memory, for instance, of having stopped to secure his hat, but he found it swinging characteristically in a hand. And now even the semblance of reasonable speech and conduct he had managed to command vanished before a panic that all but forced him into a run.

The main door of Barzil Dunsack's house was open on the narrow somber region within; he knocked sharply against the wood at the side and was immediately answered by the appearance of Kate Vollar.

" This is a great kindness, Captain Ammidon," she told him in her negative voice; " come in here, please." He

[203]

looked hastily about the formal space into which she led him, expecting to see Nettie prostrate, but she was not there. "How is she?" he demanded impatiently.

"Nettie?" her mother turned as if surprised by an unexpected twist of the situation. "Oh, why she'll mend all right, the doctor says; but it will be slow. Her arm had an ugly slithering break, and she suffers with it all the time." A pause followed, in which she met his interrogation with a growing mystification. "I suppose Edward told you," she ventured finally. The sense of being at a loss was swiftly communicated to him.

"Your brother said Nettie wanted to see me," he returned bluntly.

"Now, however could Edward do a thing like that!" she cried in deep distress. "Why, there's no truth to it. I asked him myself to see if you'd kindly stop and give me some advice. What put it in my head was that once your father offered — he told Nettie to let him know if there was anything to be done. Edward Dunsack isn't just right in his head."

Gerrit was filled with a mingling sense of disappointment, relief that Nettie was no worse, and the uncomfortable conviction that he had behaved like an hysterical fool. He, too, but angrily, wondered why Dunsack had invented such an apparently pointless lie. Probably Kate Vollar was right, and her brother's wits, soaked in opium, had wandered into a realm of insane fabrications. He composed himself — the first feeling blotting out his other emotions — to meet the deprecating interrogation before him.

" I should be glad to do what I could in my father's place."

" In a way," she continued, " it's about Edward. When he came back from China and decided to stay in Salem his father turned all the books over to him; he was to tend to everything in the way of accounts and shipments; and, he said, he would make us all rich in a year or so. But, instead, he has neglected the clerking until we can't tell what's going or coming. Edward hasn't — hasn't quite been himself lately," she paused and Gerrit nodded shortly. " Now we're not wealthy, Captain Ammidon, we never got more than just enough from our West India trade; but in the last couple of months, with Edward like he is and father too old for columns of figuring — he's dreadful forgetful now — not a dollar was made. The schooners are slow, behind the times I guess, we've had to scrape; yet it's been something. . . . They're both awful hard to do with," she stopped hopelessly.

" You must get a reliable man in charge. Some one who knows the West India shipping should go over your entire property, decide what is necessary, then borrow the money. We can find that without trouble. I'll make only one condition: That is the complete restraint of your brother. It is known that he has the opium habit, he is a dangerous —"

He stopped at the echo of a thin persistent tapping from above. " That's Nettie," Kate Vollar said; " the way she calls me. I'll ask you to excuse me for a minute." When she returned her face bore an unaccustomed flush. " Nettie heard you in the hall or through the stovepipe." She spoke doubtfully: " She'd like to see you, but I don't know if it would be right with her in bed. Still, I promised I'd tell you."

He rose promptly. The woman stood aside at the upper door and he at once saw Nettie lying with her vigorous black hair sprawling in a thick twist across the pillow. Her face was pinched, it seemed thin, and the brilliancy and size of her eyes were exaggerated. One arm, clumsy and inanimate in splints, was extended over the cotton spread; but with the other hand she was feverishly busy with her appearance. She smiled, a wan tremulous movement that again shut the pain like a leaden casket about his heart.

"Do go away, mother!" Nettie directed Kate Vollar hovering behind them. "Your fidgeting will make me scream." With an incoherent murmur she vanished from the room. The girl motioned toward a chair, and Gerrit drew it forward to a table that bore water and a small glass bowl partly covered by a sheet of paper, holding a number of symmetrical reddish-black pills. "Opium," Nettie told him, following his gaze; "I cried dreadfully with the hurt at first. It's dear, and Edward made those from some he had. You know, I watched him roll them right here; it was wonderful how quickly he did it, each exactly alike, two grains." She told him the circumstances of her accident while he sat with his eyes steadily on her face, his hands folded.

He was quiet, without visible emotion or speech; but there was an utter tumult, a tumult like the spiral of a hurricane, within him. Rebellious feelings, tyrannical desires and thoughts, swept through him in waves of heat and cold. Nettie's voice grew weak, the shadows deepened under her eyes, for a little they closed; and but for the faint stir of the coverlet over her heart she was so pallid, so still, that she might have been dead. Moved by an uncontrollable fear he bent toward her and touched her hand. Her gaze slowly widened, and, turning over her palm, she weakly grasped his fingers. A great sigh of contentment fluttered from her dry lips. " Gerrit," she whispered, barely audible. He leaned forward, blinded by his passion for her.

He admitted this in an honest self-knowledge that he had refused recognition until now. Tender and reassuring words, wild declarations and plans for the future, crowded for expression; nothing else before the immensity of desire that possessed him was of the slightest concern; but not a syllable was spoken. A sharp line was ploughed between his brows; his breath came in short choked gusts, he was utterly the vessel of his longing, and yet an ultimate basic consideration, lost in the pounding of his veins, still restrained him.

" I love you, Gerrit," Nettie said; " I'll never stop till I die." Her face and voice were almost tranquil; she seemed to speak from a plane above the ordinary necessities of common existence, as if her pain, burning out her color and vigor and emotions, had given her the privilege of truth. Curiously enough when it seemed to him that she had expressed what should have sent him into a single consuming flame he grew at once completely calm. He, too, for the moment, reached her state of freedom from earth and flesh.

" I love you, Nettie," he replied simply.

However, he speedily dropped back into the sphere of

actual responsibilities. He saw all the difficulties and hovering insidious shadows in which they might be lost. This, in turn, was pushed aside by the incredulous realization that Nettie's life and his had been spoiled by a thing no more important than a momentary flare of temper. If, as might have happened, he had overlooked Barzil Dunsack's ridiculous tirade, if he had turned into the yard where Nettie was standing instead of tramping away up Hardy Street, everything would have been well.

It was unjust, he cried inwardly, for such infinite consequences to proceed from unthinking anger! A great or tragic result should spring from great or tragic causes, the suffering and price measured by the error. He could see that Nettie was patiently waiting for him to solve the whole miserable problem of their future; she had an expression of relief which seemed to take a happy issue for granted. None was possible. A baffled rage cut his speech into quick brutal words flung like shot against her hope.

" I love you," he repeated, " yes. But what can that do for us now? I had my chance and I let it go. To-day I'm married, I'll be married to-morrow, probably till I die. Perhaps that wouldn't stop a man more intelligent — it might be just that — than I am; perhaps he'd go right after his love or happiness wherever or however it offered. There are men, too, who have the habit of a number of women. That is understood to be a custom with sailors. It has never been with me; as I say, maybe I am too stupid.

" What in the name of all the heavens would I do with Taou Yuen? " he demanded. " I can't desert her here, in

America, leave her with William. I brought her thousands of miles away from her home, from all she knows and is. If I took her back and dropped her in China it would be murder."

An expression of unalloyed dreariness overspread Nettie's features. " I wish I had been killed right out," she said. The starkness of the words, of the reality they spoke, flowed over him like icy water; he felt that he was sinking, strangling, in a sea grimmer than any about Cape Horn. He was continually appalled by the realization that there was no escape, no smallest glimmer, leading from the pit into which they had stumbled. He had the sensation of wanting enormously to go with Nettie but was fast in chains that were locked on him by a power greater than his will.

" It's no good," his voice was flat.

" I don't believe I'll see you again," Nettie articulated; " now the *Nautilus* is near ready to sail. I can't stand it," she sobbed; " that last time you went out the harbor just about ended me, but this is worse, worse, worse. I'll — I'll take all the opium."

" No, you won't," he asserted, standing, confident that her spirit was too normal, too vitally healthy, for that. His gaze wandered about the room: her clothes were neatly piled and covered by a skirt on a chair; the mirror on her chest of drawers was broken, a corner missing; there was a total absence of the delicate toilet adjuncts of Rhoda and Taou Yuen — only a small paper of powder, a comb and brush, and the washstand with a couple of coarse towels. What dresses she had were hung behind a ridiculously inadequate drapery. She had so little with which to accomplish what, for a girl, was so much.

His emotion had retreated, leaving him dull-eyed, heavy of movement. The moment had come for his departure. Gerrit stood by the bed. Nettie turned away from him, her face was buried in the pillow, the uppermost free shoulder shook. " Good-by," he said. There was no answer and he patiently repeated the short tragic phrase. Still there was no sound from Nettie. There would be none. Even the impulse to touch her had died — died, he thought, with a great many feelings and hopes he once had. A fleet surprise invaded him at the absence of any impulse now to protest or indulge in wild passionate terms; he was surprised, too, at the fact that he was about to leave Nettie. The whole termination of the affair was bathed in an atmosphere of stale calm, like the air in a ship's hold.

Gerrit Ammidon gazed steadily at her averted head, at the generous line of her body under the coverlet; then, neither hasty nor hesitating in his walk, he left the room. Kate Vollar met him at the foot of the stair. "You understood," she said, " that I only bothered you because your father . . . because I was so put on? "

" You were quite right," he replied in a measured voice; " it will all be attended to. With the agreement I mentioned."

" How they'll take it I don't know."

" In some positions," he told her, " certain persons are without any choice. The facts are too great for them. I said nothing to Nettie of Edward Dunsack's reason for my coming," he added significantly. Out in the street he stopped, facing toward Java Head and evening; but, with a quiver of his lips, the vertical bitter line between his drawn brows, he turned and marched slowly, his head sunk, to where the *Nautilus* was berthed.

IX

SEATED in the library, placidly waiting for Edward Dunsack to go, Taou Yuen studied him briefly. A long or thoughtful survey was unnecessary: the opium was rapidly mastering him. That fact absorbed all the rest. She had an immeasurable contempt for such physical and moral weakness; all the three religions fused in her overwhelmingly condemned self-indulgence; her philosophy, the practical side of Lao-tze's teaching, emphasized the utter futility of surrender to the five senses. At the same time he was the subject of some interest: he was an American who had lived in China, and not only on the fringe of the treaty ports — he had penetrated to some extent into the spirit, the life, of things Chinese; while she, Taou Yuen, was amazingly married to Gerrit Ammidon, was a Manchu here, in America.

Absolutely immobile, her hands folded in her lap, she considered these facts, each in relation to the other: there was wisdom hidden in them for her. If Mr. Dunsack had retained the ordinary blustering Western commercial mind, his knowledge of China confined to the tea houses and streets, he would probably be prosperous and strong to-day. The wisdom lay in this — that here she must remain Manchu, Chinese; any attempt to become a part of this incomprehensible country, any effort to involve herself in its mysterious acts or thought, would be disastrous. She must remain calm, unassertive, let the eternal Tao take its way.

Edward Dunsack looked actually comic: he was staring rudely, with a foolish air of flattery, and breathing in labored gasps — like a coolie who had run miles with a heavy palanquin. Then her mind, hardly reacting from immediate objects, returned to the contemplation of the deeper significance of her presence here. Bent in on itself her thought twisted like a moonflower vine about the solid fact of Gerrit. She realized, of course, that he must have had the past of any healthy honorable man of his age, and that it would have included at least one woman. However, when even the present was an almost complete puzzle his past had been so lost to her that she had not considered it until now.

" You must overlook my unceremonious speech," Edward Dunsack proceeded in creditable Chinese. " It was clumsy, but I was deeply affected. It is my niece, you see, who was hurt, and who has a very sad history. Then there are some special circumstances. I'd have to explain a great deal before you could understand why she sent for your husband and why he left so hurriedly."

" There is nothing you need tell me," Taou Yuen replied in her slow careful English. " Manchu eyes can see as well as American."

" A thousand times better." He, too, returned to his native speech. " It is delightful to talk to a truly civilized being. All that would have to be shouted at the women of Salem is unnecessary now. You see — you understand the heart of a man."

" I understand you," she said impersonally.

" I wonder if you do," he speculated. " You ought to see what — how much — I think of you. My brain holds nothing else," he declared in a low intense voice, drawing nearer to her.

She had a momentary, purely feminine shrinking from his emaciated shaking frame, the burning eyes in a face dead like a citron; then her placidity returned, the assurance that it was all ordained, that his gestures, the pumping of his diseased heart, had no more individual significance than the movements of a mechanical figure operated by strings, here the strings of supreme Fate. She even smiled slightly, a smile not the mark of approval or humor, but an expression of absolute composure. It drove him at once into febrile excitement.

" At least I understand you," he cried; " far more than you suppose! You can't impress me with your air of a Gautama. I know the freedom of your country. It doesn't shock you to realize that your husband has gone to see a woman he loved, perhaps loves still, and you are not disturbed at my speaking like this."

Here, she knew, regarding him no more than a shrilling locust, was the center about which for a moment blindly her thoughts of Gerrit and herself had revolved. His past —" a woman he loved." But it didn't in the least upset her present peace of mind, her confidence in Gerrit. There was a sharp distinction between the eternal, the divine, Tao, that which is and must prevail, and the personal Tao, subject to rebellion and all the evil of Yin; and she felt that her husband's Tao was good. Out of this she remarked negligently:

[214]

"After all, you are more ignorant of China than I thought. But, of course, you saw only the common and low side. You have not heard of the books girls are taught from —'The Sacred Edict' and 'Mirror of the Heart.' You don't know even the first rule of 'The Book of Rites,' 'Let your face and attitude be grave and thoughtful,' and the second, 'Let your steps be deliberate and regular.'" She paused, conveying by her manner that he was already vanishing and that she was relieved.

"That would do well enough if you were a scholar, or a bonze," he retorted; "but such innocence in a fashionable woman is a pretense. If you are so pure how can you explain your gold and bracelets and pins, all the marks of your worldly rank? Lao-tze taught, 'Rich and high but proud brings about its own misfortune.'" He was so close to her now that she caught a faint sickly reek from his body. It seemed to her that she could see his identity, his reason, vanish, replaced by madness in his staring eyes.

"I worship you," he murmured.

"Opium," she spoke disdainfully.

"Your own tobacco is drugged," he asserted. "But that's not important. I tell you I worship you, the most beautiful person in the world. These fools in Salem, even your husband, can't realize one-tenth of your perfection; they can't venerate you as I do. And now that Ammidon has gone back to the first, we are free too."

"You are a liar," she said with an unexpected colloquial ease.

A darker color stained his dry cheeks. "You saw him," he replied. "Did he get pale or didn't he? And did he or not rush from the room like a man in a fever? I tell you it's no use pretending with me; say what you please I know how delicate your senses are. I'll tell you this too: It's written in our progression that we should meet here, yes, and be a great deal to each other. It was written in the beginning, and we had been drawing together through a million cycles before Gerrit Ammidon stumbled across you."

Taou Yuen was surprised by a sudden conviction that a part of this, at least, was so. No living thing, however minute, escaped from the weariness of movement, either ending in final and blessed suspension or condemned to struggle on and on through countless lives of tormenting passion. All had this dignity of hope or despair; all she encountered were humble, impressive or debased in the working of the mighty law. She had been guilty, as this American had pointed out, of dangerous and wrong pride, and she accepted her lesson willingly. There was, however, an annoying conflict between Edward Dunsack, the example, the impersonal, and Edward Dunsack making violent profession of his unspeakable desire for her. Even the word seemed to soil her; but there was no other. He went recklessly on, trying to increase his advantage:

" We're made to be together."

" If we are it is because of some great wickedness of mine. If we are, then perhaps I am lost. But it is allowed to resist evil, at least, as far as staying out of its touch is resistance."

" Nothing can keep you from me," he declared. Another short step and his knees would be brushing her

[216]

gown. A stronger wave of dislike, shrinking, anger, drowned her logical and higher resignation. "It is time for you to go," she said, her voice still even.

"Never."

It seemed to her that she could feel his hot quivering touch and, all her philosophy dropping from her, she rose quickly. "If this were China," she told him, in a cold fury, "you'd be cut up with knives, in the courtyard where I could look on. But even here I can ring for a servant; and when Captain Ammidon comes back he'll know what to say to you."

She could see that the last affected him; he hesitated, drew back, his hanging fingers clasping and unclasping. That, she thought, relieved, would dispose of him. Then it was clear that his insanity persisted even in the face of the considerable threat of Gerrit's hot pride and violent tempers.

"It's our destiny," he repeated firmly in his borrowed faith, at once a little terrifying and a little ridiculous in the alien mold. His lips twitched and his bony forehead glistened in a fine sweat. Now, thoroughly roused, she laughed at him in open contempt.

"Diseased," she cried, "take your sores away! Dog licked by dogs. Bowl of filth," she was speaking in Chinese, in words of one syllable like the biting of a hair whip. Edward Dunsack gasped, as if actual blows cut him; he stood with one hand half raised, appalled at the sudden vicious rush of her anger. A leaden pallor took the place of his normal sallow coloring, and it was evident that he had difficulty in withstanding the pressure of his laboring heart. He stood between her and the door and she had a premonition that it would be useless to attempt to avoid him or escape. She could, however, call, and some one, there were a score of people about the house, must certainly appear. At that moment she saw a deep change sweep over his countenance, taking place in his every fiber. There was an inner wrenching of Edward Dunsack's being, a blurring and infusion of blood in his eyes, a breath longer and more agonized than any before, and she was looking closely into the face of an overwhelming hatred.

For a moment, she realized, he had even considered killing her with his flickering hands. Then that impulse subsided before a sidelong expression of cunning. "With all your Manchu attitudes," he mocked her, "yes, your aristocratic pretense of mourning and marks of rank, you are no different from the little pleasure girls. Your vocabulary and mind are the same. I was a fool for a while; I saw nothing but your satins and painted face. I forgot you were yellow, I had forgotten that all China's yellow. It's yellow, yellow, yellow and never can be white. I shut my eyes to it and it dragged me down into its slime." His voice was hysterical with an agony of rending spiritual torment and hopeless grief. "It poisoned me little by little, with the smell of its rivers and the cursed smell of its pleasures. Then the opium. A year after I had lost my position, everything; and when I came over here it followed me . . . in my own blood. Even then I might have broken away, I almost had, when Gerrit Ammidon brought you to Salem. You came at a time when I was fighting hardest to throw it all off. You see — you fascinated me. You were all that was most alluring of China, and I wanted you so badly, it all came back so, that I went to the opium to find you."

"Progression," she said ironically.

"Perhaps," he muttered. "Who knows? I'm finished for this life anyhow. You did that. I can't even keep the books for my father's penny trade."

His hands crept rigidly toward her. If they touched her she would be degraded for ever. Yet she was incapable of flight, her throat refused the cry which she had been debating; alternate waves of revulsion and stoical resignation passed over her with chills of acute terror. Yet she managed to preserve an unstirred exterior; and that, she observed, began to influence him. His loathing was as great as ever; but his vision, that had been fixed in a blaze of fury, broke, avoided her direct scrutiny, her appearance of statue-like unconcern.

There was a sound of quick light feet in the hall, the bright voice of one of Gerrit's nieces. Edward Dunsack fell into a profound abstraction: he turned and walked away from her, standing with his back to the room at a window that opened upon the broad green park. He was so weak that he was forced to support himself with a hand on the wall.

Taou Yuen was motionless for a perceptible space, and then moved toward the door in a dignified composure. All this had come from the utter impropriety of the life in America. Dunsack glanced at her as she withdrew, and for a moment she saw his fine profile sharp and dark against the light-flooded window. His lips stirred but she heard no sound. Then she was on the stair mounting to her room.

There mechanically she filled her pipe; but doing this she noticed that her hands were trembling. How lamentably she had failed in the preservation, the assertion, of her superiority, not as a Manchu, but in the deeper, the only true sense of the word — in submission.

" Requite hatred with virtue."

She spoke Lao-tze's admonition aloud and, in the customary devious channel of her mental processes, her thoughts returned to her early life, her girlhood, so marred by sickness that the Emperor had surrendered his customary proprietary right in the daughters of Manchu nobles.

Surrounding the fact of her early suffering, which had kept her out of the active gayety of brothers and sisters, she remembered in the clearest detail her father's house in the north; the later residences in Canton and Shanghai, even the delightful river gardens of the summer place at Soochow, were less vivid. Inside the massive tiled stone-wall the rooms — there were a hundred at least — faced in squares on the inner courtyard, and were connected by glass enclosed verandas. The reception houses of the front court, the deeply carved wooden platform with its scarlet covering, were of the greatest elegance; they were always astir with the numerous secretaries, the Chinese writers and messengers, the *mafoos* and chair coolies, the servants and blind musicians with the old songs, *The Millet's in Flower* and *Kuan Kuan Go to the Ospreys.*

[220]

The side door to the women's apartments, however, opened into a retreat, where her father's concubine, he had but one, trailed like a bird of paradise, and there was the constant musical drip of a fountain in an old granite basin. There, during the years when she was lame, Taou Yuen mostly stayed.

She had been dropped from a palanquin in her sixth year; sharp pains soon after burned in her hip, and the corresponding leg had perceptibly shortened. A great many remedies were tried in vain — burning with charcoal, the application of black plasters, sweating, acupuncture — sticking long needles into the afflicted part. The doctors declared that the five elements of her body — the metal, wood, water, fire and earth, were hopelessly out of equilibrium. Her mother had then called necromancers and devil charmers; lucky and unlucky days were explored; strange rites were conducted before her terrified eyes screwed into the determination to show no alarm.

A year, perhaps, after they had become resigned to her injury, her father, always a man of the most liberal ideas, had suddenly brought into the garden to see her an English doctor passing through China. Against the wailing protests of the women the Englishman had been given authority to treat her; and he had caused to be made a thin steel brace, clasping Taou Yuen's waist and extending in a rigid band down the length of her injured leg. After putting a high shoe on her other foot he had commanded them to keep the brace on her for two years.

It was through that period of comparative inactivity that she acquired a habit of reading and thought, a certain grasp of philosophical attitude, common to the higher masculine Chinese mind but rare among their women. She had, for instance, later, read Lao-tze's Tao-teh-king, and been impressed by his tranquil elevation above the petty ills and concerns of life and the flesh. Her father, like all the ruling class, regarded Taoism — which had, indeed, degenerated into a mass of nonsense about the transmutation of base metals into gold and the elixir of life — with contempt. But this seemed to her no depreciation of the Greatly Eminent One or his philosophy of the two Taoes.

The household, or at least the family, worshipped in the form of Confucius; his precepts and admonitions, the sacred *hiao* or filial submission, the tablets and ancestral piety, were a part of her blood; as was the infinitely fainter infusion of Buddhism; yet in her intellectual brooding it was to the Tao-teh-king that she returned. She paused to recall that, the brace at last removed, she was practically completely recovered; but the bent, the bracing, given her mind had remained.

The colorful pageant of her first marriage, the smaller but splendidly appointed house of her husband — he was extremely intelligent and had honorably passed the examination for licentiate, one of only two hundred successful bachelors out of twenty thousand — and the period following his accidental drowning wheeled quickly through her brain. . . .

Only Gerrit Ammidon was left.

She loved him, Taou Yuen realized, for a quality entirely independent of race: he had more than anyone else she knew the virtues of simplicity and purity an-

nounced by Chwang-Tze as the marks of the True Man.
"We must become like little children," the Old Master
had written. She had seen this at once in the amazing
interview sanctioned by her father-in-law. Most women
of her class, even widows, would have perished with
shame at being exposed to a foreigner. But Lú Kikwáng had expressed her difference from them in the
terms of his proposal. His words had been "finely better" although the truth was that her curiosity had always mastered the other and more prudent instincts. Yet
that alone would not have prostrated her before Gerrit
Ammidon — death was not unthinkable — nor carried her
into his strange terrifying ship and stranger life. The
love had been born almost simultaneously with her first
recognition of his character. Now her passion for him
was close and jealous. A constant shifting between such
humanity and the calm detachment which prefigured heaven
was what most convinced her of the truths of Lao-tze.

All this took body at the announcement of Edward
Dunsack about Gerrit and his niece. Certainly he might
have had an affair; that she dismissed; but the insinuated
permanence of this other affection was serious. She would
not have believed Mr. Dunsack for an instant, but, as he
had pointed out, Gerrit had undoubtedly been upset; he
had turned pale and hurried away impolitely. It was by
such apparently slight indications that the great inner
currents of life were discovered. The fact that Chinese
officials had more than one wife, or, to speak correctly,
concubines in addition, had no bearing with Gerrit; such
was not the custom with American men. It represented
for him, yes — dishonor.

She laboriously recalled his every attitude since they had landed in America, and was obliged to admit that he had changed — he was less gay and though his manner was always considerate she recognized a growing impatience beneath his darker calm. Her philosophy was again torn in shreds by sharp feminine emotions. She was filled with jealousy and hatred and hurt pride. The clearest expression of his possible discontent had marked his face when he had suddenly come into their room and saw her rising from a prayer for his father. Gerrit's lips had been compressed, almost disdainful; at that moment, she knew unerringly, he found her ugly. Of course it had been the hideous garments of mourning.

She must wear the unhemmed sackcloth and dull slippers, bind her headdress and cover her pins with paste, for a hundred days; and then a second mourning of black or dark blue, and no flowers, for three years. It might well be that by then Gerrit, blind to these proprieties, would find her unendurable. Suddenly, in the tremendous difficulty of holding him against an entire world, his own and of which she was supremely ignorant, it seemed to her that she needed every possible means, every coral blossom and gold filament and finger of paint, the cunning intoxication of subtle dress and color and perfume. With a leaden sense of guilt, but in a fever of impatience, of haste, she stripped off the coarse hemp for her most elaborate satins, her santal and cloves and carmine.

When Gerrit came in it had grown dark with night, and he explained that he had been busy inspecting the *Nautilus'* spars. She lighted a lamp, then another, all

[224]

she could find, and studied him unobtrusively. She was shocked at the worn expression of his face; it seemed as if he had aged in the few hours since he had left the library. He was uneasy, silent; and, secretly dismayed, she saw that he was indifferent to her changed appearance, too. Taou Yuen debated the wisdom of telling him about the painful scene with Edward Dunsack; against her original intent she decided in the negative. She informed herself that the reason for this was a wish to preserve him, now that they were practically at the day of departure, from an unpleasant duty. But there was an underlying dimly apprehended and far different motive: she was afraid that it would blow into flame a situation that might otherwise be avoided, bring to life a past naturally dying or dead.

She saw that he was scarcely aware of her presence in the room, perhaps in his life. A period of resentment followed. " You are dull," she declared, " and I am going down to the garden for entertainment." Gerrit nodded. He would, he told her, be along shortly. Below she found Roger Brevard, with the oldest Ammidon girl and her mother.

Roger Brevard, she had discovered, was in love with Sidsall. The latter, it developed, was to leave shortly for a party; Mr. Brevard was not going; and, when Gerrit's sister-in-law walked across the grass with her daughter the man dropped into an easy conversation with Taou Yuen. She had a feeling, which she had tried in vain to lose, of the vulgarity, the impropriety of this. Yet she recognized that there was none of the former in Roger Brevard; he resembled quite a little her dead husband, Sié-Ngan-kwán; and for that reason she was more at ease with him — in spite of such unaccustomed familiarity — than with anyone else in Salem but Gerrit.

He was, she admitted condescendingly, almost as cultivated as the ordinary Chinese gentleman. Many of his thoughts, where she could understand their expression, might have come from a study of the sacred kings. At the same time her feminine perception realized that he had a genuine liking for her.

"You'll be delighted to leave Salem," he said, leaning forward and studying her.

"That would not be polite," she answered formally. "You have been so good. But it will give me pleasure to see Shanghai again. Anyone is happier with customs he understands."

"And prefers," he added. "Indeed, I'd choose some of your manners rather than ours. You see, you have been at the business of civilization so much longer than the rest of us."

"Our history begins two thousand years before your Christ," she told him; "our language has been spoken without change for thirty-three centuries, as you call them. But such facts are nothing. I would rather hear your non — nonsense," she stumbled over the word.

"Do you mean that what we call nonsense is really the most important?"

"Perhaps," she replied. "Devotion to the old and dead is greatly necessary yet you smile at it. I didn't mean that, but moons and lovers and music." He cried in protest, "We're terribly serious about those!"

" I hear nothing but talk about cargoes and sales and money."

" We keep the other under our hats," he instructed her. She was completely mystified, and he explained.

" In China," she remarked tentatively, " it is possible for a man to love two women at once, maybe one a little more than the other, but he can be kind and just and affectionate to them both. Tell me, is — is that possible with an American? "

" No! " he spoke emphatically. " We can love, in the way you mean, only one, perhaps only once. I wouldn't swear to that, but there are simply no exceptions to the first. Men are unfaithful, yes; but at a cost to themselves, or because they are incapable of restraint. To be unfaithful in anything is to fail, isn't it? You can lie to yourself as effectively as to anybody else."

She fixed a painful attention upon him, but lost at least a half of his meaning. However, one fact was clearer than ever — that Edward Dunsack had said an evil thing about her husband. " It seems," he went on, " that even spiritual concerns can be the result of long custom." If he was trying to find an excuse for Chinese habit she immediately disposed of it. " No," she said, " you are upside down. The spirit is first, the eternal Tao, everywhere alike, but the personal spirit is different in you and in us."

A sudden dejection seized her — now the difference seemed vaster than anything she had in common with Gerrit. A wave of oppressive nostalgia, of confusion and dread, submerged her in a faintly thunderous darkness.

She felt everywhere about her the presence of evil and threatening shades. The approach of her husband, his heavy settling into a chair, did nothing to lighten her apprehension.

" How soon do we go? " she asked faintly.

" In two weeks, with nothing unexpected," he responded without interest or pleasure. It flashed through her mind that he was depressed at leaving Salem, that other woman. His present indifference was very far from the manner in which he had first discussed their leaving. Yet, even that, she recalled in the light of her present sensitiveness, had been unnaturally abrupt and clothed in a great many loud-sounding words. She told herself arbitrarily that Edward Dunsack had lied — for the purpose which his conduct afterward made clear — but her very feeling was proof that she believed he had spoken the truth.

She was a victim of an uneasy curiosity to see . . . she made a violent mental effort and recaptured the name — Nettie Vollar. Of course the latter had been the deliberate cause of whatever wickedness had threatened at the return of Gerrit with her, Taou Yuen. She had however no doubt of the extent of this: Gerrit was upright, faithful to the necessity Roger Brevard had explained; all that assaulted her happiness was on an incorporate plane, or, anyhow, in a procession of consequences extending far back and forward of their present lives.

But, she recognized, she had no excuse nor opportunity to see Nettie Vollar. Mrs. Ammidon, when she heard of the accident, had at once declared her intention of going to the Dunsacks' house; still that promised no chance of satisfying her own desire. The least politeness in the world prohibited her from going baldly in and demanding to see the woman. She couldn't, all at once, make convincing a sympathy or impersonal interest entirely contradictory to her insistent indifference. The best she could hope was for them to sail away as quickly as possible; when on the other side of the seas Gerrit would probably return to the simplicity of being she had adored.

Then a trivial and yet serious fear occurred to her — perhaps here, among all these dead-white women, he no longer held her beautiful. The word was his own, or it had been his; he had not repeated it, she realized, twice since they had been in Salem. Personally, she found the American women entirely undistinguished and dressed in grotesquely ugly and cheap clothes — not unlike paper lanterns bobbing along the ground. Their faces were shamelessly bare of paint and their manners would have disgraced the lowest servant in a Chinese courtyard. This was natural, from any consideration of the hideous or inappropriate things that surrounded them, and from the complete lack of what she could distinguish as either discipline or reverence. Yet Gerrit, a part of this, would be unable to share her attitude; she had heard him praise the appearance of women so insipid that she had turned expecting vainly an ironic smile.

Roger Brevard rose and made his bow, the only satisfactory approach to a courteous gesture she had met outside Gerrit's occasional half-humorous effort since leaving Shanghai. He stirred, muttered a perfunctory phrase, and sank back into obscurity.

Little quirks of unfamiliar disturbing feeling ran through Taou Yuen; her mind, it seemed, had become a thing of no importance; all that at one time had so largely ordered her life was superseded by these illogical emotions spreading apparently from her heart. The truth was, she told herself, that — with all her reading and philosophy — she had had little or no experience of actuality: the injury to her hip and quiet life in the gray garden at Canton, her protected existence in the women's apartments, whatever she might have learned from them neglected because of the general silliness of their chatter, the formal early marriage, had all combined for the preservation of her ignorance.

She regarded herself now with distrust; nothing could have been more unpleasant than the failure of her will, this swamping of her equanimity. She never lost for a moment the image of superiority that should be her perfect example, the non-assertion that was the way of heaven; but her comprehension was like a figure ruthlessly dragged about by an overpowering unreflective force. A sharp hatred of Nettie Vollar seared her mind and perished in a miserable sense of weakness.

Against the dark, charged with a confusion of the ten thousand things, she stared wearily and wakeful. She reminded herself again that Gerrit would soon be gone from Salem, alone with her on the long voyage to China; but he'd return to America, come back to Salem; and she knew that he would never bring her westward again. A period of depression followed which seemed to have no immediate connection with Gerrit; she had an indefinable feeling of struggling in vain against adversity, of opposition to an implacable power.

For a short while after she rose in the morning it appeared that she had regained her self-control, her reason; and a consequent happy relief irradiated her. But when Gerrit came up after she had finished her toilet and she saw, from his haggard face, that he too must have been awake, tormented, through the night, a passion of bitterness enveloped her at which all that had gone before turned pale. She could scarcely restrain herself from a noisy wailing accusation, and stood regarding him with a tense unnatural grimace, the result of her effort to preserve propriety. She told herself, at the tempest of vulgar phrases storming through her consciousness, that what Edward Dunsack had said about her being no better than the tea house girls was true, and she was aghast at the inner treachery capable of such self-betrayal. Not a quivering word, however, escaped; she managed a commonplace phrase and turned aside in a trivial pretext of occupation.

" I am going into Boston with Captain Dunsack on business connected with his schooners." The girl's grandfather! " Very well." She spoke placidly, and with a tempestuous heart watched him stride quickly about the park.

She settled herself in a long motionless contemplation, fastening her mind upon the most elevated and revered ideas conceivable. She saw the eternal Tao flowing like a great green river of souls, smooth and mighty and resistless; and she willed that she too might become a part of that desirable self-effacement, safe in surrender. Men striving to create a Tao for personal ends beat out their lives in vain. It was the figure of the river developing, like floating on a deliberate all-powerful tide or struggling impotently against it.

Later a message came up from Mrs. Ammidon — she hoped that Taou Yuen would drive with her that afternoon. She dressed with the most particular care, in blue and dark greens, her shoulders thick with embroidered garlands and silver *shou,* her piled hair ornamented in glittering silver leaves and garnets.

She went down when she heard the horses on the street below but the barouche was empty except for the coachman. "Mrs. Ammidon left a half hour ago," a servant told her; "and sent the carriage back for you." They moved forward, going, she saw, into a part of the town where they seldom drove — the narrow crowded way by the wharves — and, turning shortly into a street that ended abruptly at the water, drew up before a dingy house on her right.

The door was open, and they waited, confident that Mrs. Ammidon would hear the clatter of hoofs and come out; but a far different appeared. She gazed for a silent space at Taou Yuen seated above her, as if confused by the glittering magnificence. It was probable that Gerrit's brother's wife had come there on an errand of charity for the woman was poor, dingy like the house, with a face drawn by suffering and material struggle.

"Of course you're Captain Ammidon's wife," she said; "and you are here after Mrs. William Ammidon. Well, she's gone; but she left a message for you. She will be at Henry Whipple's, the bookseller. After she saw Nettie she went right off to send her some things; wouldn't wait for the carriage. A kind-hearted determined body."

Taou Yuen leaned out to command the coachman to drive on; but the other, plainly bent on making the most of a rare opportunity for such a conversation, continued talking in her low resigned way.

"I was glad to have her too; Nettie gets pretty fretful up there with nobody but me, really. She hasn't been so well, either, since —" here she stopped abruptly, recommenced. "I like to see a person myself of Mrs. Ammidon's kind. I've been alone all day; father's gone to Boston and Edward away I don't know where."

Taou Yuen's curiosity to see Nettie Vollar returned infinitely multiplied; here, miraculously, was an opportunity for her to study the woman who was beyond any doubt an important part of Gerrit's past, present — it might be, his future. The men were gone. . . . She got resolutely down from the barouche. "Take me up to your daughter," she directed quietly.

"Why, that's very kind, but I don't know — Yes, certainly. Mind these stairs with your satin skirts; I don't always get around to the whole house."

Taou Yuen saw at once that Nettie Vollar was far sicker than she had realized: her head lay on the pillow absolutely spent, her brow damply plastered with hair and her eyes enlarged and dull. Taou Yuen drew a chair forward and sat beside a table with a glass bowl of small dark pills which from a just perceptible odor she recognized as opium. She looked intently, coldly, at the prostrate figure. A flush like match flames burned in Nettie Vollar's cheeks, and she said in a voice at once weak and sharp:

"You're her!"

Taou Yuen nodded slowly, disdainfully.

"Oh, how could he!" the other exclaimed in what sounded like the thin echo of a passionate cry. "I knew you were Chinese, but I never realized it till this minute."

As Gerrit Ammidon's wife had feared she was totally unable to judge a single quality or feature of the girl before her. She looked exactly like all the others she had seen in Salem: in order to realize her she needed Gerrit's eyes, Gerrit's birth. Then one fact crept insidiously into her consciousness — here, in a way, was another being who had Gerrit Ammidon's childlike simplicity. That was the most terrifying discovery she could have made. Taou Yuen felt the return of the hateful irresistible emotions which had destroyed her self-control. She wanted to hurt Nettie Vollar in every possible way, to mock her with the fact that she had lost Gerrit perhaps never to see him again; she wanted to tell her that she, Taou Yuen, entirely understood her hopes, efforts, and that they were vain.

An utter self-loathing possessed her at the same time, a feeling of imminent danger as if she were walking with willfully shut eyes on the edge of a precipice above a black fatal void. Not a trace of this appeared on her schooled countenance; and once more she completely restrained any defiling speech. She deliberately shifted her point of view to another possible aspect of all that confronted her — it might be that this woman was a specter, a *kwei*, bent on Gerrit's destruction. Such a thing often happened. How much better if Nettie Vollar had been killed! She studied her with a renewed interest — a fresh question. Perhaps the other would die as it was. She was extremely weak; her spirit, Taou Yuen saw, lay listlessly in a listless body. Nettie Vollar slightly moved her injured arm, and that little effort exhausted her for a moment; her eyes closed, her face was as white as salt.

A further, almost philosophical, consideration engaged Taou Yuen's mind — this extraordinary occasion, her being with the other alone, Nettie Vollar's fragility, were, it might be, all a part of the working of the righteous *Yang*. In the light of this, then, she had been brought here for a purpose . . . the ending of a menace to her husband. She hesitated for a breath — if it were the opposite malignant *Yin* there was no bottom to the infamy into which she might fall. It was a tremendous question.

The actual execution of the practical suggestion, from either source, was extremely easy; she had but to lean forward, draw her heavy sleeve across the strained face, hold it there for a little, and Nettie Vollar would have died of — of any one of a number of reasonable causes. She, Taou Yuen, would call, politely distressed, for the mother . . . very regrettable.

Gerrit free —

Perhaps.

She had no shrinking from the act itself, nothing that might have been called pity, a few more or less years in a single life were beneath serious consideration; it was the lives to come, the lingering doubt of which power led her on, which restrained and filled her mind. A flicker of rage darted through her calm questioning; her mental processes again faded. With her right arm across the supine body and enveloping the face in her left sleeve a single twist and Nettie Vollar would choke in a cloud of thick satin made gay with unfading flowers and the embroidered symbol of long life. She felt her body grow rigid with purpose when the sound of a footfall below held her motionless in an unreasoning dread.

It was not heavy, yet she was certain that it was not the woman's. A blur of voices drifted up to her, the dejected feminine tone and a thin querulous demand, surprise. Taou Yuen turned cold as stone: the sensation of oppressive danger increased until it seemed as if she, and not Nettie Vollar, were strangling. There was a profound stillness, then a shuffling tread on the stair, and Edward Dunsack entered, entered but stood without advancing, his back against a closed door.

Even since yesterday he had noticeably wasted, there were muscles of his face that twitched continuously; his hands, it seemed to her, writhed like worms. He said nothing, but stared at her with a fixed glittering vision; all his one time worship — it had been so much — was devoured in the hatred born in the Ammidon library. Frozen with apprehension she sat without movement; her face, she felt, as still as a lacquered mask.

To her astonishment — she had forgotten Nettie Vollar's existence — a shaken voice from the bed demanded:

" Uncle Edward, what's come over you! Don't you see Mrs. Ammidon! Oh —" her speech rose in a choked exclamation. Edward Dunsack had turned the key and was crossing the room with a dark twisted face, his eyes stark and demented. Taou Yuen, swung round toward the advancing figure, heard a long fluttering breath behind her. Perhaps Nettie Vollar had died of fright. The terror in her own brain dried up before an overwhelming realization — she had betrayed herself to the principle of evil. She was lost. Her thoughts were at once incredibly rapid and entirely vivid, logical: Edward Dunsack, ruined, in China; herself blinded, confused, destroyed in America. Yesterday she had held him powerless with the mere potency of her righteousness; but now she had no strength.

There was a loathsome murmur from his dusty lips. He intended to kill her, to mar and spoil her throat, a degradation forbidden by Confucius, an eternal disfigurement. This filled her with a renewed energy of horror. . . . Here there was none but a feeble woman to hear her if she called. She rose mechanically, a hand on the table; Taou Yuen saw Nettie Vollar's deathly pallid face rolled awkwardly from the pillow, and the bowl of opium. There were twenty or more pills. Without hesitation, even with a sense of relief, she swept the contents of the bowl into her palm. The effort of swallowing so many hard particles was almost convulsive and followed with a nauseous spasm.

Exhausted by mental effort she sank into a chair and a dullness like smoke settled over her. The figure of Edward Dunsack retreated to an infinite distance. The smoke moved in a great steady volume — the eternal and changeless Tao, without labor or desires, without. . . . Hatred requited with virtue . . . attracting all honor — mounting higher and higher from the consuming passions, the seething black lives of her immeasurable fall.

[237]

X

ALTHOUGH the late afternoon was at an hour when Derby Street should have been filled by an half-idle throng in the slackening of the day's waterside employments Roger Brevard found it noticeably empty. In this he suddenly recognized that the street was like the countingroom of the Mongolian Marine Insurance Company, the heart of Salem's greatness — they were weaker, stilled in a decline that yet was not evident in the impressive body of the town.

When he had first taken charge of this branch both Salem and it had been of sufficient moment to attract him from New York; the company was insuring Boston and New York vessels; the captains had thronged its broad window commanding St. Peters and Essex Streets. Now only an occasional shipmaster, holding the old traditions and habits or else retired, sat in the comfortable armchairs with leather cushions drawn up at the coal hearth or expansive in white through the summer.

His mind shifted to a consideration of these facts in relation to himself — whether the same thing overtaking the place and marine insurance had not settled upon him too — as he made his way from Central Wharf, where he had vainly gone for prospective business. His inquiry was reaching a depressing certainty when, passing and gazing down Hardy Street, he saw the Ammidon barouche standing in front of the Dunsacks'.

Roger Brevard stopped: the Ammidon men, he knew, seldom drove about Salem. He had heard of Nettie Vollar's accident and came to the conclusion that Rhoda was within. If this were so, her visit, limited to a charitable impulse, would be short; and thinking of the pleasure of driving with her he turned into the side way. As he approached, the coachman met him with an evident impatience.

"No, sir," he replied to Brevard's inquiry. "But we were to get Mrs. Ammidon at the bookstore. Mrs. Captain Gerrit called here for her, but she went inside unexpected. All of an hour ago. I don't like to ask for the lady, but what may be said later I can't think."

He had scarcely finished speaking when a woman whom Brevard recognized as Kate Vollar appeared at the door. "Oh, Mr. Brevard!" she exclaimed with an unnaturally pallid and apprehensive face. "I'm glad to find you. Please come upstairs with me. Why I don't know but I'm all in a tremble. Mrs. Ammidon went to see Nettie, then Edward came in, and when he heard who was there he acted as if he were struck dumb and went up like a person afflicted. I waited the longest while and then followed them and knocked. Why the door was shut I'd never tell you. But they didn't answer, any of them," she declared with clasped straining hands. "Three in the room and not a sound. Please —" her voice was suddenly suffocated by dread.

"Certainly. Quarles," he addressed the coachman, "I'll get you to come along. If there is a lock to break it will need a heavier shoulder than mine."

Mounting the narrow somber stair, followed by the man

and Kate Vollar, he wondered vainly what might have happened. Obscurely some of the woman's fear was communicated to him. Brevard knocked abruptly on the door indicated but there was no answering voice or movement. He tried the latch: as Nettie's mother had found, it was fastened.

"Quarles," Roger Brevard said curtly.

The coachman stepped forward, braced himself for the shove he directed against the wooden barrier, and the door swept splintering inward. Roger advanced first and a grim confusion touched him with cold horror. Taou Yuen was half seated and half lying across a table beside the bed; he couldn't see her face, but her body was utterly lax. Nettie Vollar, too, was in a dreadful waxen similitude of death, with lead colored lips and fixed sightless eyes. A slight extraordinary sound rose behind him, and whirling, Brevard discovered that it was Edward Dunsack giggling. He was silent immediately under the other's scrutiny, and an expression of stubborn and malicious caution pinched his wasted sardonic countenance.

Brevard turned to the greater necessity of the women, and moved Taou Yuen so that he could see her features. It was evident that she was not, as he had first thought, dead; her breathing was slow and deep and harsh, her pulse deliberate and full; she was warm, too, but her face was suffused by an unnatural blueness and the pupils of her inert eyes were barely discernible. He shook her with an unceremonious vigor, but there was no answering energy; she fell across his arm in a sheer weight of satin-covered body. He moved back in a momentary uncontrollable repulsion when Kate Vollar threw herself past

[240]

him onto the bed. "Nettie!" she cried, "Nettie! Nettie!" Brevard was chilled by the possibility of an unutterable tragedy, when with a faint suffusion of color the girl gave a gasping sigh. Her voice stirred in a terror-shaken whisper:

"Uncle Edward, don't! Why — don't. Oh!" She pressed her face with a long shudder into the pillow. "Whatever was it —?" her mother began wildly. Brevard caught her shoulder. "Not now," he directed; "you'll come downstairs with me. We must have help at once and your daughter quiet."

However he was in a quandary — he couldn't trust the woman here, he would have to go immediately for assistance, and yet it was impossible to leave Nettie Vollar and Gerrit's wife alone. "You will have to wait in the room," he decided, turning to Quarles.

Edward Dunsack was wavering against a wall; Brevard went swiftly up to him. "We'll need you," he said shortly. Dunsack maintained his silence and air of stubborn cunning; but, when the other man clasped his incredibly thin arm, he went willingly followed by Kate Vollar below. There he sat obediently, his judicious detachment broken by a repetition of the thin shocking snigger.

"You must be responsible for your brother," Roger Brevard told the quivering woman. "I'll be back immediately. Now that you know Nettie's safe you must control yourself. No one should go up — keep everybody out — till you hear from me or the doctor or Captain Ammidon."

What an inexplicable accident or crime, he thought, hurriedly approaching the countinghouse of Ammidon, Ammidon and Saltonstone, the first and nearest of the places to which he must go. He could remember no mark of what had overcome Taou Yuen. How was Dunsack, who was now clearly demented, implicated? What racking thing had Nettie Vollar seen?

In the subsequent exclamatory rush, even on the following morning when Roger Brevard learned that — poisoned by opium undoubtedly taken by herself — Gerrit Ammidon's wife had died without regaining consciousness, the greater part of the tragedy became little clearer. No statement could be had from Edward Dunsack other than a meaningless array of precautionary phrases; and returning in a sliding gait toward Hardy Street he was put under a temporary restraint.

Nettie Vollar, Brevard heard, had relapsed from her injury into a second critical collapse. Yet, he told himself, entering the room that was his home in Mrs. Cane's large square house on Chestnut Street, that the Manchu still absorbed his speculations.

It was a pleasant room and a pleasant house with a dignified portico; and his tall windows, back on the right of the second floor, opened on the length of the Napiers' garden. Brevard sat looking out over a dim leafiness of evening and tried to discipline his thoughts into order and coherence. Any dignity of death had been soiled by the ugly mystery of the aspects surrounding the end of Taou Yuen.

He had liked her extremely well, agreeing with Rhoda Ammidon that, probably, they had never been permitted to know a more aristocratic breeding or greater degrees of

purely worldly and mental and personal charm than those
of Gerrit's wife.

His mind grew more philosophical and a perception,
yet without base in facts, convinced him that Taou Yuen
had been killed by America. It was a fantastic thought,
and he attempted to dismiss it, waiting for more secure
knowledge, but it persisted. She had been killed by unfamiliar circumstances, tradition, emotions. In some
manner, but how he was unable to disentangle from the
pressures of mere curiosity and conjecture, Nettie Vollar
— or rather Gerrit's old passing affair with Nettie — had
entered into the unhappy occurrence. After an hour's vain
search he gave up all effort to pierce the darkness until he
had actual knowledge — if he ever had, he was forced
to add silently. It was possible that the secret might be
entirely guarded from the public, even from the closer part
he had played and his familiarity with the Ammidon
family.

He was an inmate of their inner garden with its lilac
trees and hedged roses in season, the pungent beds of
flowers and box, the moonshade of the poplars. Roger
Brevard turned from the consideration of Taou Yuen to
the even more insistent claim of his increasing affection
for Sidsall. He stopped again both to lament and delight
in her youth — another year and he would have unhesitat-
ingly announced his feeling as love to them all. It was
that, he admitted to himself almost shyly. The obvious
thing was for him to wait through the year or more
until the Ammidons would hear of a proposal and then
urge his desire. . . . He could see her quite often mean-
while.

Yes, that was the sensible course, even in the face of his own multiplying years. They were twenty-five more than Sidsall's; yet, he added in self-extenuation, he was not definitely snared in middle age; he was still elastic in body and youthful, but for graying hair, in appearance. His birth was eligible from every social consideration; and, though he was not rich, he had enough independently to assure the safety of his wife's future. This did not come entirely, or now even in the larger part, from the Mongolian Marine Insurance Company, but took the form of a comparatively small but secure private income.

He paused to wonder if it had not been that latter fact which had prevented his being successful — successful, that was, in William Ammidon's meaning of the word. He had not made money nor a position of importance among men of affairs. Such safety, he decided, was a dangerous possession judged by the standards he was now considering. A few thousand a year for life struck at the root of activity. It induced a critical detached attitude toward life, overemphasized the importance of the cut of a trouser and the validity of pedigree. It was a mistake to dance noticeably well.

Drifting, together with almost everyone else, he had reached his present position, past forty, by imperceptible degrees, obscurely influenced by the play of what he intrinsically was on circumstances or accident or fate.

Although he had never done so before, he compared himself with Gerrit Ammidon. The other's refusal to accept a partnership in the family firm or command a California clipper was known. Gerrit and himself were alike in that they apprehended the values of life more clearly than did the ordinary mind or heart. But, in retaliation, the world they differed from curtly brushed them aside. Roger Brevard could not see that they had made the least mark on the callous normal cruelty or the æsthetic and spiritual blindness of the existence they shared. But it was always possible that something bigger than their grasp of justice or beauty was afoot.

He turned from the darkened prospect of the window and his thoughts to the room. Without a light he removed his formal street clothes, hanging the coat and waistcoat, folding the trousers in a drawer, with exact care; changing his light boots for fiber slippers he set the former in the row of footgear drawn up like a military review against the wall. Though it was quite obscure now, and no one would see him, he paused to brush his slightly disarranged hair, before — tying the cord of his chamber robe — he resumed his seat.

The year, he reverted to Sidsall, would pass; but, try as he might, he had no feeling of security in the future, however near. It was the present, this Sidsall, that filled him with a tyrannical and bitter longing. She was unbelievably beautiful now. Against the faintness of his hope, his patience, he saw the whole slow process of the disintegration of marine insurance, and with it his own fatuous insensibility to the decline: that decline with its exact counterpart in himself. Salem and he were getting dusty together.

He straightened up vigorously in his chair — this would never do. He must wind up his affairs here and return to New York. The tranquil backwater had overpowered him for a time; but, again awake, he would strike out strongly

. . . with Sidsall. Endless doubt and hope fluctuated within him. Voices rose from the Napier garden, and from a tree sounded the whirring of the first locust he had noticed that summer.

On a noon following he saw the passage of the three or four carriages that constituted the funeral cortège of Taou Yuen's entirely private interment. She would be buried of course by Christian service: here were none of the elaborate Confucian rites and ceremonial; yet — from what Taou Yuen had occasionally indicated — Confucius, Lao-tze, the Buddha, were all more alike than different; they all vainly preached humility, purity, the subjugation of the flesh. He stopped later in the Charter Street cemetery and found her grave, the headstone marked:

TAOU YUEN

A MANCHURIAN LADY

THE WIFE

OF

GERRIT AMMIDON, ESQ.

and the dates.

He saw, naturally, but little of the Ammidons — a glimpse of Rhoda in the carriage and William on Charter Street; the *Nautilus,* ready for sea, continued in her berth at Phillips' Wharf. Fragments of news came to him quoted and re-quoted, grotesquely exaggerated and even malicious reports of the tragedy at the Dunsacks'. Standing at his high desk in the countingroom of the Mongolian Marine Insurance Company, Taou Yuen's glittering passage through Salem already seemed to him a fable, a dream. Even Sidsall, robustly near by, had an aspect of unreality in the tender fabric of his visions. Captain Rendell, his spade beard at the verge of filmed old eyes, who was seated at the window, rose with difficulty. For a moment he swayed on insecure legs, then, barely gathering the necessary power, moved out into the street.

Later, when Roger Brevard was turning the key on the insurance company for the day, Lacy Saltonstone stopped to speak in her charming slow manner: "Mother of course is in a whirl, with Captain Ammidon about to marry that Nettie Vollar, since she is recovering after all, and our moving to Boston. . . . You see I'm there so often it will make really very little difference to me. Sidsall is the lucky one, though you'd never know it from seeing her. . . . I thought you'd have heard — why, to Lausanne, a tremendously impressive school for a year. They have promised her London afterward. I would call that a promise, but actually, Sidsall —."

"Doesn't she want to go?" he asked mechanically, all the emotions that had chimed through his being suddenly clashing in a discordant misery. He bowed absently, and hastening to his room softly closed the door and sat without supper, late into the evening, lost in a bitterness that continually poisoned the resolutions formed out of his overwhelming need. He was aghast at the inner violence that destroyed the long tranquility of his existence, the clenched hands and spoken words lost in the shadows over the Napiers' garden. He wanted Sidsall with a breathless tyranny infinitely sharper than any pang of youth: she was life itself.

She didn't want to go, Lacy had made that clear; and

he toĭd himself that her reluctance could only, must, proceed from one cause — that she cared for him. As he dwelt on this, the one alleviating possibility, he became certain of its truth. He would find her at once and in spite of Rhoda and William Ammidon explain that his whole hope lay in marrying her. With an utter contempt at all the small orderly habits which, he now saw, were the expression of a confirmed dry preciseness, he left his clothes in a disorderly heap. Such a feeling as Sidsall's and his, he repeated from the oppressive expanse of his black walnut bed, was above ordinary precautions and observance. Then, unable to dismiss the thought of how crumpled his trousers would be in the morning, oppressed by the picture of the tumbled garments, he finally rose and, in the dark, relaid them in the familiar smooth array.

In the morning his disturbance resolved into what seemed a very decided and reasonable attitude: He would see Rhoda that day and explain his feeling and establish what rights and agreement he could. He was willing to admit that Sidsall was, perhaps, too young for an immediate decision so wide in results. The ache, the hunger for happiness sharpened by vague premonitions of mischance, began again to pound in his heart.

At the Ammidons' it was clear immediately that Rhoda's manner toward him had changed: it had become more social, even voluble, and restrained. She conversed brightly about trivial happenings, while he sat listening, gravely silent. But it was evident that she soon became aware of his difference, and her voice grew sharper, almost antagonistic. They were in the formal parlor, a significant detail in itself, and Roger Brevard saw William pass the door. Well, he would soon have to go, he must speak about Sidsall now. It promised to be unexpectedly difficult; but the words were forming when she came into the room.

There were faint shadows under her eyes, the unmistakable marks of tears. An overwhelming passion for her choked at his throat. She came directly up to him, ignoring her mother. " Did you hear that they want me to go away? " she asked. He nodded, " It's that I came to see your mother about."

" They know I don't want to," she continued; " I've explained it to them very carefully."

" My dear Sidsall," Rhoda Ammidon cut in; " we can't have this. What Roger has to say must be for me and your father." The girl smiled at her and turned again to Roger Brevard. " Do you want me to go? "

" No! " he cried, all his planning lost in uncontrollable rebellion.

" Then I don't think I shall."

William entered and stood at his wife's shoulder. " You won't insist," Sidsall faced them quietly. " Ridiculous," her father replied. Brevard realized that he must support the girl's bravery of spirit. How adorable she was! But, before the overwhelming superior position of the elder Ammidons, their weight of propriety and authority, his determination wavered.

" To be quite frank," the other man proceeded, " since it has been forced on us, Sidsall imagines herself in love with you, Brevard. I don't need to remind you how unsuitable and preposterous that is. She's too young to know the meaning of love. Besides, my dear fellow, you're a quarter century her elder. We want Sidsall to go to London like her mother, have her cotillions, before she settles into marriage."

"They can't understand, Roger," Sidsall touched his hand. "We're sorry to disappoint them —"

"You ought to be made to leave the room," William fumed.

"That isn't necessary," Rhoda told him. "I am sure Roger understands perfectly how impossible it is. You mustn't be hurt," she turned to him, "if I admit that we have very different plans . . . at least a man nearer Sidsall's age."

The girl lifted a confident face to him. "You want to marry me, don't you?" she asked. More than any other conceivable joy. But he said this silently. His courage slowly ebbed before the parental displeasure viewing him coldly. "Then —" Sidsall paused expectantly, a touch of impatience even invaded her manner. "Please tell them, Roger."

"Why I have to put up with this is beyond me," William Ammidon expostulated with his wife. "It's shameless."

Roger Brevard winced. He tried to say something about hope and the future, but it was so weak, a palpable retreat, leaving Sidsall alone and unsupported, that the words perished unfinished. The girl studied him, suddenly startled, and her confidence ebbed. He turned away, crushed by convention, filled with shame and a sense of self-betrayal.

A stillness followed of unendurable length, in which he found his attention resting on the diversified shapes of the

East India money in a corner cabinet. It was Sidsall who finally spoke, slowly and clearly:

"Forgive me."

He recognized that she was addressing her mother and father. From a whisper of skirts he realized that she was leaving the room. Without the will necessary for a last glimpse he stood with his head bowed by an appalling sensation of weariness and years.

In a flash of self-comprehension, Roger Brevard knew that he would never, as he had hoped, leave Salem. He was an abstemious man, one of a family of long lives, and he would linger here, increasingly unimportant, for a great while, an old man in new epochs, isolated among strange people and prejudices. Whatever the cause — the small safety or an inward flaw — he had never been part of the corporate sweating humanity where, in the war of spirit and flesh, the vital rewards and accomplishments were found.

Soon after he passed Gerrit and Nettie Vollar driving in the direction of the harbor; she was lying back wanly in the Ammidon barouche, but her companion's face was set directly ahead, his expression of general disdain strongly marked. A vigorous hand, Roger noted, was clasped about Nettie's supine palm. She saw him standing on the sidewalk and bowed slightly, but the shipmaster plainly overlooked him together with the rest of Salem.

The end of summer was imminent in a whirl of yellow leaves and chill gray wind. There was a ringing of bugles through the morning, the strains of military quicksteps, rhythmic tramping feet and the irregular fulmination of salutes. That it was already the day of the annual

[251]

Fall Review seemed incredible to Roger Brevard. He was indifferent to the activities of the Common; but when he heard that the *Nautilus* was sailing in the middle of the afternoon he left his inconsequential affairs for Phillips' Wharf.

A small number were waiting on the solid rock-filled reach, the wharfinger's office at its head and a stone warehouse blocking the end, where the *Nautilus* lay with her high-steeved bowsprit pointing outward. The harbor was slaty, cold, and there was a continuous slapping of small waves on the shore. Darkening clouds hung low in the west, out of which the wind cut in flaws across the open. The town, so lately folded in lush greenery, showed a dun lift of roofs and stripping branches tossing against an ashy sky.

Close beside Roger stood Barzil Dunsack, his beard blowing, with Kate Vollar in a bright red shawl, her skirts whipping uneasily against her father's legs. Beyond were the Ammidons — William, and Rhoda in a deep furred wrap, and their daughters. Rhoda waved for him to join them, but he declined with a gesture of acknowledgment.

The deck of the *Nautilus* was above his vision but he could see most of the stir of departure. The peremptory voice of the mate rose from the bow, minor directions were issued by the second mate aft, a seaman was aloft on the main-royal yard and another stood at the stage rising sharply from the wharf. Gerrit and his wife had not yet arrived, and the pilot, making a leisurely appearance, stopped to exchange remarks with the Ammidons. He climbed on board the ship and Roger could see his head and shoulders moving toward the poop and mounting the ladder.

The wind grew higher, shriller, every moment; it was thrashing among the stays and braces; the man aloft, a small movement against the clouds, swayed in its force. There was a faint clatter of hoofs from Derby Street, Brevard had a fleeting glimpse of an arriving carriage, and Gerrit, supporting Nettie Ammidon, advanced over the wharf. The shipmaster walked slowly, the woman clinging, almost dragging, at his erect strength. They went close by Roger: Nettie's pale face, her large shining dark eyes, were filled with placid surrender. Her companion spoke in a low grave tone, and she looked up at him in a tired and happy acquiescence.

The two families joined, and there was a confused determined gayety of farewell and good wishes. Out of it finally emerged the captain of the *Nautilus* and the slight figure upon his arm. He wore a beaver hat, and, as they mounted the stage, he was forced to hold it on with his free hand. When the quarter-deck was reached they disappeared into the cabin.

" Mr. Broadrick," the pilot called, " you can get in those bow fasts. Send a hawser to the end of the wharf; I'm going to warp out." There was a harsh answering clatter as the mooring chain that held the bow of the *Nautilus* was secured, and a group of sailors went smartly forward with a hemp cable to the end of the wharf's seaward thrust. The *Nautilus* lay on the eastern side, with the wind beating over the starboard quarter, and there was little difficulty in getting under way. Strain was kept on the stern and breast fasts while the mate directed:

"Ship your capstan bars."

The capstan turned and the *Nautilus* moved forward to the beat of song.

> "Low lands, low lands, hurrah, my John,
> I thought I heard the old man say.
> Low lands, low lands, hurrah, my John,
> We'll get some rum . . . .
> , ... Hurrah, my John.
> Then shake her —"

"Vast heaving," Mr. Broadrick shouted.

The intimate spectators on Phillips' Wharf moved out with the ship. Gerrit Ammidon was now visible on the quarter-deck with the pilot. He walked to the port railing aft and stood gazing somberly back at Salem. The stovepipe hat was not yet discarded, and the hand firmly holding its brim resembled a final gesture of contempt. The pilot approached him, there was a brief exchange of words, and the former sharply ordered:

"Stand by to run up your jib and fore-topmast staysail, Mr. Broadrick. Put two good men at the sheets and see that those sails don't slat to pieces.

"On the wharf there — take that stern fast out to the last ringbolt. Mr. Second Mate . . . get your fenders aboard." The wind increased in a violence tipped with stinging rain. "Give her the jib and staysail." She heeled slightly and gathered steerage way. Roger Brevard involuntarily waved a parting salutation. An extraordinary emotion swept over him: a ship bound to the East always stirred his imagination and sense of beauty, but the departure of the *Nautilus* had a special significance. It was the beginning, yes, and the end, of almost the whole sweep of human suffering and despair, of longing and hope and passion, and a reward.

"Let go the stern fast. Steady your helm there."

"Steady, sir."

A mere gust of song was distinguishable against the blast of storm. Under the lee of the stone warehouse, on the solidity of the wharf, the land, Roger Brevard watched the *Nautilus* while one by one the topsails were sheeted home and the yards mastheaded. "A gale by night," somebody said. The ship, driving with surprising speed toward the open sea, was now apparently no more than a fragile shell on the immensity of the stark horizon.

The light faded: the days were growing shorter. Alone Brevard followed the others moving away. Kate Vollar's red shawl suddenly streamed out and was secured by a wasted hand. Just that way, he thought, the color and vividness of his existence had been withdrawn.

THE END

A NOTE ON THE TYPE IN
WHICH THIS BOOK IS SET

The type in which this book has been set (on the Linotype) is Old Style No. 1. In design, the face is of English origin, by MacKellar, Smith and Jordan, and bears the workmanlike quality and freedom from "frills" characteristic of English old styles in the period prior to the introduction of the "modern" letter. It gives an evenly textured page that may be read with a minimum of fatigue. Old Style No. 1 was one of the first faces designed and cut by the Linotype Company, and it is still one of the most popular.

SET UP AND ELECTROTYPED BY THE
VAIL-BALLOU PRESS, INC., BING-
HAMTON, N. Y. · PRINTED AND
BOUND BY H. WOLFF ESTATE,
NEW YORK · PAPER MANUFAC-
TURED BY S. D. WARREN COM-
PANY, BOSTON, MASS.